EVIL'S UNLIKELY ASSASSIN

AN ALEXIS BLACK NOVEL

JENN WINDROW

rreverent
publishing

Cover Art © 2017 by Erica Petit Illustrations
Title Art © 2018 By Mariah Sinclair
Layout and Book Production by Jenn Windrow
Second eBook Edition July 2018

Irreverent Publishing
PO Box 11371
Chandler, AZ 85248

To my READerlicious girls…eleven women rocking the writing world.

Chapter One

Tonight's job had me sitting in a shadowy corner of a dead-end dive watching the unfortunate, the hopeless, and the degenerates. Had I known this is how I'd be spending my one hundred and seventy-third birthday, I would have called in sick.

An aging cocktail waitress hustled to over-serve society's misfits. An ex-con, a dealer, and an addict pissed their lives away at the far end of the bar. A trio of prostitutes circled the room, their knock-off stiletto's clicking on the wooden floor. And a single cockroach scurried for cover before being squashed.

How would the humans feel about me, the vampire, hiding in their shadows?

One of the battered bar stools toppled, throwing its occupant to the filthy concrete. The man, in a faded red and black flannel shirt, picked himself up off the floor. Dingy jeans slid down his hips, revealing a pair of boxers far past the expiration date for a wash. He bumped and weaved his way through the crowd, ignoring the spilled drinks and curses he left in his wake, and cut a crooked but determined path right to my table.

He collapsed into the booth next to me, blocking my only chance at escape. "How's 'bout a drink?"

I wrinkled my nose at what had to be three days' worth of sweat and grime, raised my bottle and sloshed the liquid from side to side. "Still nursing this one." I focused on a faded picture of the Blues Brothers nailed to the wall and hoped he'd take the hint. A sharp tap on my shoulder told me this guy was either clueless or didn't give a shit. My money was on clueless.

"What's your name, sexy?"

Oh how I wanted to ignore his question, but the last thing I needed was Mr. Drunk and Stupid to cause a scene and blow my cover. "Alexis."

His grease-coated fingers played "Get the Buggy" up my arm. I slapped them away before they got past my elbow. "How's 'bout we get to know each other better?" He gave me a lopsided wink and ogled my breasts.

When he looked at me, he saw what every other human did, a twenty-three year old, petite brunette with large, light blue eyes. But if he leaned in close, he would see what lurked below the exterior, something sinister and scary, with sharp fangs and a deadly personality.

I placed my finger over the throbbing vein on his wrist, tempted to sink my fangs in and make him regret hitting on me, but I settled for a hastily spoken, "Not interested."

He nudged deeper into the booth, his arm snaking its way across my back, until his hand settled on my shoulder. "Bet I can change your mind."

Bet I could eat you before you can remove that dirty appendage.

My inner vampire, the unwanted passenger that shared my body, who I lovingly called Eddie, spoke up, always hoping I would give in and reward him with the human meal he craved. Every night I let him starve.

I tapped my lilac-coated nails on the scratched tabletop, and searched for my angel-appointed human partner, pain-in-my-fangs, and self-assigned babysitter. On my second pass of the smoke-filled room, I found him tucked between Pac-Man and Centipede, arms crossed over his bulldozer-like chest, the usual happy-to-see-you scowl on his face.

Reaper.

I caught his gaze and silently begged him to run interference. "Stop screwing around," he mouthed.

I blew him a kiss. Reaper sneered and turned his head.

Sleazy bars were a hazard of my vampire-dusting occupation. Working with Reaper was another. Had I known the details before I signed away my undead life for a chance to become human again, I might have driven a stake through my own heart. Before I turned my attention back to Mr. Can't-Take-A-Hint: the stench hit me.

The smell of blood, the smell of death, the smell of a predator, the unmistakable smell of another vampire.

My fingers tightened around the beer bottle in my hand. Fangs forced their pointy tips through my gums. Eddie stretched and a fiery pain traced every curve of the branded angel wings on my hip. The intensity would render any other vampire useless, but after two years I had learned to suck it up and get the job done.

I searched the small crowded room and joined every other female eye that watched the undead Don Juan strut to the bar. In his designer jeans and gleaming shit kickers, he stood out like a diamond in a pile of crap. He located a stoned working girl, and after a few words and a smile, he placed his hand on the small of her back and guided her down a hallway.

Vampire. Eddie pushed against my defenses, ready to take the lead. Anxious for the kill.

Not yet.

Why not?

Too public. After two years, Eddie still needed the reminder.

Eddie raged, using my insides as his own personal punching dummy. He wanted death, food, and release. He didn't care that we were in a public place, but I did. And I controlled the beast. It didn't control me.

I took a deep breath and attempted to tamp down my inner Mr. Hyde.

I pushed past my foul-smelling friend, anxious to confront my prey. "Excuse me, need to use the restroom."

He grabbed my wrist and jerked me onto his lap. "Can I join you?" He waggled his eyebrows at me. "I could put the motion in your ocean. Know what I mean?"

I shot out of his lap like someone lit my ass on fire and swallowed back the urge to remove his heart from his chest cavity.

Instead, I reached down and gave his nuts a painful twist, grabbed him by the collar, and lifted him off the booth. "You don't have what it takes to put the motion in my ocean." I shoved, and he hit the back of the booth, eyes going wide, mouth opening and closing like a ventriloquist's dummy.

One minor annoyance taken care of, one major annoyance left to go. A quick nod in Reaper's direction and I followed the mixed smell of copper and blood down the hall.

Stopping in front of the men's room, I leaned my ear against the door; muffled moans came from the other side. Hopefully he was into quickies because I could only hold Eddie back for so long before he exploded out of me in a fit of rage.

I slipped into the women's room to wait and grimaced. Lemony-scented rot polluted the air, and a nuclear bomb wouldn't remove the filth. The stalls wore graffiti and the walls recited limericks from amateur poets. I leaned against the door and promised myself I would burn my shirt when I got home.

The ten minutes it took my prey to feed felt like a hundred lifetimes, thanks to the amped-up bloodlust raging a battle I was sure to lose, a wonderful by-product of my cursed existence. When he finished, the hinges on the men's room door creaked, and two sets of footsteps left. The click of hooker heels went back into the bar, but the soft clunk of boots stopped close by.

Had he sensed me waiting? Was *he* waiting for *me*?

Of course. Running into another vampire out of the Underground was rare these days. Unless it's your job to assassinate them, and then you found one in every rat hole in the city.

I reached down and patted Revanche, Reva for short, the silver dagger that hung at my side. The smooth bone handle a comforting presence that reminded me why I spent my evenings hunting and killing my own kind. Revenge, for the mother, father, sister, and twin brother that Xavier had ripped from my life.

I counted five heartbeats of the nearest human, opened the door, and searched the hall. The vampire leaned against the wall next to a payphone, the words *for a good time call* written over his head. The tips of his blood-tinged fangs peeked over his too-rosy lips. He gave me a cringe-inducing leer.

He. Must. Die. The close proximity of the vampire drove Eddie insane. He Freddie Kruegered my insides, demanding control, demanding to be set free. I lost the fight and Eddie's blood lust took over. The multi-colored world faded into shades of red. Heat rushed through my veins like a blazing inferno through a water-starved forest. My fangs elongated, cutting my lower lip, and a warm trail of blood ran down my chin.

My ironclad contract with the angel of attitude was very specific. The death of one supernatural creature every night for fifty years, or the blood of a human. Any human. The only two ways to satisfy my blood lust, and the only chance I had to survive.

I locked eyes on my prey. Tonight it would be Rico's death.

One look at my unusual red eyes and the dagger at my hip, and a spark of recognition turned his wanna-fuck-grin to a holy-shit-frown. No one wanted to get up close and personal with Evil's Assassin. He ran toward the emergency exit and pushed the bar on the door, setting off an ear-piercing siren.

Run. Chase. Kill. Eddie urged from the abyss.

Half a second behind, I pursued him like a newly turned vamp pursues her first meal. I rushed into a back alley. A single light bulb blinked on and off, doing an inadequate job of cutting through the dark.

The vampire scrambled to a nearby dumpster and hooked his hands over the top. I grabbed him by the boot and pulled him down. *Ca-thunk.* His head bounced off the concrete.

Before he could recover, I pinned him to the ground, one knee on his chest, one hand wrapped around his throat. I reached into my knee-high, silver-studded boot, and pulled out a five-inch long redwood stake, my never-fail-me vampire killing tool.

I clenched the smooth familiar wood and drove it forward.

The point was just millimeters from his heart when he arched his back and knocked me off. I stumbled but didn't let go. I lifted him by the collar of his Brooks Brothers shirt and forced him against the brick wall, stake against his neck. He scratched my face, clawed my arms, and knocked off my hat. A hunk of my hair fell free and he wrapped it around his fist. A silver dagger appeared from behind his back. He held his weapon high, aimed at my heart, ready to strike.

With my stake threatening to pierce the base of his throat, and his weapon aimed at my ticker, we were locked in a stalemate.

"I heard you were dead." He pushed the words out with such venom spit peppered my face. I really needed that shower now.

"Guess you heard wrong."

"Does it weigh on your conscience to kill your own kind?"

"Does it weigh on yours to use humans as your personal blood bank?"

"I only drink from the willing." He pulled my hair tighter. I felt the roots giving up the good fight but swallowed down the pain.

"I bet you do." I pushed the stake harder into his flesh.

His eyes flickered over my shoulder, and his lips spread into a smile far too confident for a man who had a piece of pointy wood adding a drainage hole in his throat. Before I had a chance to react, something prodded me in the small of my back. Now what? I pushed against the vampire's chest hard enough to tear my hair from his grasp, most of it, anyway. A hunk of my jet-black waves remained tangled around his fist.

I turned and confronted my intruder.

Three men stood behind me, bodies swaying from side-to-side, led by my horny friend from the bar. He held an aluminum baseball bat, the words 'Vampire Basher' written on the beat-up metal in thick black marker.

The clueless wonder cleared his throat. "Leave him alone,

Bloodsucker." He held the bat high on his chest, but his words were laced with tremors.

The hunger was out of control, and the blood of Larry, Curly, and Moe would satisfy the craving more than the death of a vampire. My mouth salivated at the thought of blood fresh from the vein slipping down my dry throat, but I fought off the thirst.

I. Don't. Drink. From. Humans.

But they taste so delicious. Eddie purred from his prison.

"You need to leave. Now." There was nothing in my tone that hinted my words were a suggestion.

The vampire knocked the stake out of my hand and sent it flying to the other side of the alley. It landed in a pile of garbage. He pushed against my chest, knocked me to the ground and leapt to the roof of the four-story building next to the bar. He took off into the inky blackness.

"What the hell was that?" Moe asked.

Blood or death. The only way to tame the beast, and the option of death just left.

The angrier half of my sparkling personality rejoiced. *Blood was back on the menu.* But I wouldn't, no, couldn't, let Eddie feed.

I stalked over to the trio and stopped close enough to smell the cigarettes and the stale beer and whisky that stained Moe's teeth yellow. "That was the vampire you let get away to suck another innocent human dry." The two without weapons glanced at each other and took a step back. One look from Moe and they took two steps forward.

"Don't move." Moe pointed at me with the blunt end of the bat.

I looked at his useless weapon and gave him a lethal grin. "Or you'll what? Attempt to kill me with aluminum?"

His gaze traveled along my barely five foot six frame. "Three men against one tiny vampire. We're not afraid." He rubbed the stubble on his chin and turned to his buddies. "Don't you agree, boys?" Larry and Curly stayed silent, obviously the brains of the operation.

I bared my fangs. "Tiny but lethal."

"Well, if you give us too much trouble we can always call the VAU."

Hearing the words caused cold fingers to grip my spine and shake my bones. No vampire wanted to tangle with the Vampire Apprehension Unit, a highly trained unit of former military and police who made it their mission to find and destroy any vampire brave enough to peek their head out of the gutters.

Grisly images of televised executions swarmed my brain, but I coated my words with confidence. "Call the VAU. By the time they get here, you and your buddies will be lying in a pool of your own blood, and I'll be long gone."

The stupid human leader didn't back down. Didn't he understand that I was wrestling for control? For his life? Eddie didn't care if he lived. I did, but I wasn't in charge anymore. If it was up to me I would be chasing the vampire that got away, but my feet were rooted to the floor and wouldn't budge. I needed to scare some sense into this lower-than-shit-on-my-shoes human.

I slapped the bat out of his hand. The clang of metal and concrete connecting rang through the alley. I grabbed him by the throat and my nails punctured his flesh. "You're pissing me off."

Larry and Curly got out fast, taking the only functioning brain with them. They left their not-so-fearless leader in my clutches. The odor of freshly released urine mixed in with the pungent aroma of garbage.

"I'm sorry." His words finally shook with the fear I expected from any semi-intelligent human. "Please let me go."

"You're only sorry because you realize you've made a fatal mistake."

"I'm just drunk and stupid."

"Being stupid is no excuse for confronting a vampire. Did

you forget why they tried to wipe us off the planet? Why the Eradication took place?"

"I remember." He swallowed over the lump in his throat. "But you looked harmless."

"No vampire is harmless." He obviously needed a reminder. I released the tight leash that controlled my hunger, allowing him a peek of the true monster that lived beneath the surface. "Don't let my pretty exterior fool you. I *am* the monster they warned you about."

Moe's mouth sagged open.

The smell of his fear called to my inner monster, the predator. I fought Eddie, tried to control him once again, but Eddie was strong. Stronger than me. I couldn't stop myself—I sank my fangs into the soft skin of his throat. The first drop of blood landed on my tongue.

More. More. Eddie begged. *Blood gives you strength. Blood will quench the hunger. Tame your blood lust. Tame me. Blood will allow you to be the creature you are meant to be.*

One sip. One draw. One gulp. That's all it would take to satisfy the urge. To kill the craving.

To destroy everything. To turn me into the monster that I have fought to become.

I released my grip, and Moe fell from my hands, landing at my feet, limp and pale. Twin rivers of blood ran down his neck and dripped onto the asphalt.

You will never win this battle. I meant every word.

Eddie growled, frustrated, beaten once again. *One day you'll be too weak to deny me.* Then he settled into the background.

A large hand shoved me out of the way. Reaper rushed past me and knelt next to my victim. I backed against the wall. Terror that I had almost drank from the man jump-started my cold, dead heart. *No. No. No.* Two years. I hadn't touched a human in two years.

"Is he okay?" My voice trembled under the weight of fear, guilt, and shame.

"He'll be fine. Just passed out." He looked up at me and disappointment marched over his features before it was replaced with his perma-scowl. "His buddies called the VAU from the bar. Get out of here. I'll clean up your mess."

I turned and followed the same path over the dumpster as the vampire who had escaped.

I ran away from my guilt, away from my fears, and away from my pain. I leapt from one rooftop to another, feet pounding on the exposed tarpaper and kicking up bits of gravel, hoping to outrun the life I had been forced to live.

There was one thing I couldn't outrun: the consequences. I let the vampire escape. Eddie needed payment and satisfaction or he would tear me apart from the inside out or even worse, force me to feed from the first human I came across.

The roof of my warehouse apartment was in sight, two blocks away, an eyesore of a building nestled among other buildings the city had forgotten long ago. I jumped from the roof to the empty sidewalk below.

Before my feet fully connected with the ground, my supernatural sonar let me know I had a second chance to satisfy my monster within.

There was a creature near my home. A creature that wouldn't live to see sunrise.

Chapter Two

The creature darted and clung to the deep shadows cast by the skeletal rail cars. I stalked, studied, watched. Waiting for the opportune moment to attack, ideally in an isolated area, no witnesses.

Every vamp, werewolf, and creepy crawly in Chicago knew where I lived. Hell, they probably had my address listed on an undead city tour. "Next up, Evil's Assassin's house." There were two explanations for someone to be around my place. They were new to the area. Or they had a death wish.

My prey's identity was hidden underneath a heavy, black cloak. I didn't know what flavor of creatures-that-go-bump-in-the-night I stalked. Not that it mattered. After tonight's disaster I needed a good fight.

I knew just the place for our confrontation, and my prey headed right for it. An abandoned train station on the corner of Wells and Polk, two short blocks from my home. The empty parking lot in the rear was the perfect place for a moonlight execution.

I picked up speed, rounded the corner of an empty caboose, a short cut that would bring me out ahead, and slipped underneath a rickety stairwell. I pulled out my redwood stake and dug my nails into the wood.

The angel wings branded on my hip, another by-product of my contract, pulsed with fire. The growing intensity let me know the creature was close, even before I heard its shoes slapping on the pavement.

Pain sliced through my insides, a thousand tiny knives carving into my bones, my organs. I bent over and clutched my stomach. I didn't have long before the beast took control, and I became the monster I loathed. The monster I feared.

The black-clad figure rounded the corner and passed my hiding spot. I leapt out and yanked off its cloak.

My blood curdled like rotten milk. It couldn't be. Not him. Not tonight. Not ever. Not Nathan.

My heart high-dived into the pool of bile in my stomach.

"'ello, China Doll." His British accent had thickened in the past two years.

He looked exactly the same—amber eyes surrounded by thick charcoal eyeliner, spiked bleached blonde hair, silver hoops hanging from his earlobes, and an old ratty Ramones t-shirt I'd given him for Christmas five years ago. He was the vampire Billy Idol, and damn proud of it.

Nathan. Father-figure, friend, mentor all rolled into one flamboyant vampire. God, I missed him.

And tonight he will sacrifice himself to help you fight for another day.

I won't do it. I wasn't sure if I was telling Eddie or myself.

There's no other option. Eddie always liked to state the obvious.

Fangs ripped through my gums, fire raced through my veins, and red bled into my eyes. Eliminating the creature in front of me pushed all rational thought to the dusty cobweb corners of my mind. All I could think about was death.

For the second time that night the beast demanded to be fed. I wrapped my arms around my stomach and squeezed. Squeezed hard, hoping it was enough to keep myself in control, or at the very least keep Eddie at bay long enough to dig us out from under this mountain of shit.

I bent over, placed my hands on my leather-clad knees, and pulled deep breaths through gritted teeth. *Come on Alexis. You've been in worse situations than this. You're strong. You're in control. You're not a monster. Not. A. Monster.*

Are you sure about that? Eddie interjected.

Positive.

My pep talk swept the pain, the hunger, and the need to kill under the rug, like the dirt hidden from an unexpected house-guest, which would eventually creep back out. I estimated we had five minutes before my personal beasty bust out. Five minutes to figure out how to get Nathan out of here alive.

"You okay, Luv?" His voice snuck through my concentration.

"Not even a little." There was a sharpness to my words. Sharp enough to ram a stake through my heart. "What are you doing here? We had an understanding."

"I heard you were dead. I needed to see for myself."

"That's twice tonight someone's informed me of my own demise, but I'm very much alive, and now we're screwed."

"I cocked up, but I had to know. I had to say goodbye." He lifted his shoulders in a half-assed shrug. "What's the plan? I bugger off into the night, and you find some poor unsuspecting bastard to replace me?"

"There are no unsuspecting bastards." I shot my thumb over my shoulder, and pointed out the deserted area behind us. "Everyone knows to stay clear of my turf. Especially you."

Nathan flinched like I had just thrown holy water on him. "What are our options?"

"Blood or death," I said through clenched teeth, repeating the mantra out loud that had been constant in my mind for the past two years. "In order for you to live, I have to feed."

"Off a human?"

I shot him my best what-do-you-think look.

"Sorry." He lowered his gaze and his voice shook just enough to let me know he was afraid.

The memory of sinking my fangs into the drunk at the bar surfaced, so did the revulsion and shame and terror. The truth was, I knew what I had to do to get Nathan out of here alive, but could I do it? At the bar Eddie had been in control, I hadn't attacked of my own free will. But here. Right now. It would be my choice. Could I live with that on my conscious? It'd be hard, but living with Nathan's death in my heart would be worse.

"Yeah. Me too. It seems I'll be falling off the wagon twice tonight." I shut out the background noises that accompanied all big cities, and searched the area for a beating heart or hammering pulse or warm body.

Damn. No one. No vagrants, street thugs or drug-addled idiots.

This was Chicago for Christ's sake. Where were all the warm blooded-humans? I glanced at the gold watch on my wrist: two forty-seven a.m. Tucked away for the night.

My head rolled back on my shoulders, my eyes pinched shut. "Shit."

"Problem?"

"No humans."

Nathan laid his hand on my shoulder. The touch of the creature my curse considered the enemy sizzled through my flesh, my blood, my bones. "Now what?"

My hard-won control slipped through its carefully built barrier. I pushed his hand away. "Don't touch me."

Nathan backed away, both hands up in the air. One step. Two steps. Three steps, but it wasn't far enough for me to regain control. Eddie rammed against my insides and tore through his prison of weak flesh. He demanded the vampire in front of me die. Tonight. By my hand.

Tears stung my eyes when I looked at the pointy hunk of wood and then at Nathan. Nathan. The one who found me. Saved me. Protected me. How could I drive a stake through his heart when it would break mine?

Pain crashed through me like a wrecking ball through Wrigley Field. Our time was up.

"I can't control the beast." I clamped my teeth so tight I was afraid they were going to shatter.

"I know." His words carried a heavy dose of pity. "Your eyes are shining like rubies."

It's the vampire in front of you or the humans you love so. Your choice.

I lowered my chin and eyelids, ashamed of the monster Caleb the-asshole-angel turned me into. How did I get us out of this mess? The rules were simple. In order for one to live, the other had to die. But who'd be sacrificed? I swore I would do anything for the return of my humanity, and I meant it, but looking at Nathan I knew that wasn't a promise I could keep.

There was only one solution I could live with.

"Go." I pointed to a break between two buildings, an escape that led to his survival.

He stayed put. "What happens to you?"

"Just go."

"What happens to you?" The concern in his voice ricocheted off my heart.

"I die." The full force of my anger pushed the words out. I lunged forward, stake raised high, aimed at his heart. "Get the fuck out before I do something we'll both regret."

His soft soles crunched the gravel slowly at first, then picked up speed. I looked up to see him turn the corner. Tears of relief and dread and fear rolled down my cheeks. The beast lunged against my inner flesh prodding me to give chase. I ground my teeth against the pain and refused to give in to its demands.

Without the satisfaction of the vampire's demise or blood to satiate its thirst, the beast turned its anger on me. I welcomed the swift death.

You chose wrong. I detected a hint of satisfaction in Eddie's tone.

A hot poker traced every curve, every line, and every detail of the angel wings on my hip. It burned its way like scorching lava through my veins, slowly consuming me from the inside out. The beast tore at my heart and ripped through my muscles, forcing me to drop to my knees, my hands, and roll onto my side.

A mix of raw terror and suffering ripped through my vocal cords and ended in one single blood-curdling scream.

I lay in a heap on the ground unable to move, the life draining out of me. The cicadas' buzz, shrill to my sensitive ears, the smell of an over-ripe dumpster, toxic to my nose, the cold pavement underneath me, harsh to my feverish flesh. This was the end, but instead of regret I found peace. Peace because unlike so many other things in my life, this was my choice. My opportunity to make the right decision. I looked up. A blanket of stars covered my pain-ravaged body.

The scuffing of shoes on the blacktop let me know I wasn't alone. My head fell to the side. A pair of faded fire engine red Dr. Marten's stopped next to me. Only one person I knew owned shoes that ugly.

Nathan.

"I can't let you do this." He bent down, wiped away my tears, and placed my head on his lap. The physical contact sent a jolt through my extremities that arched my back and rendered me silent. He wrapped his hand around mine, and closed my fingers tight around the stake.

Eddie reared his ugly head and begged me to do something. Try to resist. Try to fight back. Try to survive.

Kill. Kill. Kill.

Instead, I let my head sink back into the deep V of Nathan's thighs, and hoped my life would be over soon.

"Listen, Luv." He played with the dark waves of my hair. "I've looked after you since the day I found you on that cargo ship." He raised the stake. Pinching my eyes shut, I mentally prepared for the pain that would accompany the smooth wood on its way to my heart. "And I'm not stopping now." My eyelids sprang open.

The tip didn't rest over my breastbone. It hovered over his.

The beast kept the words I wanted to say locked behind their cracked lips. I wanted to tell him to let me go, to make him understand I couldn't live with his death on my conscience. Instead, all I could muster was one shaky word and a half-ass attempt to pull the stake away from his heart. "No."

His hand cupped the side of my face, and he tilted my head so our eyes met. "It's okay. I've lived for almost three hundred years. You've got a purpose. A chance to get your life back. I want that for you."

I searched his face. His heavily outlined eyes said he didn't want to die. His firm grip on the stake said he would…for me.

My hand shook—his was steady. My eyes were moist—his were dry. He gave my fingers a quick squeeze. "Close your eyes?" His fingers touched my forehead, but I couldn't shut my eyes, couldn't blind myself from what the beast was about to force me to do.

Nathan pulled the stake back at arm's length and drove it toward his heart. The sharp tip drilled through his flesh, but caught on his breastbone.

I pushed with all the strength my body could muster on the wooden handle, until it broke through the bone and went straight into his heart.

He smiled at me one last time, a smile of pure love I'd never forget.

The skin that touched the stake glowed red and dissolved. The heat continued outward until all Nathan's flesh and bone was reduced to a smoking pile of ash, which swirled in one last dance with the late summer breeze. Bits of it landed on my hair and clothes, covering me in a light grey layer. A gruesome reminder of what I had done to survive.

Smart vampire. Content, Eddie slipped back into the abyss without another word.

The all-encompassing pain disappeared once the last piece of flesh dissolved, only to be replaced with something worse. The emotional pain gripped my heart and ripped it in two.

I focused on the pile of ash, the only thing left of my best friend. Silver sparkled under the dim streetlight, a flickering object buried in the center of Nathan's remains. I sifted through and found the platinum band he'd worn on his left ring finger, one of the few mementos from his human life. Blowing on the shiny metal to cool it off, I slipped the circle on my thumb, and clutched my hand to my chest.

Slapped with grief, I fell to the ground. Silent sobs wracked my body before the anguished sounds left my lips. My fist slammed into the concrete and then I threw the stake across the parking lot.

Tears tumbled down my cheeks. Trembling fingers reached out, not quite touching Nathan's remains. "I'm sorry, so sorry." My vocal cords rattled with despair.

Nathan's death. Another scar on my already battered heart. Another person I couldn't save. Another failure to add to a long list of failures.

I grabbed the rail car and pulled myself to my feet. Locking my emotions behind my black heart, knowing they wouldn't stay there for long, but I needed to hide them. I walked the same path that Nathan had taken earlier; headed to a place I knew I couldn't hurt another soul.

Squeaky wheels on the pavement made me pause and look back. An older man in a shredded coat and filthy clothes pushed a wobbly shopping cart through the parking lot on his way to a garbage can in a corner. The man arrived ten minutes too late to save Nathan's life.

Fate was a fickle bitch.

Chapter Three

The crumbling graffiti-covered walls of my abandoned warehouse lay ahead. I walked quickly, chin to chest. Wanting sanctuary, safe haven, isolation.

Wanting somewhere I could fall apart.

The sight of Nathan's ashes floating away on the wind had brought a new kind of despair to my already lonely life. His death plunged my non–beating heart into the sewer of my soul. A sewer filled with anger and regret and self-loathing.

You are the most morose vampire I have ever encountered. Eddie poked at my wounds, trying to goad me into fighting back, but I let his wisdom-less words turn into white noise.

Every half-peeled concert sticker stuck to the light poles, and every discarded Marlboro pack along the cracked sidewalk reminded me of him. If only the homeless man had shown up a few minutes sooner, I'd have sucked him dry to save Nathan's life. Hell, I'd already broken my oath once tonight. Guess I needed to flip my "it's been seven hundred and twenty-six days since an accident" sign back to zero.

Tiny cyclones of guilt twisted through my stomach and kicked debris over my heart, burying the useless organ in a heavy blackness. Blood and a hot shower would erase the physical pain, but the memory of what I was forced to do settled deep in my soul. Hidden away from any type of healing. Maybe I should skip the blood and shower, hold on to the pain a little longer, like a scarlet "SB", for selfish bitch, nailed to my chest.

I yanked open the three-inch thick steel door that separated me from the welcome sight of scratched concrete and chipped walls. An old service elevator waited to take me to the loft on the second floor. I slammed my hand into the red up button and waited for it to lurch upward.

The smell of pine cleaner and ocean breeze potpourri, mixed with the unwelcome aroma of a familiar musky male, slipped in between the metal diamonds of the elevator cage. A warning that an overly hostile Reaper waited for me on the other side.

What the hell was he doing here? And how did he get in? It's not like he had a key. Or manners. The only other time he had stepped foot in my apartment was the night he introduced himself and announced his extreme dislike for anything of the vampire persuasion.

Reaper and I didn't have conversations. We had shouting matches with punches for punctuation. Something told me tonight's conversation would be laced with exclamation points.

The elevator stopped. I pushed back the cage and drew a deep breath, bracing myself for what was sure to be a chilly reception. I stepped into the loft.

Nice. He'd made himself at home. Butt comfy on my cream-colored leather sofa, black combat boots propped on my coffee table, my black and orange cat curled on his lap.

I ignored Reaper, but crouched and made kissy noises to entice my kitty. "Come, Raja."

Raja opened an eye, yawned, arched her back in a stretch, and curled up even tighter. Reaper reached down and stroked her fur. No Friskies for her tonight.

Reaper stood with my traitorous animal in his arms, petting her one last time before placing her gently on the floor. She purred and wound in and out of his legs, but he ignored the cat and focused his it's-time-to-talk gaze on me. His fists pumped at his sides. "What the hell happened tonight?" The softly spoken words sent a missile shaped icicle to my core and scared me more than if he had screamed.

You should have eaten him years ago. Reaper's crappy attitude, the only thing Eddie and I agreed on.

And even though I felt as if death stared at me from behind

Reaper's green eyes, I figured a few more minutes wouldn't kill him.

I removed my black leather duster, tossed my keys on the cherry wood entry table, and walked to the kitchen. Grabbed a bag of "O" positive from the fridge, and popped it in the microwave. I leaned against the black granite counter and waited out the forty-five seconds it took to heat a pint of blood.

Reaper paced behind the couch, one hand on his hip, the other rubbed his forehead. Back and forth. Back and forth. Back and forth. The heavy thud of his boots on the wood floors got louder with each step.

Beep. Beep. Beep. Dinner's ready. I shoved a straw in the vampire Capri-sun, and planted myself on a leather ottoman in front of Reaper. I sucked down the blood until the bag flattened and wrinkled, then licked my lips. Half of Reaper's upper lip lifted so high even Elvis would have been impressed.

I picked up my fuzzy security blanket before she scurried away and buried my face in her fur. Finally ready, I answered my partner. "I lost control. It happens." It was a crappy explanation, but all I felt Reaper deserved.

"Not around me it doesn't." He took a step back, gaze moving up and down my body. "I thought the vampire got away."

I shut my eyes before he noticed the anguish etched in the depths of my pupil's. "He did."

He ran a finger along my thigh and through the ash clinging to my leather pants. He held it up for me to see. "Who's this?"

Nathan's ash on Mr.-I-Hate-Vampire's finger drove a stake into my heart. "What do you care?"

"I don't. I'm just glad tonight wasn't a total waste." He wiped Nathan's remains on his army green cargo pants, a long grey smudge wrapped around his thick thigh.

I started counting in my head. One-one thousand. Two-one thousand. Three-one thous... Oh, who was I kidding. "Fuck you, Reaper."

"Not on your life, princess." He sat back on my couch and crossed one ankle over his knee. "So, who'd you dust?"

The casual tone he used toward a vampire's death really pissed me off, always had, but tonight it caused an eruption at my core. An eruption that spewed foul language and bad choices all over my living room.

I leapt off the ottoman, my foot knocking into the table, sending the candles and remote controls scattering to the floor. Reaper found himself pinned to the sofa, my fingers wrapped tightly into the fabric of his shirt. I pulled him forward until we were nose to nose. "When it's any of your fucking business who I dust, I'll fucking tell you."

He pried my fingers free and pushed me off his lap. The back of my legs smacked into the coffee table sending the last few remaining items to the ground. He pointed a finger at my chest, the tip just barely touching me. "I don't give a shit if it's your father you staked. Killing vampires is your job. Spare me the tortured theatrics."

The angel of gloom and doom stuck me with Mr. Personality. That didn't mean I had to take his crap. I grabbed his finger and bent it back. "I never wanted this job."

"No one forced you to take it." He yanked his pointer from my grasp and rubbed the knuckle.

"I had two choices. Death or Curse."

"You could have chosen death." Reaper's cold tone matched his frigid demeanor.

"I could have, but you'd be out of a job."

"So why'd you take it?"

I've wondered the same thing for the past two years. It's not the they-should-be-reported-to-OSHA working conditions or crappy co-workers that keep me around. Nope. The only thing that kept me going night after night was the big bonus at retirement. The return of my soul. Humanity.

"You know what, I don't give a shit." He pointed his finger at my face this time. "You don't drink from humans. Period."

Reaper was the last person who needed to remind me. I promised myself when I became Evil's Assassin that I wouldn't take human blood from the vein again. I'd broken that vow tonight and it scared the shit out of me. The fear that one small taste, one miniscule drop, would tear through my carefully built defenses and trigger my inner beast.

I didn't need a reminder that a killer lurked just below my flesh. A killer who waited for the opportunity to ruin everything I've worked for. "I know. Trust me. I know."

"Make sure you do. I won't have a partner who can't control herself."

"I never agreed to a partner." If my words had been a gun, Reaper's ass would be full of lead.

"Don't think of me as your partner, think of me as a babysitter. A guard to make sure you don't slip and make a snack out of an innocent bystander." He paused. "And neither of us is getting rid of the other until one of us dies."

"That could be arranged." Spoken nice and clear so he'd understand I meant every word.

His gaze settled on the stake sticking out of my boot. "Better watch it. I won't hesitate to stake you myself."

I pulled out the pointy wood and handed it to him. "Go ahead." I tugged down the edge of my tank top and exposed the flesh that covered my heart. "Here's your target."

He rolled the wood in his palm then gripped it in a tight fist. The corners of his mouth lifted just a fraction and his eyes twinkled. Reaper's grudge against vampires made the Grand Canyon look like a roadside ditch.

I hoped his hatred ran so deep that he'd slam the stake through my flesh and bone and into my heart. A stake through the heart brought me peace. A stake through the heart erased the guilt. A stake through the heart ended my miserable existence.

My only regret is that he hadn't killed me sooner. At least then Nathan would be alive.

He held the stake high over his head, the skin over his knuckles blanched under the pressure. His lips pinched into a thin line and his eyes focused on my chest.

I smiled and made sure to show a lot of fang. "Don't fuck this up. You've only got one shot."

His hand shot forward, the point of the stake aimed for its target. But stopped just before the tip touched my flesh. "Too easy." He let the stake fall to his side and tapped the dark colored wood against his leg. "You deserve to die, but not until the job's over. For now at least you're being useful and not sucking the world dry."

"That's me: Alexis Black, the useful vampire."

I had forty-seven years, thirty-eight weeks, and ten days left as Caleb's guided missile. By the time my contract ended, Reaper would be just another annoying patient in Shady Hills nursing home.

"One day." Reaper tossed the stake on top of the coffee table.

"Is that a warning or a promise?"

"Warning for you." He looked me straight in the eyes. "Promise for me."

There's an old saying. With friends like you, who needs enemies? That's where Reaper and I stood and always would. I could sit here all day and try to convince him I'm not a monster, but that would be a waste of my undead life. Reaper considered me a means to an end. What end I didn't know. We both had our secrets.

I went to the elevator, and slid the cage open. "Leave. Now."

Reaper grabbed the remote control off the black and tan rug and pushed the button, the television flickered on. "Watch the news. The vampires are getting brave, reckless. There are reports of attacks all over the city, even in the burbs." He bent down and picked his keys up off the floor. "Don't forget that it's our job to keep them from slaughtering the innocents. Every time you kill one of those monsters, it's one more human life saved." He brushed past me, and stepped onto the elevator. "By the way, I came to tell you that *your* victim is perfectly healthy." He crossed his arms in front of his chest and leaned against the wall.

I pushed the button and watched the top of Reaper's blond crew cut disappear down the shaft.

The front door slammed and I called the elevator to the upper floor, then sat down, flipping through news channel after news channel. Reaper was right—report after report of vampire attacks. The VAU couldn't keep up. The hospitals were over-loaded with victims. Why now? Why four years after the start of the Eradication? What had brought the vampire's back out of the shadows? A little voice in my head told me I wasn't going to like the answer to those questions.

Turning off the T.V., I picked up a purring Raja, got a box from the top shelf of the hall closet, and headed to my room.

After stripping out of my uniform of black leather pants and deep red tank top, then kicking my boots across the room, I wiped dust from the lid and dumped the contents on the red brocade comforter and sifted through the mementos. I picked up a stub from the last concert Nathan and I saw together, The Smiths, three years ago in Texas. A playbook from a production of Les Miserable I dragged him to. And photo after photo after photo of our almost fifty years together. Each and every one a stick-a-knife-in-my-heart memory of Nathan.

Pathetic. Wasting your time mourning over death. I'm going to bed. The connection to Eddie went blissfully quiet.

The first rays of the morning sun snuck through a small crack in my black-out shades. I placed Nathan's memories back in the box and set it on the floor, curled around my already snoozing kitty, and attempted to fall into a deep slumber.

Sleep didn't come easy. It came on the heels of dark memories, dark thoughts, and an even darker mood. But I needed the rest because tomorrow night I anticipated an ass kicking of monumental proportion.

Chapter Four

R eaper slammed my head into the blue gym mat—*hard*. Hard enough that my brain bounced around in my skull and my fangs cut through my lower lip. I stared at the row of punching bags that hung from the ceiling like the bats I imagined circling my head, and let my body recover.

The past two years of training with Reaper never prepared me for the brain rattling assault he pulled out of his beat-Alexis-to-a-bloody-pulp arsenal.

Every single day I cursed Caleb for forcing me to spar with Reaper. I mentioned this to Reaper once. His answer: "Being a blood sucking leach isn't enough to defeat the monsters." So, early every evening, Reaper spends his time training me in hand-to-hand combat, and the proper handling of guns and knives.

I rolled to my side, and surveyed the gym. It was one of those old-time boxing gyms, something that you would see in Rocky. No fancy machines, just free weights, a sparring ring, and bench press off in the corner.

Reaper was strong and fast for a human, and most nights we were evenly matched. So evenly matched I wondered if Caleb had given him super powers to go along with his super-annoying attitude. But tonight was different. Tonight my body was his Alexis-shaped punching bag, and his goal was to turn my innards into outtards. I didn't want to stand up and face him. In fact, lying on the ground for the rest of the night sounded like a good plan. Too bad it wasn't Reaper's plan.

He pounded his fist into the mat and missed my head by centimeters. His eyes radiated with hatred and rage. "Pay attention, blood sucker, or I'll use you as a mop, wipe up the floor, wring you out and hang you on a wall."

He yanked me to my feet by my braid, placed his hand on my back and shoved me across the room. I tripped, but turned my stumble into a somersault that ended in a ten-point dismount.

Reaper was a tank in tennis shoes and camo pants. Two hundred and forty pounds of hard-earned muscle. All it took was one look and a sensible person peed their pants and scrambled to get away.

I'm not sensible. I'm not human either.

"You may be bigger. But I'm faster. Stronger."

Reaper curled his finger inward, his smile smug. A smile that my fists ached to wipe off his face.

I bee-lined for him. At the last second I flipped over his head, and landed behind him. In the moment it took him to turn around, I sent a roundhouse kick to his ribs. He grabbed his side, but stayed standing.

My fists flew. One connected with his jaw. The other he batted away. His right fist came at my chest. I dodged to the left and it missed its target. His left one didn't. Four sharp knuckles hit my face with a holy-hell-the-pain-might-kill-me crunch. One broken nose. Blood gushed down the back of my throat and puddled on my tongue. I spit a wet glob on the floor. More blood dripped from my nostrils and ran down my lips and neck and cleavage.

Tilting my head back a notch, I wiped away the blood running down my face with the back of my hand. "That's the last hit you're getting in tonight." I attacked.

My speed caused him to go on the defensive, but I wasn't fast enough. Every punch he blocked. Every kick he dodged. Every move he anticipated.

Pain and anger made me sloppy, and being sloppy would get me hurt…again. Sweat mixed with blood dripped down my face and fell to the mat. I glanced at my opponent. Reaper's forehead was as dry as his personality.

I tightened my fists at my sides, nails digging into my palm, and ground my teeth against each other. His smug smile forced me to kick high at his chest, but never made contact. Reaper grabbed my heel with one hand, my toes with the other and twisted. My body followed the same direction as my foot and I ended up face first on the mat. I battered the ground with my fists.

This was pathetic, and the butt beating was my fault. My heart and mind were preoccupied with other things. Nathan's death. It weighed on me like a coffin tied to my ankle.

What the hell was I still doing here?

Jumping up, I gathered what was left of my pride and walked to the exit. And almost made it. Almost. But a pair of strong arms wrapped around me, one across my chest, and the other between my legs. He lifted and tossed me to the ground. The impact evacuated my breath in a loud *whoosh*. I pushed to my elbows, but Reaper positioned his full weight on my chest, and pinned my arms over my head.

He leaned so close I could see the faint flecks of gold in his eyes and smell the coffee on his breath. "Here's your lesson for today." The chill in his voice iced my bones like the Chicago streets in January. "Don't ever turn your back on your opponent. Unless they're passed out or dead."

I obviously needed the reminder.

I may be pinned under a Reaper-shaped dumb-bell, but I still had my vampire strength. I raised my hips and knocked him to the ground. Stood up, dusted off my yoga pants, and headed to the door.

"We're not done," Reaper called after me.

I lifted my arms high and gave him a double one-finger salute.

"Don't make me come get you."

Don't turn around. Do. Not. Turn. Around.

"The tough, little vampire can't take a beating?"

His words wiggled their way into my blood, my ego, my brain. Damn, he was good.

I stopped, sighed, and spun around. He leaned against the rope of the sparing ring and picked his nails. "You know I can."

"Prove it." The crooked smile he wore told me he couldn't wait for me to do just that.

So I did.

AN HOUR LATER, I walked out my front door. Reaper's 1970 SS Chevelle waited at the curb. Midnight blue with two white stripes on the hood, the car demanded attention with the rumble of its engine and the growl of its exhaust pipe. The perfect car for Reaper.

The passenger side door opened with a creak. "You're late. Get. In."

I slid into the seat and glanced at the seething human. His jaw tight, teeth grinding. One hand clutched the steering wheel, and the other held an ice pack over his newly blackened eye.

I thought about suppressing my smile at the sight of his bumps and bruises but didn't. Let him see it. "Ready?" My word was happy and high.

"Don't talk." The quiet fury in Reaper's voice told me I was about to push his patience off a cliff.

Alexis twenty-three. Reaper twenty. Not that I was keeping score.

The too-chirpy voice of the GPS unit led us through the maze of downtown Chicago. Eminem played on the radio, looking for the "Real Slim Shady", and I sat and watched the world go by at forty miles per hour. A glimpse of humanity speeding past through a thin layer of glass.

I coveted their lives. Men, women, and children with the freedom to live how they wanted. No angelic contract or mysterious vampire body snatcher or prejudiced partners.

I clung to my dreams like a five year old clings to their mother's leg on their first day of kindergarten. The dream of a beating heart. The warmth of the sun on my skin. A family of my own. The return of what was stolen from me—my humanity.

Those are the dreams. And the reason I put up with Reaper each and every night.

The landscape changed from the urban nightlife of the city streets to the tall pine trees and dense evergreens of the suburbs. The city water tower announced we were in Oak Park, just one of the many suburbs that surrounded the city.

Reaper turned into a small paved parking lot attached to a neighborhood park. Loose gravel crunched under the tires. He parked the car and the engine rumbled to a stop.

"I've started researching areas with high assault rates. This used to be a quiet community, now it's not." He pulled the keys from the ignition. "Thought it was worth checking out."

Between Reaper's instincts and the police scanners he used for back up, my partner was usually right. "Then let's see what's disturbing the good people of Oak Park."

I opened my door and took a deep breath. Clean air. Wet grass. Spilled blood.

Vampire.

Eddie woke up with a jolt. *More than one.*

I got out of the car and followed the coppery smell along a well-worn path of pebbles, lined with maroon and yellow mums, and past a row of wooden benches, straight into the middle of a playground.

Pink and grey Nike's peeked out from underneath the slide.

I rushed to the slide and fell to my knees next to the body of a girl, maybe nineteen, in black running shorts and tank top. Arms spread wide, legs spread wide, mouth spread wide in a scream that would never be heard.

Eddie rushed to the surface, tried to gain control, at the sight of her too-still lifeless body, but I fought it back and refused to let it come out and play.

I knew before my hand touched the side of her neck there

wouldn't be a pulse, but I still had to check, in case there was a bit of life left in her battered body. There wasn't. With the tip of my fingers I slid her eyes closed. What a wholesome place for such a horrific act. Swings, slides, and monkey bars all witness to the carnage. Desecrated by brutality and death and horror.

Then I heard it. The sound of a struggle, of someone fighting for their life. The slurping of a vampire stealing what didn't belong to him. I stood up and looked and listened. The sounds were coming from a break in the evergreens off to the left, just a few feet away.

Silently, I snuck up on two vampires kneeling over a second girl. Her legs shook and she pushed with her hands to fight them off, but they held her down. One attached to her neck; the other feeding from her inner thigh. They were so focused on their meal that they didn't hear me come up.

Looks like you get to have some fun, I told Eddie before letting him loose on the unsuspecting bloodsuckers.

I pulled my stake from my boot and stabbed the one feeding at her leg through the back. The point punctured his heart. His body glowed red, burst into flames, and then dissolved to ash.

The second vampire looked up, a piece of skin he'd torn from the girl's throat dangling from his mouth. He spit her flesh on the ground and charged me. I punched him. He hit the trunk of a tree a hundred yards away and slid to the ground.

Time froze when I looked at his victim. Her curly blonde hair and scared blue eyes reminded me of another girl, another time. Reminded me of my little sister, Lysette. Gone. Killed by the very monster who turned me into a vampire. I failed to save Lysette, but I wouldn't fail this poor girl.

I knelt next to her. Her breath was labored, blood pumped from her wound, a growing puddle of red circled her head like a morbid halo, and her heartbeat slowed. She needed help or she wasn't going to make it. I stepped closer, wanting to do what I could to save her, but the brand on my hip flared.

Kill the vampire now. Play nursemaid later. Eddie had a point.

Anger turned me toward the monster who had hurt her. Judging by his still rosy complexion, itty-bitty fangs, and pinprick pupils he was only a few days old, three at the most. I pulled Reva out of the sheath strapped to my hip, and waited for him to attack.

"Terrance told us you were dead." The vampire eyed me from the base of the tree.

I really needed to find out who started that rumor. "Don't know Terrance, but he lied."

He pushed away from the tree and came at me. Fangs and claws bared. He didn't have the experience to fight me and win. But he wouldn't be around long enough to figure it out.

The bottom of my boot connected with his stomach. He went down, arms wrapped around his torso and puked up the girl's blood.

The dying girl didn't have time for me to waste playing with her attacker. With one swift move I swung my dagger, taking his head off. It slid from his shoulders. His body slumped to the ground, not fully dead until I drove a stake through his heart. Once the wood pierced his ticker, his body burned away leaving a pile of ash in the grass.

Eddie purred like Raja after a good scratching under her chin.

I sheathed Reva and rushed over to the girl. With an outstretched hand, I put pressure on her wound, but her blood called to Eddie. I scurried away, hand covering my mouth and nose. I wanted to help her, needed to save her, but the monster inside of me wanted to consume her.

She had one chance at survival and I wasn't it. "Reaper," I yelled, my voice full of desperation. "Help."

Chapter Five

I raced to the nearest blue plastic swing and planted my hiney on my hands. "Don't eat the girl. Don't eat the girl. Don't eat the girl." I rocked back and forth and chanted over and over and over again.

The death of the bloodsucker controlled the lust, but I was a vampire and blood still called to me like cheap paper bag booze calls to a wino. By the time Reaper's boots crunched up the path I followed earlier, I wanted to run screaming from the site of the blood pooling under the poor dying girl. But Eddie wanted to force me to my knees, to run my tongue over her wounds, to drink. I stayed on the swing and prayed for control.

It would taste so good. The strength you'd have. The power. You'd be unstoppable. I could almost feel him licking his lips.

I don't want to be unstoppable.

You're no fun.

Reaper knelt next to her, looked at the wound, and then looked at me. "Half the skin is missing from her throat." There wasn't any accusation in his voice, but I still felt the need to explain.

"The vampire did it after I killed his friend."

He gently lifted her wrist, placed two fingers over the veins and searched for a pulse. "It's faint, but still there."

Reaper placed her hand back on the grass and tore off the edge of his shirt. He wadded the fabric and held it to her neck. Once satisfied, he reached into his back pocket and pulled out his cell phone. "She's not going to make it unless we get her help." He tossed the phone in my direction. "Scroll through my contacts. Find James Coleman. Tell him you're a friend of Reaper's, where we are, and that we need an ambulance ASAP."

I dialed the number, thankful to have something to do to keep my mind off my hunger. Seconds later a bored voice answered and announced I'd just called the VAU. My words caught in my throat and I took a moment to clear the large boulder they were stuck behind. I asked for James Coleman and, while waiting, I glared at the back of Reaper's head and counted all the ways I could hurt him. When the Detective answered I relayed the information and quickly hung up.

I tossed the phone back to Reaper with a little more force than necessary. "You had me call the VAU?"

He picked it up and stuffed it in his pocket, his hand never leaving the girl's throat and his eyes never meeting mine. "I have connections. Plus, this is a vampire-related incident. They need to know."

The girl moaned and Reaper lifted the blood-soaked cloth. "It may be too late anyway. Her pulse is barely there."

"Let me help." I knelt on the other side of her and licked my fingertips.

Reaper removed the cloth and I rubbed my saliva over a few of the shallow cuts. The puncture holes knitted together, scabbed over, and within seconds healed. The skin around the wounds turned purple, yellowish-green, pink, and then finally flesh colored as the bruises disappeared.

I sat back on my heels and wiped the blood from my hands onto my pants. "Just a dab'll do ya."

Tonight wasn't the first time Reaper had seen the healing power in my spit, but today he looked at me like I had grown a second pair of fangs. "You should have thought of that sooner." This time his voice was filled with accusation.

"You wanted the vampire with super blood lust to stick her finger in the bleeding woman without someone here to make sure she didn't eat her? Next time I'll remember."

Reaper waved me over to the next wound, the worst of all of them. "Stop wasting time. Put some on this wound, just enough to keep her from bleeding out."

The VAU was on the way, I didn't think this was the best idea, but the girl needed help or she wouldn't be alive when help arrived. Kneeling down, I barely wet the tip of my finger, and placed it in the center of the blood-filled wound. Being this close to her pulsing veins sent Eddie into a frenzy. I swallowed, took a deep breath, and forced him to comply. My finger slid over the slick surface, finding the artery, and the bleeding stopped, but I couldn't even begin to heal the gaping holes left behind.

Just one lick. A small taste. I wouldn't ask for more. We both knew it was a lie.

Eddie would never be satisfied with just a taste.

No chance.

Her blood coats your hands, such a simple thing to let me feed.

I ran my hands through the grass to remove as much blood as I could.

Weak.

The dead vampires were your payment. That's all you will ever get.

Eddie stayed silent.

Reaper and I stood guard over the injured girl. An uneasy quiet formed between us, until the high-pitched wail of the cavalry broke through the night.

"Get out of here." Reaper pointed in the direction of his car. I hated getting sent away like a naughty child.

"Now."

I had to go. But I wanted to watch them save her. Needed to see her survive. I'd lost my baby sister to a monster; I couldn't lose this girl too. Far enough away, that I wouldn't endanger my life, but still close enough to watch, that's where I'd be. I took off and ducked behind a group of tall bushes, safely concealed by the thick evergreens.

Footsteps, voices, and squeaky wheels moved closer to my hiding spot. The fear of being caught played kick-the-can with my insides. I hunkered down farther and waited until the black and red uniforms of the VAU agents passed by before peeking my head out.

Five years ago, before the start of the Eradication, I would have lent a hand to the humans to save her life. That was before a few greedy vamps started their own all-you-can-eat blood buffet and all of humanity turned against us. Now vampires weren't allowed out of the shadows. If you were found, you were executed. No questions asked. No slaps on the wrist. No second chances. No begging for mercy, because mercy didn't exist for creatures of the night.

"I did what I could to help her. Now it's their turn," I reminded myself and leaned out farther from between the heavy foliage.

The medical experts hurried to the injured girl's side and officers closed off the area with yellow crime scene tape. A stout man in his late thirties, dressed in a charcoal grey pinstriped suit, with a cockeyed red tie, ran his hand through his short wavy dark hair before stopping in front of Reaper. They shook hands, and patted each other on the back, the way old friends do.

"James, it's been too long." Reaper's voice carried over the hustle of the emergency team. Both men turned and watched the paramedics work around the girl, checking her pulse, heart rate, and wound. "I wish it were under better circumstances."

"I've called. You haven't answered." The detective's words were laced with concern.

Reaper looked at his gleaming black combat boots before answering. "It's been difficult."

The detective placed his hand on Reaper's shoulder then slowly let it fall away. "What happened here, Reaper?" The detective's baritone voice switched from concerned friend to the commanding tone of a man who was used to being in charge.

"My friend and I were out walking and found her like this."

The detective looked around the park.

"Where's your friend now?"

"Sent her home. The blood was too much."

The detective pinched the bridge of his nose, and blew out his breath. "God damn it, Blake."

Blake? Must be Reaper's real name. File that away for future torment.

"You did this for three years. You know I need to talk to every witness. Immediately."

Reaper had been a VAU agent? Shit. Maybe I shouldn't work so hard to piss him off.

You should never put your trust in a human.

I don't have a choice. Caleb stuck me with him the same day he stuffed you into my subconscious.

I went back to listening to Reaper's conversation. "I can give you all the information you need."

The detective's narrowed eyes said he wasn't buying it. "She's a witness. I need to talk to her too. Hear her side of the story. Find out if she saw anything. Heard anything. You know the protocol."

"I don't think I can bring her in."

"What are you hiding?"

"Nothing" The word left Reaper's mouth like a bullet from a gun.

"I've known you since we were eighteen years old." The detective put his hand on Reaper's shoulder and gave it a shake. "We've been through war and tragedy together. I can tell when you're feeding me a line of shit. Bring her to the station tomorrow night."

No way. He can't bring me in the station. Tell him, Reaper. "I'll try." He'll try? Was he insane? Had he lost his marbles?

The paramedics loaded the girl on a stretcher and covered her face with an oxygen mask. A large bandage covered her neck and a mobile heart rate monitor beeped at her side.

They stopped next to Detective Coleman. "The scene's all yours."

He rested his hand on the girl's calf and closed his eyes. Moments passed before he reopened them. "Thanks. Please keep me posted on her condition." He nodded to the paramedic.

They wheeled her toward my hiding spot. I hid deeper in the bushes, and pushed aside the limbs and leaves, hoping to see her wound, check if it was still healing, but it was covered tight. I worried that my decision to help her would bite me in the ass.

"Tomorrow night?" I couldn't tell if Coleman's words were a question or a command.

Reaper shrugged.

"Don't brush me off." Coleman rubbed the back of his neck. "I need your witness. This isn't the first girl attacked, but she's the first we found alive."

I didn't have to hear Reaper's next words to know that we would be making a visit to the VAU. "I promise, we'll be there." Reaper extended his hand and the detective shook it. "I'll leave you to your job." Then Reaper turned on his heels and walked away.

"See you tomorrow," Detective Coleman yelled after him.

Reaper passed my hiding spot. "Meet me at the car." He didn't even turn his head in my direction, just issued his order and continued walking.

I took a different trail through the trees and bushes because I was afraid I might have a close encounter with one of the many VAU agents lurking in the area.

Fifty feet away Reaper leaned against the hood of his muscle car, arms crossed over his chest, head down, lost in thought. When I approached he glanced up. The look on his face wasn't anger, or rage; it was despair, sadness. A look I wasn't used to associating with Reaper. Sometimes it's easy to forget he had a life other than our nightly vampire hunting expeditions.

He pushed off the car, and opened the passenger side door for me. His act of chivalry caught me off guard. "We need to talk." He slammed the door after I got in.

I fidgeted in my seat. Reaper with emotions made me nervous. On edge.

He didn't say anything until we pulled out of the parking lot and picked up speed on a deserted rural road. "We're going to the VAU tomorrow night."

"The hell we are." I crossed my arms over my chest.

"In the two years we've worked together I've never asked you for one single thing."

I flipped my hands out, palms up. "Why start now?"

"Because, I made a promise and I intend to keep it."

"Why should I get involved?"

"Don't you want to catch the monster who did that to those girls?"

And he got me. There still had to be an easier way than walking into a vampire execution chamber. "Why didn't you tell me you were a VAU agent?"

Because the vampire hating human would love to see you fry like the ones he helped fry before you.

I hated to admit it, but Eddie had a point.

"You never asked." Reaper responded.

"Are you setting me up?"

Reaper showed his pearly whites like he had a secret. Frankly, it was frightening. "What makes you think that?"

I help up my hand and began ticking off the reasons, starting with my middle finger. "One, you had me call the VAU tonight. Two, you neglected to tell me you are an ex-VAU agent. Three, You're insisting I visit the one place that could get me killed." I moved my fingers closer to his face. "Three very good reasons for me to be concerned."

Reaper smiled again. "Guess you'll have to wait and see."

"Asshole."

"So, you'll do it? For her?"

Damn him to hell. Of course I'd do it for her, for the young girl who looked like my baby sister. Saving girls like her was the reason I teamed up with Caleb in the first place. "Fine. But you owe me."

We pulled up to my place, but before opening the door, I said, "Meet me at the VAU station one hour past sundown."

"Can you pull this off?"

"Does it really matter to you if I can?"

"No."

"Then, just meet me at the station."

I slammed the car door and Reaper took off. Gravel kicked up from his tires and showered my shoes. There was no time to worry about Reaper's rude departure. I had a costume to prepare.

Chapter Six

Reaper was fucking late. Reaper was *never* late. The clock on the bank across the street from the VAU station read 7:32. One hour past sundown. When he finally showed up he better be bleeding profusely.

If he wasn't he would be.

I waited far back in a shadowed corner, hidden behind a large stone pillar and a potted fern, and rested my shoulder against the chipped brick wall and waited. My only company a daddy longlegs spinning a silky web in a corner.

Where the hell was he? The six bags of blood I guzzled to give myself a nice rosy complexion would only last so long. After all, I had to put on my best human disguise to walk into the VAU.

I tapped the toe of my gold sandal against the chilly concrete, and looked at the clock for at least the hundredth time that evening. 7:33.

The VAU. The one place any semi-intelligent vampire stayed away from, and here I was waiting to walk past the heavily guarded doors. I was beginning to question my own intelligence.

That makes two of us.

I gave Eddie the internal middle finger.

I wanted to believe everything would be okay. That I wouldn't end up as a pile of ash on the over-waxed linoleum floors or as the star of my own televised execution. But the annoying tremors that ran up and down my spine wouldn't let me.

Even hidden from the eyes of the agents walking in and out of the building I felt naked and exposed. I missed my leather and weapons.

My finger slid over the soft cotton of my red sundress and traced the branded angel wings on my hip. The familiar loops and curves of the raised skin comforted my frayed nerves.

The guards at the door stopped a man and pulled him off to the side. They patted down his exposed flesh, checked his canines, and searched his wrist for a pulse. Great, the VAU equivalent to the TSA.

I clenched my jaw, gritted my teeth. "Where the hell is he?"

Screw this. I don't care how much Reaper needed me to go in and talk to his old friend, I wasn't putting my life on the line.

I pushed against the wall, ready to leave my hidey-hole, but something held me back, refused to allow my sandal-clad feet to move from this spot.

The girl I saved and the one I couldn't. I owed it to them. The vampires I killed had been babies, probably out on their first hunt. That meant there was a Sire creating them. The escalated attacks meant there were more where they had come from. I needed to locate and stop them, and Coleman was my best option. I leaned back against the wall and continued to wait.

Coleman had knowledge that Reaper and I couldn't get from the scanners.

Hopefully he was in a sharing mood. Hell, hopefully I made it past the sniff test.

My vampire enhanced hearing heard the rumble of the Chevelle's engine come up the ramp of the parking garage. Seconds later, Reaper parked and slammed the door. When he was within arms reach I grabbed the back of his shirt and yanked him into my hidey-hole.

"You. Are. Late." Each word hissed through my clenched teeth.

Reaper shrugged and took a step back. His gaze traveled up my body, then back down and settled on my cleavage.

I placed my finger under his chin and lifted until his eyes met mine. "Up here." When he was once again focused on my face, I asked, "Are you sure this is necessary?"

"Did you watch the news? Do you want another girl attacked? Almost killed? This is your chance to help others like her." Dirty. Rotten. Bastard.

"Anyways, you're already here, and you look…" His eyes went on another journey before finishing his sentence. "It'll do."

"Can't we just call Coleman?"

Reaper stared at my breasts. "No, we…" his words trailed off.

"Reaper, focus."

"You look so…alive." He placed his hand over my heart. "Still not beating." His hands rested on my shoulders, their warmth seeping into my skin. "Cold as usual."

I shoved his hands off my body. "Knock it off. I'm not a science experiment."

"Is this what you looked like before you turned?" He started touching my arms.

"If I didn't know you were a blood sucker…"

This was ridiculous. I bared my fangs and growled.

Reaper's eyes widened and his heartbeat took off in a gallop. Spell broken. "We need to find another way." I turned and started to walk off.

He grabbed my arm, pulling me back into the shadows. This time when he looked at me the hatred seeped back into his eyes. I was once again Alexis the vampire. His hands fell away from my shoulders, taking their heat with them.

"You'll be fine."

"Says the human."

"All we have to do is make it past the guards at the entrance and the front desk."

"How are we going to manage that?"

"Just follow my lead."

I'm glad one of us was confident because every second closer to walking through the doors unnerved me. If I had a beating heart it would be ramming against my flesh.

"Anything I should know?"

"Keep your story simple. James is good at picking up on lies. The rest I'll help you with."

He placed a hand on the small of my back. I pushed back the last bit of doubt and walked one step closer to a vampire's nightmare. Even Eddie stayed silent.

We stepped out onto the sidewalk and started walking the thirty paces to the entrance. Guards flanked the doors, their machine guns loaded with silver bullets. Canisters of holy water hung from their utility belts and their eyes were covered with visors made from a special lens to keep them from being glamoured. The humans made it their business to know all our secrets.

Reaper pulled me close. "Pretend to cry." He pushed my face into his shoulder and patted the top of my head.

Who needed to pretend? I buried my face deeper into Reaper's neck and pretended to sob. Loud enough that every guard would hear.

"You're not trying to win an Oscar. Tone it down." He wrapped his arms around my shoulders and led me past the guards. "Poor thing, lost her fiancé to a vampire," Reaper said to the guards. I cried harder.

"Evil bastards." The guard answered and waved us past. They didn't even pay attention to the mountain of snot leaning on Reaper for support. Men hated dealing with tearful females.

The revolving door welcomed us into its octopus-like embrace and deposited us into the lobby. Every square inch of the puke green walls covered with vampire-hating propaganda. Emergency contact information in case of a vampire sighting. Human Only posters, advocating for an all-human society. And my personal favorite, 10 Safety tips to ward off a hungry vampire. I might have stepped closer to read their advice if I hadn't been afraid for my life.

A balding man sat behind a tall counter, a phone receiver at his ear. He looked up, smiled, and held up his index finger.

Reaper leaned over close to me. "Johnson. Family man. Desk jockey. Harmless."

Johnson placed the receiver back on the cradle, and stood. "Blake. How the hell are ya?" He offered his hand. "It's been what? Three years?"

"Almost. How are the wife and kids?" Reaper didn't understand that this was not the time for small talk.

Johnson picked up and placed a hand-made picture frame on the desk. Reaper picked it up and showed it to me. A red-haired woman and four red-haired kids smiled back at me.

I didn't care about his family, but pretended to be normal. "You have a beautiful family." He beamed like I told him he won the lottery.

Their small talk faded into white noise. I wanted to focus on what they were saying, but it was hard with the sound of the rubber on the bottom of the revolving door scraping along the floor. With each new turn I expected a pair of fangs to walk through and blow my cover. Because nothing said innocent human woman like glowing red eyes, fangs, and the personality of a serial killer.

Flumph. The door turned again. Just another VAU agent.

Flumph.

Man in a business suit.

Flumph.

Holy hell, get me out of here.

My hand inched toward Reaper's shirt to force him to move on, but I pulled it back before touching him. I didn't want to appear rude in front of Johnson.

After several moments, Johnson said, "Coleman's expecting you. Go on back." He reached under the desk and a shrill buzz sounded from the glass door off to our left. I jumped at the noise.

Reaper leaned in. "Relax. Employee entrance."

With a wave to Johnson, Reaper pushed open the door and the buzz stopped. I hesitated, unable to force my feet forward.

Reaper reached for my hand and for once I was happy to feel his flesh against mine. He pulled me over the threshold and led me past rows of desks filled with VAU agent after VAU agent. Reaper greeted some of the agents on our way through, but didn't stop to chit-chat. We entered a long hallway of doors and stopped at the second to last one. He knocked twice and then opened it.

Keep your lips zipped, I warned Eddie before we walked into Coleman's office.

I won't utter a syllable.

Detective James Coleman sat behind an old metal desk, surrounded by mountains of manila file folders. Two diplomas hung on the faded beige wall behind him, one from the police academy, the other from the VAU. There were no personal effects in the office, nothing to tell you who the man sitting across from us was. So far all I perceived was a man buried in work, who didn't mind clutter.

The detective looked up from his paperwork and glanced briefly at Reaper, but then turned his attention to me. Studying me. These guys were trained to notice anything out of the ordinary human appearance. I hoped my disguise held up under the scrutiny.

His facial expression didn't give any indication of his thoughts. He turned to Reaper and his smile turned friendly. "I can't tell you how happy I am to see you."

"Didn't want to let you down."

"Appreciate that." His attention turned back to me, the smile he gave Reaper wiped away.

"Who's your friend?" He walked around the desk and held out his hand. I really didn't want to touch his flesh, but I had to remember that whole acting normal thing. I rubbed my hand on my dress hoping to warm it up and placed it in his.

"I'm Alexis Black. So nice to meet a friend of Blake's." I was trying for harmless girl next door, but it sounded more like guilty suspect.

He let my hand drop. "It's nice to meet you, Alexis." He studied me for a moment. "You've got the most unusual eyes. Purple's not a color you see often."

Fuck. There was no way to hide my damaged retinas, the blood that mixed in with the blue of my eyes whenever I got nervous, turning them more periwinkle than blue. Thank the fates it wasn't a vampire trait, just another present from Caleb. Hopefully he didn't get any closer. "Contacts," I explained.

He gestured to a pair of beat up blue plastic chairs in front of his desk. "Mind if I ask you a couple of questions about last night?"

Guess the pleasantries were over. How disappointing. I was looking forward to making Detective Coleman my new best friend. "Not at all." I plastered my best I've-got-nothing-to-hide smile on my face.

He shuffled some files, pulled one out from the stack and placed it on the desk in front of him. He grabbed a pad of paper and a pen and leaned back in his chair with a creak. "Did you see any vampires last night?"

What a lead in. "No. None."

"Are you positive?"

"I'd remember if I saw a vampire."

The detective's eyes shifted back and forth between us. He leaned forward and tossed the paper and pen on the desk. "I find it hard to believe you didn't see one. Especially since vampires rarely leave anyone alive."

I crossed and uncrossed my legs. Settled my skirt around my thighs. Detective Coleman watched my every move. I willed myself to stop fidgeting, but the thought that Coleman suspected something had me on edge. "Maybe we scared them away."

"Two," he paused. Coleman's gaze tick-tocked between us. "Humans?"

Time for a quick change of subject. "Did the girl make it?"

"She's in the ICU and expected to make a full recovery."

I snuck a glance at Reaper. He was composed, like a robot, no emotion at all. "Has she said anything?" he asked.

"No. She can't remember a thing after the first bite."

Thank goodness for vampire pheromones and their ability to wipe a memory. "That's a shame." I lowered my eyes hoping to conceal my excitement that something had gone our way.

"We need to find the vampires responsible." Detective Coleman stared directly at me again. "Anything you'd like to share?"

I shook my head because my voice had packed up and gone on a trip with my nerve. Some big, tough vampire I was.

Reaper spoke up. "You mentioned other attacks last night. Same M.O.?"

Detective Coleman sat back and steepled his fingers under his chin, his eyes locked on mine. "We're keeping that information confidential, but yes. Two others in the past week. Only their victims didn't survive."

Damn. Three attacks in less than a week. Vampires didn't dare create a pattern, it draws attention, and attention in a post Eradication world is the last thing you'd want.

The detective nodded. "You know any vampires, Ms. Black?"

Ha! Eddie broke his vow of silence.

"Not a one." Besides the one sitting in front of him.

"Is there anything else you can tell me? Anything that will help the VAU catch the vampire responsible?"

I shook my head, mostly telling the truth. I didn't have any information that would be useful to Detective Coleman or the VAU, but I had learned something that would help me.

The detective slammed his fist on the desk, the impact causing the stack of folders to wobble, but they didn't topple. He stood and ran a hand through his hair. "Thanks for coming." His dismissal was abrupt.

Reaper stood and I pushed back my chair, moving next to him. Thankful this meeting was coming to an end. The farther I got from Detective Coleman, the VAU, and their arsenal of death, the better.

Detective Coleman pushed Reaper aside and stepped closer. Close enough to see the freckles I'd always hated. Close enough to see the frown lines my current life-style etched around my lips. Close enough to see the flecks of blood that swam in the ocean of my eyes. Close enough to learn my secret.

One step back gave me distance. Two steps back kept my secret safe.

I saw it in his eyes the moment he caught my unease, my discomfort. That look confirmed I'd never be able to hide my true identity.

The smile he gave said he knew all my deep, dark secrets. He held out his hand. I didn't want to shake it, but didn't have a choice. If I refused his suspicions would be confirmed. I knew what was coming the moment I slipped my palm into his. We were screwed. And here I was without my trusty dagger.

His index finger slid over my wrist and pressed down. He held it there for five seconds, just enough time. Shit. If he didn't suspect I wasn't human before, he did now. No pulse always gave it away. That's why they taught the VAU that handy maneuver.

"She doesn't seem like your type." His brown eyes hardened before he looked at Reaper. His grip on my hand tightened. I thought about yanking it away. Hell, I thought about tearing out his throat. But, acting on impulse would end badly for both of us. How did I get out of this mess with my fangs intact?

We could eat him. Problem solved. Eddie liked to think he had all the answers.

"Would Lorelei approve?" Coleman asked Reaper.

In half a second he was going to have a close encounter with Eddie if he didn't back down. I'm positive whoever Lorelei was she wouldn't approve of that either.

"Don't bring her into this." Reaper's voice was low, almost a growl. He reached down and grabbed Coleman's wrist. "Let her go."

While Coleman and Reaper worked through their Mexican standoff, I fought to tamp down my inner monster who wanted to turn them into human sushi rolls.

Coleman finally released my hand and took a step back. "I think we should get a beer sometime, Blake." Guy-code for, we need to have a talk.

"Sure, I'll call you." More guy-code for, not a chance.

"No. I'll call you." Reaper wasn't getting off that easily.

Reaper grabbed my hand. "Ready?" I nodded and he led us back through the maze of desks. I was tempted to turn and see if Coleman was watching us, but I fought against it, choosing to pretend he wasn't.

The ride home was quiet, both lost in our own thoughts. Mine a jumbled mess. Detective Coleman had rattled me, unnerved me, scared me. Would he turn me in? Hunt me down? Would I have to kill him?

"Coleman knows." Reaper's words surprised me out of my thoughts.

"What will he do?"

"Depends."

I wanted to strangle him, but instead I urged him on with a wave of my hand. "On what?"

"How useful he thinks you are."

"If I'm not?"

"I won't save your ass when he comes gunning for you."

What a reassuring thought. I hoped Detective Coleman caught his vamp and didn't need any further assistance.

And no matter how shitty that situation was, it wasn't our biggest problem. "We've got a nest," I said.

Eddie murmured in agreement.

"What makes you say that? Don't Sire's control the nest and all the vampires in it?"

Reaper's question reminded me of my time spent in the

world of nests and Sires. A time I thought I left behind when I fled Xavier, my Sire, and his land of twisted morals, but it looked like the universe wanted to pull me back in.

I rubbed the back of my neck and gave it a tight squeeze to release the tension that had built up in the muscles before I started with my explanation.

"Usually, but I think we have a nest that's missing its Sire. Those vampires we encountered the other night, they were newly turned, maybe three days old." My raised eyebrows wrinkled my brow. "If I'm right then they were hunting for the first time. Without a Sire they're surviving by instinct. They don't know the rules."

"The VAU knows the minimal amount about nests, but you were in when you were newly turned, you've got to know more. Know how they operate."

"More than I want to." I thought back to my time as a newly turned vampire and what it was like to hunt that very first time. Xavier teaching me the in's and out's of the undead hunting rituals. My reluctance, horror, and disgust of what it took to survive.

The humans are not to know this.

They have to if we want to find out who is doing this.

Then you will doom your race.

But protect another.

Eddie snarled in my head and I felt him fade back into the abyss that he lived

"A nest is the baby vampire's home, where a newly turned vampire is safe, secure, and totally protected. When a Sire takes his baby vamps out hunting, it's just the Sire and one protégé, never a pair or a group. The Sire uses that time to teach the vampire how to hunt, drink, and what rules apply to cleaning up after your meal." I slumped back into my seat, the cool leather offering me comfort from memories best forgotten.

"They never venture far from home, choosing to only hunt in a circle around the nest. That way they can always get back to safety if they are in danger. To find the nest, we just have to locate the center. Find an area with a large rate of sightings or attacks in all directions and follow the path to the middle."

Reaper nodded his head. "I'll start checking the scanners, reports, and maps. Tomorrow we'll start searching for the nest."

Reaper and I had a volatile personal relationship, but when it came to our working relationship we got shit done. I knew when he picked me up tomorrow night we'd be on our way to search for our rogue vampires, and one step closer to taking them out.

But our night wasn't finished I still needed to kill a supernatural and feed the beast.

Reaper and I agreed to make it fast, and headed to our good ol' stand by. A corner populated by willing blood donors, attached to a dark alley, perfect for a quick game of hide the fangs.

We parked the Chevelle a few blocks away and headed to the alley on foot. Past rows of businesses with protective gates over their entrances and windows, beggars sitting on the corner waiting for some loose change to fall into their gloved hands, and rows of homes the rest of the city would love to see torn down. Then we turned the corner and entered a pocket of the world that most of polite society didn't know existed.

It always surprised me, the sheer number of men and woman who volunteered to play cattle to the vampires. All addicted to the high and euphoria they experienced from a vampire's bite. Not just the bums and the homeless, but businessmen, homemakers, and college kids looking for a thrill.

Before the Eradication, Sanguine houses populated the city, legal places for the willing donors to live and vampires to feed. When the undead population became public enemy number one, the houses closed, but that didn't stop the humans from feeding their addiction. Nope, like any other addict, they just moved to secret locations. Locations like this one.

All I needed was one misbehaving vampire, and then I was free to leave.

Eddie stirred at the first whiff of blood and vampire. Creeping to the surface, anticipating payment.

My favorite time of day.

That makes one of us.

I slipped into the shadows at the back of the alley and waited for the sounds of struggle. It didn't take long before the sound of fabric ripping, and frightened protests filled the cramped quarters.

I focused on the sounds and found my target not more than twenty feet away. Pulling out my stake, I casually strolled past the vampires who were behaving, and moved closer to my target. Standing behind him, I plunged the stake through his back, straight into his heart, and watched him disintegrate into flames and ash.

One less undead asshole in the world.

Eddie settled deep into the background, satisfied with the single kill that my contract required.

The girl, not more than seventeen, clutched her ripped shirt to her breasts. "He hadn't paid me yet." Her unappreciative tone angered me.

I dug deep into my purse, pulled out a few crumbled bills and threw them at her feet. "Next time get payment up front," I shot back and stormed out of the alley.

I didn't talk on the way home, and Reaper didn't ask about my shitty mood. I wanted to forget everything that had happened tonight, starting with the VAU visit, ending with the ungrateful blood whore.

We pulled up to my apartment. I left Reaper and went upstairs to my home, happy to have the rest of the evening to be able to sit and relax. A very rare occurrence in my life, and I was taking advantage of it. Hot bath, cheesy movie, bag of blood, and then off to bed at a decent hour.

The rickety service elevator arrived at the second floor. I

pulled back the cage door, but before I stepped off I knew something was wrong. The hunched back, hissing kitty was my first clue.

The ghost hovering in the middle of my living room was my second.

Chapter Seven

Holy fucking shit! There was a ghost in my living room. And not just any ghost. Nathan.

A rocket-propelled lump plopped into my stomach. *Plunk.*

I wanted to run to him. Wrap my arms around him. Hold him. I wanted to do all that, but my feet were frozen to the floor and my jaw hung open.

My fangs clicked against each other when I snapped my mouth closed to stop the drool from running out of my mouth, and I forced my brain to process words. Speech eluded me unlike the stake that I drove through Nathan's heart. What are the appropriate words when faced with the apparition of the vampire whose death you were one hundred percent responsible for? Unpeeling my fingers from the elevator cage, I twirled the platinum ring, Nathan's ring, on my thumb and walked closer.

How was it possible that Nathan was here? In my home. In the…well, not flesh.

Nathan's ghostly form was unlike anything I'd ever seen before, and not at all what I thought a ghost would look like. Sure, he was transparent, and hovering two feet over the wood floors, but a small part of him was solid, still very corporeal. His heart.

"It's not possible." I reached out and touched his arm, surprised when my fingers rested on his wrist.

Tiny sparks of blue and purple shot out from where we touched. His body became solid. It started around his heart, a wave that spread out until every inch of him looked like it did when he was alive. I jumped, pulling my hand back, and he began to fade away again.

"How…" I stuttered. "How did you do that?"

"No. Bloody. Idea." His words slow and enunciated, but his

wide, round eyes showed that he was at freak-out level seventeen.

I placed my hand over his heart. It beat under my touch, a slow thump that shouldn't have been there. More sparks shot out from under my palm. A jolt of energy ran up my arm, lifting the fine black hairs. It raced through my body, sending a hum of electricity though me. Crackles and pops, like a bursting campfire filled the room.

"How did you get here?" I walked around Nathan's ghostly form, astonished that I had a second chance to tell him how sorry I was. How much his death scarred me.

Nathan turned to face me. "This is just where I appeared when I woke up."

"Where have you been for the last two days?"

"Two days?" His voice entered teenage girl at a sleepover territory.

"You die…" The word tripped over my tongue. I cleared my throat and forced it out. "Died two nights ago."

He shot straight up from the couch, his head going through the ceiling leaving his legs dangling over my head. Once he extracted himself, he began floating around the room. "Not possible. Right after the stake pierced my heart I came here."

"No you didn't."

"Then where was I?"

I didn't have the energy to figure out the mysteries of the universe so I ignored his question. "Have you tried to go anywhere else?"

He stopped in the middle of the room. Closed his eyes, scrunched his nose, and made some grunting sounds. His body began to fade, starting at the edges and moving inward, slowly, all the way to the solid area around his heart that beat in a slow rhythm, something it hadn't done in over three hundred years. The last bit of transparency disappeared and all that was left was the Ramone's logo on his shirt, then that disappeared too.

Pop.

The light fixture shook, bottles of blood clinked in the refrigerator, and my apartment had a tiny Nathan-induced earthquake, then he returned.

"Where'd you go?"

"Nowhere. Maybe I'm not doing it right." His loudly spoken words shook with panic. "It's not like being a ghost came with an instruction manual."

This time Nathan settled his smoky form over the couch, crossed his legs, made with his best "I dream of Jeannie" pose and took two deep breaths. His eyelids closed over his golden pupils, lips pursed, hands gently placed in his lap. The edges shimmered, blurred, faded.

Pop.

Back again. Biting his bottom lip between his teeth. Chest rising and lowering. Fist clenching and unclenching. All that was missing was the puffs of smoke coming from his ears. I wondered if he was counting to ten in his head.

"Why can't I fucking go anywhere?" If his word were any shaper they would have cut me to shreds.

"What happened?"

"Weren't you watching?"

My eyebrows lifted and I nailed him with my best don't-get-pissy-with-me look.

"I can't leave."

I placed my hand on his shoulder and our personal firework display started right up.

"Why does that happen when we touch?"

"No sodding idea. Every time you touch me it's a jolt to my heart."

My fingers left his body and he returned to his ghostly form. I flopped on to the couch and played with the ring again. Stressed. Confused. Exhausted. On top of being a freaky vampire I was also some sort of ghost jumper cable. Could my life get any more complicated?

"We'll get it figured out." I tried to sound optimistic because

Nathan looked like he was about to lose whatever sanity he had left. "Until then it looks like we'll be roommates." I placed my hand on his knee. He solidified.

"Just like old times, except this time I'm dead. Well, dead, dead, not just undead."

This seemed like the best opportunity to acknowledge the eight-thousand pound elephant sitting on my chest. "Nathan, about your death…"

He touched his finger to my lips and shocked me. I pulled back and rubbed the flesh that the electricity had run through. He held his hand up and turned it from side to side. "What's done is done. At least I bit it in my favorite t-shirt." Nathan pointed to the platinum circle on my thumb. "Is that my wedding band?"

"I pulled it out of the ashes."

"I was looking forward to seeing her again." His voice lowered. "Main reason I wanted to die." He cleared his throat and settled next to me on the couch. "Let's watch the tube."

He was taking this pretty well. I picked up the remote and began channel surfing.

Living with Nathan wouldn't be that bad. Hell, it wasn't the first time either. I stayed with him for ten years when I first came to Chicago. Having company would be good for me. And best of all, I had Nathan back, even if he was transparent, and I didn't have to kill him again.

Yeah. This could be fun.

"Do you get any porn channels?" Okay, maybe not.

The morning light crept into the room. Time for bed. I didn't know if ghosts slept, but I needed to. I said good night to my friend. Happy to have him back in my life, although I'm not sure he felt the same.

———————

I SPENT the next evening on my small bricked-in balcony

surrounded by foliage and flowers; it overlooked the world around me. Twenty minutes of peace. Twenty minutes of contemplation. Twenty minutes of assault rifles and Sigourney Weaver blowing alien guts up all over space.

Sounds blared from my surround sound and Raja's body tensed with each gunshot. I stroked her fur to reassure her. Finally, she curled into a tight ball and started to purr. Wish I had someone to rub my fur.

I tried to ignore the sounds coming from inside and took a sip of my mug o' blood. The city skyline kept me company while the human world below prepared to settle in for the night.

Mine was just getting started.

A horn blared from below and I glanced over the railing and watched the cars play chicken on the abandoned streets. I downed the rest of my breakfast and slid back the sliding glass door and peeked in at my roommate. His ghostly form sprawled across the couch, eyes focused on the big screen hanging on the wall, hand securely tucked down his pants like a ghostly Al Bundy.

"Hey, Nate. I'm going to get ready for work." When he didn't acknowledge me I added, "You going to be okay today?"

He brushed me off with a wave of his hand.

Half an hour later, showered, dressed, and ready for a night of hunting, I walked out of my room. The couch was empty. I wandered through the living room and into the kitchen, searching for Nathan the friendly ghost. He hovered in the middle of the room, fading in and out, over and over again. Every time he came back the room shook.

"Nathan?"

He popped back in. "Thought I'd try again."

"No luck?"

He rubbed the back of his neck and shook his head. "None."

I laid my hand on his shoulder, the sparks shot between us. I wanted to comfort him, like he had done a thousand times for me in the past, before the stake pierced his heart, but I didn't know how. "We'll figure this ghost thing out. I promise."

His lopsided smile didn't meet his eyes.

"I'll be back before sunup." I walked to the elevator and pulled back the cage.

With one last look at Nathan, I pushed the button and started down. I shouldn't feel guilty about leaving him, after all he was older than me by one hundred and fifty years, but I did.

The night was beautiful, full of stars, so I decided to walk the eight blocks to the gym. I'd taken ten steps when I heard a familiar pop.

Standing in front of me, wearing the same what-the-fuck expression I imagined mirrored my own, was Nathan.

"Aw. Bloody hell."

And there went the tiny bit of hope that the situation with Nathan would be easy. "Looks like you go where I go."

"But the next movie was just about to start."

For eight blocks I listened to Nathan grumble about the injustice of being a ghost who couldn't do as he pleased. By the time we got to the gym my eye twitched and I contemplated finding an exorcist.

I needed to punch something.

Reaper greeted me at the door and I wondered if he could see Nathan, who now floated in and out of the punching bags hanging from the ceiling, like it was his personal obstacle course, but Reaper never glanced in his direction. "Let's get this over with," he said.

Without any warning I attacked. Fist headed right at his nose, but the fast bastard grabbed it and pushed me away. I went back for more. We sparred back and forth, kicks, punches, and blocks. The workout was just what I needed to get rid of the edge.

When I felt more in control I said, "There have been some developments."

"About the attacks?"

"No."

Reaper turned his back on me, and walked to the other side of the gym. Obviously un-interested in my developments. "I've got a ghost attached to me."

That earned me a you've-completely-lost-it look from across the gym.

"I'm serious. The vampire I...um..." I stopped to think about the next words that would leave my mouth since the vampire in question was right across the room. "The vampire I killed the other night, Nathan. He turned up in my apartment yesterday."

Reaper started working a punching bag in the corner. "A ghost that used to be a vampire now lives in your apartment?"

"Yes, and he's right here." I pointed to where Nathan was standing.

Reaper stopped beating up the bag and massaged his temples. "Did you drink some bad blood today?"

Fine, he needed proof. I placed my hand on Nathan's shoulder. The sparks flew and he appeared.

Reaper's head jerked back. "Shit."

"This is Nathan."

Reaper walked around Nathan, head bobbing up and down while he checked him out. "He looks like a bad imitation of Billy Idol."

"And you're the tosser she's stuck working with?"

I didn't have the patience for male posturing. "Knock it off." I steeled my gaze at Reaper, and then at Nathan. "Both of you." Once I was sure they would behave I continued on with my explanation. "It seems Nathan is tied to me some how. Where I go he goes."

Nathan gave Reaper the finger over my shoulder. Great, the ghost wanted to antagonize the hot head. This situation had disaster tattooed all over it. There was no way I was going to spend every night refereeing the two of them. I took my hand off Nathan's arm. Problem solved.

"Hey." Nathan protested.

I turned to him. "We don't have time for a pissing match. We have a Sire-less nest to locate."

Reaper shot a last glance in Nathan's direction. "I've been researching the police records of the area surrounding the park. There are several with high attack rates, so I chose one at random to start with. Make-Out Creek is our first stop, lots of activity in the area. No deaths yet, but a lot of vampire related injuries."

I grabbed my leather duster off a pile of gym mats. "Sounds like a good place to start."

Reaper grabbed the rest of the gear and headed to the car. A vampire, a human, and a ghost. Sounded like the beginning of a bad joke.

Chapter Eight

Bare breasts and butts. That was the view on our walk through Make-Out Creek, as the humans liked to call this little section of dense forest that ran along one of the many streams that made up the Illinois landscape. The tall pines and oaks provided the perfect camouflage for the sex-starved teenagers to get hot and heavy under, behind and in-between.

Nathan and I followed Reaper through the woods. I tried to shield my eyes from the sights, unlike Nathan who didn't have a problem with PDA. He pointed to a couple half a second away from penetration. "Why weren't girls this slutty when I was young?" he whispered, even though I was the only one who could hear him.

"In the 1700's? Not likely."

"Damn shame," he muttered, and left to enjoy the rest of his little private peep show. I guess I should be happy he couldn't join in, unless he figured out how to possess a body. Let's hope that never happened.

Reaper stopped and waited for me to catch up. "Getting anything?"

I waited for any sign from Eddie, but he stayed quiet in his corner of my mind. "Not yet. But that doesn't mean they aren't out there."

We continued to walk along the rock-covered ground in silence. Nathan popped in and out causing slight tremors that none of the teenagers seemed to notice. Probably thought they were making the earth move with their naughty bits.

I turned a corner and Eddie gave me a poke that kicked the breath out of my lungs. I smelled the vampires before I saw them, held up three fingers behind my back and waited for

Reaper to back away. Eddie was ready to fight and clawed at my insides for control.

Not yet.

You must release me. I must fight.

Pain flared through my chest as I held him back just a moment longer.

A trio of vampires turned the corner and stopped when they saw me blocking their path.

A burly vampire, who looked like Arnold Schwarzenegger, if Arnold was a foot shorter and suddenly sprouted fangs, spoke up. "Hey, pretty lady, want to play?"

Either I hadn't gone full beast mode yet or the steroids had shrunk his brain instead of his balls.

One of his buddies, wearing a letterman jacket and a pair of jeans with holes in the knees, pointed at me and he cleared his throat. "Dude, that's the assassin." But no amount of vampire bravado could hide his fear.

Arnold looked at me and then at his friend. "Can't be. Sire told us she was dead."

I was going to kill the person who started that rumor.

"What do we do?" Arnold asked.

"Kill her." A third vampire spoke up, this guy didn't belong with the others, he was a hard goth, piercings and tattoos on every available inch of skin, and a Mohawk that stood at least a foot from his head. He stuck two fingers between his black lipstick colored lips and let out a long high-pitch whistle.

Two more vampires stepped out of the foliage. That made five. I've seen worse. Hell, Eddie was looking forward to a work-out. I turned and sized up my opponents. The two that joined the party were dressed in business suits. What a mismatched group of misfits. But they all had one thing in common—the looks of a newly turned vampire, just like the ones at the park. The nest had to be close.

Another loud whistle and three more vampires walked up

the path behind me, dressed in the finest homeless attire the streets had to offer. Eight. Not the best odds, but still doable.

Reaper moved to step forward and join the fight, but I waved him back. All his presence would do is distract me.

The whistle happy vampire raised his fingers to his lips again. There was no way he was making another sound.

Get ready. Get set. I let Eddie free.

I moved faster than their eyes could track me, grabbed his neck and twisted. Without the help of his spine to hold his head up, it flopped to the side and his body slid to the ground, before another sound left his mouth. I pulled out my stake and stabbed him in the heart. He dissolved into a pile of ash at his friend's feet.

"She killed Raymond," Arnold said, his jaw hanging open. "I didn't even see her move."

I spun in a slow circle to get a good look at the seven vampires who now surrounded me. All young. All hungry. All eager to die. I expected Eddie to settle down now that my contract had been fulfilled for the evening, but instead the beast clawed at my insides, fighting to get free, and ready to rip them to shreds.

This had never happened before, usually when I killed one, the beast went back to his rotten depths and I was free to move on with my night. Tonight he wouldn't settle for less than eight dead piles of ash decorating the leaf-covered ground.

I closed my eyes, took five deep cleansing breaths, and hoped the urge to kill would dissipate. But, the smell of the seven leftover vampires pushed the beast to the surface.

Death. The only thing that would push the beast into submission. But could I take on seven vampires and survive?

Seven vampires is nothing compared to the power that flows through your body. If only you would learn to work with me instead of fight me, we would never fail.

A brave, or stupid vampire, depending on how you looked at it, reached into the back pocket of his faded jeans and pulled out a switchblade. Two inches of silver glistened in the moonlight. He'd have to do better than that, but a game of whose blade is bigger sounded like fun. I reached back, pulled Reva out of her sheath and held my dagger up high. His eyes widened and the other vampires snickered from the sideline. Probably thanking the fates for not stepping up first.

Even after seeing my weapon he charged, fangs bared, claws extended. I swung my sword and left a large gash across his chest, right over his heart. Blood pumped from the wound and drenched the front of his t-shirt. The switchblade fell from his fingers and landed on the pine needle covered ground. He glanced down and I used the distraction to shish kabob his heart with my stake. His body fell next to his blade and turned into a pile of ash.

"Who's next?" I asked his stunned buddies.

Two vampires walked into the middle, empty-handed, so I put Reva away to give them a fighting chance. They came at me, one from the front, one from the rear. The vampire behind me grabbed my arms and wrenched them behind my back. The one in front threw a punch at my stomach, but before his fist connected with my midsection, the bottom of my boot connected with his chin. He went down and stayed down. He was either stunned or feeling foolish, it was impossible to tell. I slammed the back of my head into the other's nose. Blood gushed all over my hair, which immediately started a case of dry heaves. He released his hold and I spun around, stake in hand. I slammed the stake into his chest, but I didn't stay to watch him disintegrate. Instead, I walked over to his wounded friend and slammed the stake through his heart.

Four down. Eddie sounded proud.

I didn't have a chance to turn around before I heard a war cry that would make Braveheart proud, then felt the vampire cling to my back. The momentum sent my dagger and stake skittering out of reach. He wrapped his hand around my throat, knee deep in my back, holding me down. I reached up and grabbed any part of his shirt that I could hold on to, flipped him over the top of my head and onto the ground. He landed with an *oomph.*

But he didn't stay down. He charged again, head hitting me in the stomach, taking us down in a tangle of limbs. He sat on my chest and wrenched my hands over my head. One of the remaining vampires stepped close, but the vampire holding me down snarled. "My kill."

I like him.

Of course, Eddie liked him, he thrived on killing and mayhem. The other vampire backed away, leaving him to his prize.

Without Reva or my hands, I seemed to be out of options. The vampire leaned close, fangs snapping, aimed for my exposed neck. Making a grave error.

I raised my head, grabbed his ear between my teeth and tore it from his head. Blood gushed over my face, the vampire let go, hand covering the missing chunk. I scurried out from under him and collected my fallen weapons.

I rushed him, stake in line with his heart.

"Bitch." He managed to utter that single word before I staked him and moved on to my next victim.

The last three stood in a line. They looked from one to another, clearly working out who was going to take me on next. Eddie scraped his claws along my spine. Time to kill these three worthless vampires and save the day.

No one stepped forward, so I made the first move. One second I stood ten feet away, the next Reva made Swiss cheese out of two of the vampires' hearts until they were nothing but smoldering piles of ash on the ground.

That left one little vampire in my clutches, Arnold. My stake aimed at his heart, just about to send it home.

"Stop." Reaper walked out from the bushes and stood next to me. "Let's get some information." He pushed my stake so the tip pointed to the ground.

Eddie growled.

I lowered my hand, but didn't let go of his shirt.

Nathan popped in at that exact moment, bumping into my side and lighting up the surrounding area with tiny sparks. Arnold almost fainted. He pointed at Nathan. "What the fuck?"

"The bloke can see me." A big grin spread across Nathan's face.

"Is that a ghost?" Arnold stuttered.

"Damn skippy I'm a ghost."

"Ghosts are real?" he asked. I was beginning to believe he was dropped as a baby.

Nathan answered for me. "You're a vampire, but you don't believe in ghosts?"

"I've only been a vampire for three days. Tonight was my first night out."

What he was saying made sense. It took one night for vampire blood to annihilate the human blood, and then another night for all the organs to die. By the third you were so hungry you'd naw through your own arm to get your first sip of blood.

"This was your first hunt?" I asked.

He nodded. Bad luck for him. First night out and he ran into me. "Why did you come here?"

"I used to come here when I was human. I was hoping to find my ex-girlfriend, you know since I was a bad ass vampire now. Plus,"—He flashed some baby fangs —"we were told to stay close."

This meant we'd just stumbled into their Sire's recruiting ground. I looked at Reaper and he looked at me. There was no reason to tiptoe around the question we wanted answered so I just came out and asked. "Where's your nest?"

"I'm not supposed to tell anyone." He turned his head to avoid my eyes.

"I'll let you live if you tell me." The lie hidden behind my sugar-coated voice.

"Really?"

"Really." Thank the Fates I let the clueless one live.

He looked back and forth between Nathan, Reaper, and me. I gave him a little shake to encourage him to make up his mind.

"It's a pale green house on Martin Street. The number's fifteen-six-oh-two."

I watched as Reaper typed the information into his phone. I just had one last question for our little friend. "Who told you I was dead?"

"Our Sire, Terrance."

My fingers clenched around the stake at my side. "Did he say who killed me?"

"Called the guy Delano."

Reaper stiffened at my side. Nathan stopped floating. I stood slacked jawed. And Eddie. Well, Eddie laughed. If this young vamp was talking about Delano Melazi, we were fucked.

All that aside, why would Delano claim to have killed me? And why would he lie to his protégé? Those were questions for another time. Right now, I was getting sick of holding onto my muscular friend and Eddie was itching to finish him off. "Reaper, any more questions?"

"Nope."

The vampire relaxed. I raised my hand and drove the tip of the stake through his heart. I felt bad for killing such an innocent creature, but leaving him alive would cause us more problems. Vampires were loyal to their Sires, which meant he would be required to tell him about what happened and what he told us. I needed the element of surprise on my side. Arnold had to die.

Nathan watched his body turn to ash. "Bloody duffer, that one was."

Now that Eddie was satiated, he settled into the background with a purr of contentment, making me feel like myself again. "Obviously, Terrance isn't considering IQ's when he chooses them."

Reapers pocket started to vibrate. He pulled out his phone,

and immediately his face paled. "Coleman." He pushed the talk button and walked deeper into the trees.

While we waited for Reaper to come back I explained who Detective Coleman was to Nathan.

"You willingly walked into the VAU station?" Nathan seemed impressed. "You've got some big cajones, Alexis Black."

Before I could bask in Nathan's compliment, Reaper came back looking like someone had just pissed in his morning cup of coffee. "He wants us to meet him at the City Morgue. He specifically asked that you come too."

And here I was thinking he just wanted to have that beer with Reaper. "Did he tell you why?"

"He didn't get into details, just said, and I quote,"—He did the annoying finger quote thing—"'I need your pointy tooth friend at the morgue, a.s.a.p.'"

Shit. I really didn't want to go to the morgue, nothing good could come out of this visit. "Can we ignore his request?"

"We can." He looked around at the still smoldering piles of ash. "But it might be an opportunity to learn more to keep the innocents safe."

And once again my need to save anyone else from a forced vampire life-style, from years of pain, anger, and unwanted blood sucking, bowled over by my sense of self-preservation. "Looks like we're going to see my favorite VAU agent again."

After a few more trips through lover's lane to ensure we eliminated all the vampires, and kept the horny teenagers of the Chicago land area safe for another night, we made a pit stop at my place so I could work my magic and make myself look a little more human. Jeans and a Ting Ting's concert T-shirt, instead of the usual black leather seemed more human and less creature of the undead. Not that it mattered, Detective Coleman already knew my secret, but I wasn't ready to announce it to the rest of the VAU.

Chapter Nine

I must have lost my damn blood-sucking mind. Here I stood outside the morgue, waiting to meet the VAU agent who suspected I was a vampire, and I wasn't scared at all. In fact, I felt an eerie sense of calm.

Reaper, Nathan, and I walked through the double metal doors of the plain brick building and entered a lobby decorated in various shades of dull beige and not much else. It was as depressing as...well, a morgue.

Nathan moved around the room peeking behind doors and under the receptionist's desk. "Never thought I'd see the inside of a morgue."

Technically it was just the waiting room, but who was I to burst his bubble?

Detective James Coleman sat in one of the uncomfortable chairs. He placed his outdated copy of Sports Illustrated on a veneer coffee table, stood, and smoothed the creases out of his black dress pants. "Glad you could make it." Since his gaze never met mine, I was sure it wasn't me he was glad to see.

"Follow me." He walked toward us, making sure to give me a wide berth. Fine with me. I'd rather he keep the stake that hung from the holster on his belt to himself.

Reaper and I followed him into the elevator. He pushed a button labeled with the letter "M" and leaned against the wall. There was an uncomfortable silence as we descended into the lower levels.

Nathan floated close to Coleman's face. "He's got a real stick up his arse."

I disguised my laugh behind a cough that caused Coleman and Reaper to look in my direction. After a few more fake coughs Coleman went back to ignoring me, but Reaper continued to look at me like I was having a seizure.

"Nathan," I mouthed, and pointed in the ghost's direction.

Reaper reached up and rubbed his temples.

Thankfully the elevator opened and we followed Coleman into a long hallway with one single door at the end. As we got closer I saw the word morgue printed across the front, and the words "meat locker" written on a piece of duct tape just below that. The detective pushed the doors open and we went in.

A gurney sat in the center of a sterile looking room. Metal drawers filled one wall and various instruments that looked like they could inflict some serious damage filled another. A tall man with eyes so blue the ocean would be envious, and ruggedly handsome face covered with a few days worth of stubble, stood next to the gurney. I allowed myself a moment to admire his nearly perfect physique; it was unfortunate that his white lab coat covered all the good parts.

"This is Doctor Julian Monroe, head M.E for the VAU." Hot and smart, good combo.

The doctor stepped forward and shook Reaper's extended hand, but when I offered mine he looked down, hiding the fear that flickered in his eyes, and turned away.

If I had any interest in getting laid, the good Doctor would have jumped to the top of my to-do list, but judging by the fear that now permeated the small room, I wasn't his type. He probably went for short blondes with big tits and a beating heart. The exact opposite of me.

"Why is she here?" The rhythm of the Doctor's heart picked up and his hand trembled when he pointed in my direction.

He was terrified. But why? I usually only got that response from the supernatural. A quick sniff test told me the only stench of the non-human variety was coming from me. Had Coleman told him I was vampire? Probably. I gave him a reassuring smile, hoping to calm his nerves, but the moment his eyes met mine he lowered his gaze and stared at his scuffed loafers.

"Someone doesn't like you," Nathan sing-songed, going from one torture device to another. I ignored him because I didn't think talking to a ghost would make this situation any less tense.

"This is Ms. Black. She's a witness," Coleman said in my defense.

"Not to this girl's death," Monroe said.

"Let's just say I believe she's an expert when it comes to vampires." Coleman lowered his chin and looked at me through lowered lashes.

I kept uncharacteristically quiet.

He approached the gurney with the body shaped lump under the white sheet. "Doctor, would you please."

Doctor Monroe reached out and grabbed the edge of the sheet, but before he pulled the heavy fabric back he looked right at me. I was lucky the daggers in his eyes were imaginary otherwise the cleaning crew would be sweeping up a pile of Alex ash off the floor tonight. Once the silent death stare was over, he pulled the sheet back to reveal the dead girl from the park I failed to rescue.

"Can you explain to Blake and his *friend* what you noticed during your examination?" The emphasis on the word friend was not lost on me.

The doctor shot one last look in my direction and cleared his throat. "Happy to." Dr. Monroe's now fear-free deep voice sent tingles to my nether regions.

He lowered the sheet and pointed with the tip of a pen to the inside of her thighs. To the human eye the fang marks were barely detectable, but to my vampire-enhanced sight they stood out like a homing beacon. Tiny punctures, at least twenty-four, ran up and down her thigh like someone had used her as a pincushion and then tried to heal the wounds.

Some vampires had a bit of fun. Eddie's words disgusted me.

Nathan popped out of one of the drawers where they stored the dead bodies and floated next to me. He drew his breath through his teeth. "Bloody hell. I've never seen anything like that."

I agreed. Even the blood whores at the Sanguine Houses were treated better.

"What am I supposed to be seeing?" Reaper asked.

Doctor Monroe pulled a thin, black flashlight from his pocket. "Detective, would you get the lights." The room went dark and an ultraviolet ray lit up the tiny pinpricks for the humans to see.

"We discovered these during a routine exam. Twenty-six sets to be exact. " He used the end of a pen and pointed out each-and-every set. "There are also bites on her breasts and neck. She died from extreme blood loss, but not an ounce was found on her clothes or skin. In other words, she was drained completely."

Detective Coleman's eyes fixed on me for the first time. "That's too many bites for one vampire. Don't you think?"

"Why are you asking me?" I held out my hands, palms up. Totally innocent.

"Because I think you know more than you're telling me."

I had to applaud him for his honesty, but why didn't he just come out and say what he was thinking. "The first time I saw this girl was in the playground and she was already dead."

"That brings up another point," Doctor Monroe interrupted the tension. "She wasn't killed at the park. Her death occurred at least two days prior to the night you found her."

Shit. The girl had been the main course at a feeding frenzy. Brought back to the nest and served up as dinner. But why dump her body at the park? It didn't make sense.

"Are you ready to tell me the truth?" Coleman asked.

"I've told you all I can."

Coleman walked closer to the body and pointed at the marks. "In all my years with the VAU I have never seen an attack like this." The anger in his voice fully directed at me.

He obviously hadn't been raised in a nest of newly turned

vampires. Hunger is the driving force when you wake up. Without a Sire to control the urges, something like what happened to the girl on the gurney could happen easily.

I stole a glance at Reaper, hoping for some assistance, but he didn't or wouldn't meet my gaze. "What makes you think I have?"

He left her side and leaned next to my ear, his voice barely a whisper, just loud enough for me to hear, but not anyone else. "You and I both know the answer to that question."

I didn't know what to say. There was no way I was admitting to being a vampire, not here, not now, and certainly not to him.

He stepped back when he realized I wasn't going to answer him. "You told me you didn't see anyone at the park, but Doctor Monroe found vampire ash on her clothes."

"That could have happened when the vamps were feeding from her. Maybe things got rough, one of them died," I countered.

"I thought the same thing, but then I had them examine the survivor's clothes and she was covered with ash as well."

"What does that prove?" I knew he was leading me down a slippery slope, but all I could do was follow.

"Forensics says the ash belongs to two different vampires." He allowed me a minute to digest this new information before he continued on. "The DNA confirms it."

That dropped bomb exploded in my stomach "Vampires leave DNA?"

Doctor Monroe answered me this time. "They were human once and DNA doesn't change." Well shit, I guess it was still possible to learn something new, even after one hundred and seventy-three years.

Vampire DNA. The humans are learning more about our race then they should be allowed.

We know all their secrets, shouldn't they know ours?

No.

Detective Coleman came closer. "You know what else we found?"

"No clue, but I'm sure you're dying to tell me." My nerves were shot and my inner smart-ass decided to pay a visit.

"More DNA in the wound of the survivor's neck."

"Probably from the vampire bite."

"Nope. And it didn't match the DNA from the other bite wounds either. In fact, this sample was deep in the wound, mixed in with another. It's a good thing forensics is so advanced or we might have never found it."

Yeah for forensics.

Doctor Monroe handed me a sheet of paper. Black dots and letters filled one side of the long page, colored waves filled the other. To the uneducated eye it looked like nonsense.

"What's this?"

"A DNA sequencing run." He leaned in, and his clean, woodsy smell distracted me. "This here is the DNA from the ash collected at the scene." He moved his finger down the page. "This row is the DNA extracted from the survivor's neck." His shoulder bumped mine, and tiny tingles fluttered through my stomach. He met my gaze and gave me a tight-lipped smile before he moved away and finished his thought. "They don't match, and neither sample is in the Vampire DNA Database…"

"You have a data base of vampire DNA?"

He nodded. "A pet project of mine." He folded the paper and laid it on the table. "I added this new sample right before you came in. If this vampire is involved in any other killings I'll be able to verify that they are a threat."

Oh. Shit. Just what I needed, my DNA on file. I knew healing her was going to bite me in the ass. This is what I get for trying to do the right thing. I needed to know what Coleman knew. "Why are you telling me this?"

"Because either you killed the vampires at the park or you had a hand in her attack." There it was, the real reason we were here staring at a dead body.

I looked at Reaper again before I answered, wondering with my eyes if he knew anything about DNA and databases, but he continued to focus on the girl on the gurney. He was no help at all, and Nathan, well, Nathan kept popping up from inside the drawers explaining what every dead body looked like. "I didn't have anything to do with the attack." I purposely ignored the other accusation.

"How do you explain the two piles of ash?"

"I can't." I plastered a sugarcoated smile on my face. "How do you explain them?"

"I think you stumbled upon them just like you said, but that's where the truth to your story ends." He started pacing around the room, his hand on the top of his stake. If he was hoping to intimidate me he was doing a good job. "Then I think you killed the vampires and tried to help the girl. But why would someone like you save a vampire victim?"

I wasn't going to let him rattle me. "That's one theory," I said. "But here's another. Stop worrying about what I did and do your job."

The detective's jaw fell open and he narrowed his eyes at me. I looked deep and what I saw was a man on the edge. Too much stress and too many bad things had hardened him through the years. He was dangerously close to his breaking point and grasping at straws. Right now, I was the only lead he had. I could help him, throw him a bone, but I was afraid of getting bit.

Doing the right thing really sucked.

I opened my mouth, knowing what I was about to do was stupid, but the knowledge didn't stop me. "Detective Coleman, the vampire responsible for this will pay. I promise." That was as close as I was going to get to admitting I was a vampire. He'd have to be satisfied.

Reaper, Nathan, and Doctor Monroe all stared at me. Eddie groaned from his cozy home inside me. I'm guessing the words, "She's gone completely insane," marched through their minds.

Coleman looked at the M.E and motioned to the gurney between them. "I think we're done here."

Doctor Monroe covered the body, walked to the door, and held it open. Before I passed by, he grabbed my hand and gave it a shake. The warmth of his skin seeped into my flesh and spread out through the rest of my body. "It was interesting to meet you, Ms. Black." I slid my hand out of his and nodded as I passed.

Coleman walked through the door and quickly caught up to me. "I'll be watching you," he said, and then walked to the elevator.

Wasn't that a comforting thought.

Reaper, Nathan, and I walked out of the morgue and piled into the Chevelle. Once we were settled Reaper started. "Fuck. You just told Coleman you were a vampire."

"No, I didn't."

"The hell you didn't," Nathan piped up from the back seat.

I turned and looked at the ghostly traitor. "Shut it, ghost."

"What'd the spook say?"

"He agreed with you."

"Because he knows I'm right."

The conversation continued on like that all the way back to my place. At least Reaper and Nathan were finally in agreement on something. They both thought I was a complete and total idiot.

I hopped out of the car the moment it came to a stop in front of my building, thankful to be leaving one of the nagging ninnies behind. I opened the door and there he was, sitting on my foyer floor, legs stretched out, t-shirt pulled out of the waist of his pants, and a few curls of light brown chest hair peeking out of the top of his t-shirt.

Doctor Julian Monroe, M.E.

Chapter Ten

My first thought. I wanted to lick him up and down like a lollipop. My second. What the fuck was he doing here? My priorities were really messed up. That's two break-in's in five days. I needed a guard dog.

When he saw me come through the door he stood. Without his lab coat, I got a better look at his toned chest and a hint of six-pack abs through his thin black t-shirt. He wiped the dirt off the back of his cream-colored dress pants, and I watched as his hands traveled over the curve of his well-defined ass.

Fear filled the room when I first walked through the door, but after a few seconds, Doctor Monroe's heartbeat slowed and the smell of fear was replaced with something savage and sexy.

"I'll just go upstairs and leave you to your drooling." Nathan's voice broke through the cloud of lust that had fogged up my brain.

I waved my ghostly partner off and then realized what I must look like and forced my arm back down to my side. "Can I help you, doctor?" I hoped my voice sounded calm and not like a love-struck teenager.

He walked closer, but still kept a good ten feet between us. "I need to talk to you."

I pushed the call button on the elevator and leaned my hip against the wall. "How did you find me?"

"I followed you when you left the Morgue and snuck in while you talked to Reaper in the car." He glanced around my dingy downstairs, the walls that had been painted too many times, and couldn't decide what color they were anymore, the chipped and yellowed linoleum, the dirt that accumulated in the corners, and grimaced. His high eyebrows and slightly down turned lips told me he wasn't impressed. "You live here?"

"Is there something wrong with my home?" The elevator creaked to a stop and I pulled back the cage, got on and waited for him to follow.

He hesitated, but then stepped on. "Not what I expected is all."

I ignored him. Silence was the only way to control my slutty urges. Something about this man shouted do-me-now, and my mind was already imagining him naked. If I wasn't careful, I'd jump him and we'd end up having sex on the elevator floor. What was it about Julian Monroe?

We exited the elevator, and he took a moment to take in the polished hard wood floors, gleaming granite counter tops, and a Degas collection that took me most of my long life to collect.

"Now this is what I was expecting." He walked close to one of my paintings and touched the slight brush strokes.

"You know what they say, don't judge a book..." I tossed my keys on the entryway table. "What do you want to talk about?" I didn't feel like beating around the bush.

"I know you're not human." Obviously neither did he.

Eddie growled and clawed, ready to take charge and put an end to Dr. McHottie. I took a deep breath, held it, and then slowly let it out. "If that's a new pick-up line, it needs some work."

"I know who you are too."

I made my way over to the sofa and scooped Raja off the arm, my fuzzy coat of armor. "Who and what do you think I am?"

He followed me to the couch and lowered himself onto the soft leather seats. "You're the vampire they call Evil's Assassin." He reached out to pet Raja. She hissed, growled, scratched at his hand and then wiggled out of my arms and hid in her cat tree. I'd never seen her act like that before. Figures. First hot guy I bring home and the cat hates him.

I glanced back at my perturbed kitty to avoid his eyes. "I don't know what you're talking about."

He moved closer, so close that I lost all ability to think coherently. "I think you do."

Our knees touched, the contact sizzled through the layers of denim and cotton that separated our skin. I jumped off the couch and sat down in the leather armchair a safe distance away. Talk about mixed signals. An hour ago, he was deathly afraid of me, now he was playing touchy feely on my couch. "Enlighten me," I said when I found my voice again.

He sank back into the cushions and placed his elbow on the back of the couch and his hand on the back of his neck. Nice and relaxed. "There's a rumor among certain circles I'm familiar with about a vampire, beautiful and deadly, at least to the supernatural world. They call her Evil's Assassin."

My heart jumped when he said I was beautiful. Well, okay he said others said I was beautiful, but his comment implied he did too. "What makes you think I'm her?"

"Just a hunch."

When a gorgeous man tells you he thinks you're a deadly assassin the best thing to do is change the subject. "Why are you really here?"

His lips lifted in a knowing smile. He leaned forward and placed his elbows on his knees. "I need your help."

"With what?"

"Finding someone."

"Call the police."

"They can't help me. I need someone with your special skills."

If by special skills he meant dealer of death then he had his girl. "Why do you think I can help? I'm not a private investigator."

He scrubbed his hands through his hair then rubbed his eyes before looking at me again. "I've exhausted all my other resources. I figured fate brought you into the morgue tonight."

Fate or a pain-in-the-ass detective. Either way, Doctor Monroe was convinced he knew my true identity. Did Batman have these problems? Tonight seemed to be the night for guess-what-Alex-is and I was sick of playing. But one look at Doctor Monroe and I knew I couldn't just show him the door.

"Who's missing?"

"My sister." He pulled out his wallet and opened it. I leaned over and studied the picture of an attractive young girl, not more than twenty-eight. They shared the same dark brown hair, pale blue eyes, and slightly wide nose.

"Pretty," I said because I lacked the appropriate response.

He closed the wallet and tossed it on the coffee table. "She's my twin."

Pain speared my heart at the word twin. Memories of the last time I'd seen Andre, my twin, who I'd been separated from for over fifty years, surfaced, bringing with them fresh heartache. Andre who had risked his own life to give me mine, to help me escape from Xavier. My twin brother, I didn't know if he was dead or alive. If I could spare Julian the hurt, the loss, the devastation of losing someone so close to him, I would. Looks like my decision to help the good doctor has been made.

"I'm not saying I'm going to help you, but if I decide to what other information can you give me?"

"The vampires have her."

"How do you know that?"

"She's dating one."

A human dating a vampire? Not unheard of, but she looked to white bread to be the type. This good-looking guy and his missing sister seemed to know a lot about the world of the supernatural.

"Do you know his name?"

"Terrance. Some big shot in the Underground."

And the surprises just kept coming. Doctor Monroe's sister was dating the vampire I was looking for. Maybe fate did intervene. And now I had a second location to find him. The Underground. The vampire's answer to Disneyland. Created as an unlimited source of food, fun, and fetishes.

A place I made sure to avoid.

I'm sure plenty of humans knew about it, even with its spelled entrance and glamoured building, but he seemed to be well informed about a world he shouldn't know much about. "How much do you know about the Underground?"

"More than I want to."

"How'd you find out about it?"

"Same circles that told me about you." The good doctor had some strange friends.

"How long has she been gone?"

"Almost two weeks."

I didn't want to be the one to tell him, because sex would pretty much be out of the question after I did, but I had my doubts his sister was alive. No human could survive two weeks with vampires; the blood loss alone would kill them. If they were lucky.

I looked up ready to give him the bad news, but the worry that creased his brow made me hold my tongue. Instead, I said, "Where did Terrance hang out?"

"At the club my sister worked at. Cuff's."

"Have you checked it out yet?"

He looked down at his feet. "I'm banned from the premise."

"Banned?"

He lifted his head and gave me a lazy smile. "I might have started a brawl the last time I visited."

I let out a loud unladylike laugh, happy I didn't snort.

"Alexis, I need your help." His tone switched from a man answering my questions to a man who stayed up late at night worrying about his loved one. "I can't get to the people who can give me the information I need. You're all I've got."

My decision had already been made, but I didn't want Doctor Monroe to think I was too eager or easy, so I let him sweat. He started fidgeting. Playing with the cuffs of his shirt, the hem of his pants, the buckle of his belt that sat just above his…

This man will get you killed. Eddie interrupted my oogling.

What makes you say that?

More years of experience than all your human and vampire years put together. Remember if you die. I die. Eddie just made death seem way more appealing.

"Fine. Leave the picture with me, and I'll help you find her," I blurted out to keep Eddie from voicing any more of his unwanted opinion.

"Really?"

I sighed, a sigh of someone who knows when they've made the wrong choice, but can't make the right one. "Really."

Julian removed the picture from his wallet and placed it on the coffee table. He rose from the couch and started walking to the door, but stopped mid-way. "I should warn you Detective Coleman suspects you're not human."

"He made that quite obvious tonight."

"He's a good man. A good detective. Unless you do something to change his mind I think he trusts you."

I wasn't sure trust was the right word, more like tolerated until I helped solve his case, then we'd see how he felt about me. "Then I guess I shouldn't do anything to change his mind."

He turned to leave, but before he got to the elevator I caught up. "Doctor Monroe, what's your sister's name?"

He leaned in until his lips practically touched my earlobe. "Her name's Julia. And please call me Julian."

The warmth of his breath tickled my neck, sending chills from my nose to my toes. Damn those slutty urges.

He got on the elevator and pushed the button, but his eyes never left mine. I watched him go down, disappointed he was leaving. The front door closed and Raja hopped off her perch and wound in and out of my legs. I scooped her up and rubbed under her chin. "Silly cat, you've got to be nicer to company."

"Especially when they're as hot as that man." I hadn't noticed Nathan floating next to me.

"He's not interested," I said.

"I wouldn't be too sure. His eyes never left your ass when you walked him to the door."

"Were you eavesdropping?"

"Does the queen have a crown? Of course I was."

Nathan and I were going to have to have a talk about boundaries. "That's not polite."

"Like I care, I'm a ghost, we're supposed to sneak around." He had a point.

I placed Raja on the floor. "I'm off to bed."

"Sweet dreams, although I have a feeling they'll be more randy than sweet." Nathan positioned himself on the couch. I helped him with the remote and wandered back to my room.

I wanted to tell him he was wrong, that the only thing on my mind was finding Terrance, the nest, and now Julia, but I knew I'd be lying and so did the throbbing between my legs.

Chapter Eleven

I was in the middle of a very erotic dream involving the delicious Julian Monroe, a bathtub full of chocolate syrup and unlimited cans of whip cream, when the loud clunk of my phone vibrating across the nightstand woke me. I was going to kill whoever was on the other end.

I reached down and rubbed my hand along the cold wood floor, where the offending hunk of plastic and glass plunked after it had fallen. I picked it up and read the screen, Reaper. Worst. Timing. Ever.

"What," I barked.

"Meet me in front in thirty," Reaper barked back and hung up.

Not my ideal wake up call, I might have to make Reaper's evening extra unpleasant.

Half an hour later, Nathan and I climbed into the Chevelle. Reaper hit the gas and the car took off at warp speed, or something that felt like it. Good thing his passengers were a vampire and a ghost, and not prone to whiplash.

"Are we checking out the address Arnold gave us?" I asked.

Reaper looked confused. "Arnold?"

"That's what I named the vampire last night."

He turned his head and concentrated on the road in front of him. "When I got home I plugged the address into the police databanks. There have been several complaints about the property."

"What kind of complaints?"

"Noise and unusual odors."

"Have the police investigated them?"

"Nope. The overworked police department hasn't gotten around to it yet."

It paid to fight supernatural crime in a big city. The police only got to a crime scene on a timely manner if someone was still alive. If you were already dead, well, there wasn't any rush now, was there? And if you were just a nosey neighbor causing problems, you fell right to the bottom of the list.

The car headed into the rural part of the state. All grassland, cows, and horses. It was peaceful, and quiet, reminded me of home. Not the home I've known for the past one hundred and fifty-five years, but Province France, where I lived before Xavier stole me away and turned me into a vampire.

Reaper pulled the car into a long weed-lined gravel driveway and followed it up until two buildings came into view. A weather-beaten barn, missing a door, and quite a few planks of wood, and a house in desperate need of a few gallons of paint. Boards covered the windows and the front door barely hung by a hinge. There was an overgrown pasture off to the left and the wooden fence that surrounded it was knocked over. No one had called this place home in years except for cockroaches and rats.

I stepped out and took a good sniff of the air. The initial smell of vampire nearly knocked me on my ass. I gagged and swallowed back the bile that now coated my esophagus. The smell was off. Like decay and rot and blood and death.

Even Eddie stayed subdued. Sure the blood lust circled like a hungry school of sharks, but the sharks were tiny and afraid of what was causing the noxious odor.

Something's not right.

Thanks for the warning, Captain Obvious.

I pointed to the front door and wrinkled my nose. "Whatever's in that house is bad. Really bad."

Nathan floated up beside me. "Maybe I should go in and take a look around."

I'm supposed to the big, bad vampire hunter, but I was relieved I didn't have to be the first one to go in the house of horrors. "That's a great idea."

"What's a great idea?" Reaper asked.

"Nathan's going to see what we're walking into."

"That bad?"

I waved my hand in front of my face. "I've never smelled anything like it."

Reaper and I leaned against the Chevelle's hood and waited for our ghostly partner to make an appearance. "What do you think he's going to find?" Reaper asked.

"Nothing good. There's no Sire, otherwise we wouldn't have gotten this far."

Reaper went to the trunk and pushed a button on the side. A panel slid off to the side, revealing a secret compartment. He pulled out a camouflage bag big enough to hide a body in. He proceeded to unload an arsenal of guns, stakes, and knives, and shove them in pockets of his cargo pants and in his boots.

He'd just finished arming himself when Nathan came back looking like he could use his happy place and a puke bucket. "Bloody fucking hell."

His reaction didn't build my confidence. I placed my hand on Nathan's arm so I didn't have to interpret. "How many?"

"Dozens. Alive and dead. It's like the seventh circle of hell."

I pulled out my stake. "Ready?"

Reaper nodded. Nathan backed away. "No chance I'm going back in." Damn. Must be bad to spook the spook.

Eddie didn't flare to life. Something was wrong, seriously wrong. The house was full of vampires; the beast should have been forcing its way to the surface.

Want to explain why you're not shredding my insides to be let loose?

There is nothing in there that will satisfy my hunger.

I wasn't sure if that was good or bad.

Armed and ready to play, I pushed past Reaper and kicked in the door, or attempted to. Something blocked it halfway and it closed again. I tried for the more subtle approach, and pushed it open with Reva's hilt, making a gap big enough to stick my head through.

My eyes couldn't make sense of the sight laid out in front of me. Bodies, in various stages of the changing process, were scattered all over the room. There had to be thirty-five men, women, children, writhing in pain as the vampire disease ripped through their flesh and bone, stopped organs, poisoned their blood, and changed their bodies to adjust to a far tougher lifestyle. Still, there was something odd about their flesh. Open sores covered them from head to toe. Now, it's been awhile since I was forced to become a vampire, but I'm sure I'd remember oozing pockets of blood and pus.

Some were farther along in the process, the final rest before being reborn. Others were just starting the change. But they had one thing in common, all-encompassing pain. Pain that ripped through your organs, burned your flesh, and ignited your blood. Pain so severe that it drove you mad and pushed you past your limits. It's a living hell. I squeezed through the narrow opening and stepped over the body of a young boy, maybe early twenties, with a hypodermic needle sticking out of his arm, acting as a doorstop. With the tip of my boot I pushed him carefully aside and opened the entrance wide enough for Reaper.

"What the fuck?" My sentiments exactly, but Reaper said it first.

For once, I have to agree with the He-Man want to be, Eddie said from his hiding spot.

"There are no words." I wasn't lying. Vampire Sires would never leave a protégé unprotected. They're their children. And no vampire would ever create so many. Most vampires went their whole undead life without turning anyone, but if they did it was maybe one or two. This was wrong. Unheard of. Sick.

"We have to find the monster doing this," Reaper said from behind.

"First we have to put these creatures out of their misery." The thought made me sad, but most of the people in this house hadn't chosen to live like this. A feeling I knew first hand.

I moved farther into the room, kicking discarded needles out of my way, careful to step over the bodies in my path. How many other places like this were there? How many people were being forced into this life? Judging by the sheer number in this room I imagined quite a few.

My foot landed next to the head of a skinny man who looked like he had a hard life living on the streets before he was turned. My other foot was just ready to come down when a hand wrapped around my ankle, claws poking through my leather boot. I looked down and one of the resting vampires growled. Lips pulled back. Fangs bared. Hungry. Looking for a fight.

Eddie awoke with a fierce determination that kicked the air out of my lungs.

Unnatural beasts need to return to hell. Then he proceeded to use me as his own personal weapon.

I reached down and yanked the vampire up by the throat, avoiding the spit that flew from his mouth. He growled and hissed until I squeezed his larynx and cut off his ability to make noise. The last thing I needed was for him to wake up the rest of his friends. Sharp claws dug into my skin and scratched deep furrows into my flesh. I might have felt some sympathy for him if he didn't start causing bodily harm; after all, I knew how he felt. That complete lack of control, and insatiable hunger you woke up with. Everyone is your enemy or food. You're more animal than person at this point. I wish I could tell him it got better, but that would be a load of crap.

"Alexis." Reaper's pained cry, combined with a scream, came from deeper in the house. I plunged the stake into the young vampire's heart and dropped him to the ground. Rushing past the rest not caring who I kicked on the way, I went in search of my partner.

On my way, I kicked more needles out of the way. Telling myself that once things were under control I'd take a closer look.

I entered the kitchen and there was Reaper. Backed against an avocado green refrigerator, with a pair of fangs dangerously close to his jugular. Dinner was about to be served for the female vampire at his throat. I snuck up and plunged my stake through the vampire's back and into her heart. She screamed loud enough to alert the others before the hand holding Reaper's neck fell away. The body dropped to the floor and started to smolder.

Nathan rushed in. "There's about fifteen awake and looking for dinner."

"You ready to fight our way out of here?"

Reaper pulled a Beretta out of the small of his back and held it high in answer.

Eddie, I'm going to need a little help here.

My fangs elongated. Blood boiled. Brand burned. I was ready to fight. Kill. Destroy.

I pulled out Reva and went through the door first since I had the best chance at survival against a mob of hungry vampires, but Reaper wasn't far behind. Two vamps blocked the entrance so I sliced and diced my way through. Heads rolled. I continued on into the melee.

For every vampire that I sent back to the gates of hell, two more took its place.

Shots reverberated through the room. I glanced back to see Reaper filling two vampires with lead. I turned away confidant he had things in hand and fought the enemy in front of me. A *thud* sounded from behind, and something hard hit my heel. I looked down, Reaper's gun rested by my foot.

Reaper was on the ground, three vampires clawing their way up his legs. Across his stomach. To his chest. I moved fast, but not fast enough. He screamed when they sank their fangs into the tender flesh of his neck, sucking and feeding.

Four vampires surrounded me, but Reaper needed help, and no matter how much he pissed me off he was still on my team. Holding tight to my dagger, I forced my way through the mob of the undead, leaving a trail of severed heads behind.

I rushed to Reaper, stake in hand, and pierced the hearts of the vamps that held him down, turning them into nothing but ash.

Reaper's clothes were torn and he was covered in bite marks and gashes. Blood pumped from a large, deep, wide cut on the side of his neck that looked extremely painful.

I knelt next to him, licking my finger and placing my saliva over the worst of his wounds that was hemorrhaging. "We've got to get you out of here."

He grimaced and then pointed over my shoulder. I turned. The room was full of vampires. All awake, all headed our way.

"Nathan," I screamed. He appeared in an instant. "What's the exit look like?"

"Surrounded by blood suckers."

Shit. How many were in this house? "I've got to get Reaper out of here."

Reaper pushed up off the floor and used the wall for support. I was amazed he was standing at all. "I can make it, just clear the way."

Playtime was over…time for some vamps to die.

Eddie sent me another surge of vampire-ass-kicking power

With Reva in one hand and Reaper's gun in the other, I shoved my partner behind me and mowed through any vampire who was unlucky enough to be in my way. Blood flew, sprayed, splattered and the bodies piled up.

The sorry excuse for a front door was just ahead. Five, maybe six feet, and thanks to the gun and the dagger only three vampires stood in the way. I rushed forward and made a crossing motion with Reva. Three heads hit the ground and I stepped over their bodies, watching Reaper limp his way down the stairs. He stopped on the bottom step. "Come on, Alexis."

I'd already made the decision that not one creature in that house of hell could make it out alive. There was no way I was leaving until I left Terrance a calling card and a message. "Get to the car," I yelled before walking back in the house and slamming another clip into the Beretta I retrieved from the ground.

The scene was gruesome. Dead bodies. Piles of ash. Blood dripping from the ceiling and walls. And about fifteen vampires still alive and kicking. But not for long. I squeezed the trigger.

Fifteen shots left a smoking gun, empty clip, and fifteen vampire carcasses on the ground. I followed the trail of dead bodies and stabbed anything that wasn't already ash.

Smoke from the smoldering bodies filled the small room and made it difficult to see, but I found the stairs and took them two at a time, dreading what I would find on the second floor. I searched the four bedrooms and two closets, but the vampires were all gone. I went back down and did a second pass of the first floor just to make sure. For a brief moment, I considered leaving Terrance a note in blood on the wall, but looking at the carnage I doubt it was needed.

Before I ran out the door, I scooped up one of the needles for evidence, and headed to the car. Reaper was slumped in the passenger seat, chin on his chest. His neck covered in multiple bite marks, his arms scratched up.

Nathan looked at me when I got in the car, relief written all over his face. "He needs help and I'm useless."

I searched Reaper's jacket for his keys, put them in the ignition, cranked the engine, and drove like a bat out of Dracula's castle back to my place.

Reaper moaned beside me, his eyes pinched shut. Staying and healing him in the house from hell wasn't an option, who knew how many other vampires were on their way home. So, I headed to my place. But I had to make it fast, or I'd be down a sidekick.

Chapter Twelve

When you're leaving a vampire massacre with a bleeding man, fate makes it a point to stick bumpy potholes in your path. And I managed to hit every one on our getaway. I'd just like to know what I did to get on her bad side.

The bumps on the road tore moans and groans from Reaper's throat. I had to choose between comfort and speed; one look at the bloody mess passed out in the passenger seat and I used my black leather stiletto boots to push the pedal to the metal. To hell with comfort, I had a pain-in-the-ass to save.

The Chevelle's tires sprayed loose gravel when I fishtailed into my parking lot and came to a stop. Reaper's head bounced off the window.

"Hey, Mario, careful of the patient," Nathan grumped from the backseat.

I ignored him, went to the passenger side and lifted Reaper out of the car. He put all his weight on me and we slowly shuffled to the building. I couldn't handle anymore of the old man pace so I picked him up, hiking him over my shoulder.

It was times like these I was grateful I didn't live in a fancy high-rise. How do you explain a five-foot-five woman, weighing no more than one hundred and ten pounds, fireman carrying a two hundred and forty pound man covered in blood through a gleaming condo. You don't. That's why I live in an isolated piece of shit. I leaned Reaper against the wall and called the elevator. His eyes rolled back, thanks to the vampire pheromones rampaging through his blood stream. Short shallow breaths raised his chest and his skin tone gave me a run for the money in the pale department.

Once we were upstairs, I carried Reaper to my couch and carefully laid him down. I ran to the kitchen for my first aid kit, a damp cloth, and container of water. Then gently wiped away some of the blood that covered his skin to get a better look at the deep fang marks that marred his neck, throat, and shoulders. Three vampires left ten bite marks in a matter of seconds. They sure didn't waste any time getting their first meal.

Those weren't true vampires.

You can explain that remark after we save Reaper's life.

After I cleared away enough of the blood to see what I was dealing with, my bucket of water looked like the punch bowl at Carrie's prom. Only two bite marks were deep enough to be problematic and wept red drops down Reaper's neck that settled in his collarbone. The sight and smell of his blood made Eddie twitchy. Hungry. Surly. I really was the wrong girl for this job, but it had to be done. A few cleansing breaths and the beast retreated, but not far, he still lurked just under the surface. Always under the surface.

I licked the tip of my finger, stuck it in the deepest gash, and swiped it side to side, hoping I'd hit the spot. The hole stopped filling with blood, so I repeated the process on the other. It looked like the worst was over, but I still had to stitch up the wound.

I needed a second pair of hands. "Nathan, I need some help." The ghost hovered in the background watching me work. He floated closer. "Get close to the ground." I had an idea, but wasn't sure it would work.

I kicked my boot off and slipped my foot over Nathan's. The sparks shot in the air, and he became corporal. I handed him the damp towel. "Can you hold this over the wound while I thread the needle?"

Nathan pressed the cloth to Reaper's neck. Once I was satisfied he had it under control, I dug through the first aid kit and looked for antiseptic and bandages. I laid everything out on the couch next to Reaper's head, and nodded to Nathan.

He took it away, and started cleaning the blood off the other cuts. The needle was threaded and I was just about to puncture Reaper's skin when Nathan said,

"Alexis, you might want to see this." I stopped what I was doing and turned my attention to Nathan.

The ghost's fingers hovered over one of Reaper's cuts. Tiny sparks flew from his finger tips, the area around the cut glowed in the same deep blue and purples as the sparks that shot between us when we touched. But that wasn't the what-the-fuck sight. Where the skin glowed it knitted back together and the cut disappeared.

"How are you doing that?"

"No fucking clue." Nathan seemed a little freaked out by his new power, but it made sense to me. He was a vampire when he died, he had the ability to heal through his saliva, and now through our weird connection his power was amplified.

I pulled my foot off of his and watched the sparks, glow, and healing come to a stop.

"Touch me again," Nathan demanded.

I sat up and placed my hand on his thigh and everything started back up. My mouth gaped open in disbelief. "Holy shit."

"I know, right? Look how cool I am."

"Do this one." I pointed to the worst of the bunch.

He laid his fingers over the deepest cut on his neck, lightly touching the puncture marks. We both watched in amazement as it closed up and the cut healed to nothing but the tiniest pale pink line. He continued to work on the others, while I sat with my hand on him and observed.

When Nathan moved to the last of the wounds I pulled his hand back. "Wait on that one. I want Reaper to see this for himself."

Releasing Nathan's leg I stood up and leaned over Reaper. Grabbing his chin, I gave him a gentle shake, just enough to rouse him. His eyes slowly opened, and he looked up at me. His hand pushed against mine, so I let him go.

"I feel like I've been run over by a semi." He pushed himself up into a sitting position.

"Three vampires, but close."

His hands flew to his neck, and throat, searching for the bite marks. The only one left was on his shoulder.

"They're all gone,"—I pointed at the last one—"except that one. I want you to see something." I dug through the first aid kit and pulled out a compact mirror, handed it to Reaper and tilted it so he could watch.

I looked back at Nathan. "Ready?" He stepped forward.

I grasped his shoulder, and watched him take form. When he was solid he winked at Reaper and laid his hand over the last remaining wound. Just like the others, it started healing immediately.

Reaper's eyes widened. "What the hell?"

"It seems Nathan has the ability to heal through our shared energy."

Reaper didn't answer me, he just watched as Nathan worked a miracle. Once the cut disappeared, Nathan removed his hand and admired a job well done.

"Better watch it or you're going to turn into a useful member of society, spook." Reaper really needed to work on his thank-you's.

"How many bites?" Reaper asked.

"Ten."

"Fuck." That about summed it up.

We walked into a mess tonight. Unprepared and outnumbered. Reaper paid the price of our carelessness. Thank god for Nathan and his newfound talent or my human-sidekick would be out for the next few days.

Reaper pushed off the couch with a grimace and a groan. "What the hell was that place?"

"An abomination," Nathan interjected.

Both heads turned and looked at me. I didn't know why, it's

not like I had anything to add. "It was a nest, but not like I've ever seen."

Nathan floated close to me. "Alexis," he paused and looked at me. His mouth downturned and his eyes filled with concern. "You lived in a nest when you were turned. I mean Xavier had one. Was it anything like that?" Now I understood the concern.

Hearing the name of the sadistic bastard who stole everyone, and everything from me, made my blood steam. And even though I counted down the moments until I could plunge a stake through his evil heart to show my gratitude for my undead life, I knew even he wouldn't be sick enough to do anything like we encountered tonight.

"Xavier was many things." Like a kidnapping piece of shit. "But he wasn't a monster. When he turned Andre and I, we were given the best of everything. What we encountered tonight was perpetrated by a twisted fuck."

Reaper began pacing the room, back and forth, back and forth, only stopping to scratch under Raja's chin. "What was with the blood and pus?"

I beckoned Nathan closer and grabbed his arm because I didn't want to repeat the conversation. "Nathan, you've been around longer than me, have you ever seen anything like that?"

"Not since my mate died of the Black Death."

"I doubt we're dealing with the vampire equivalent of the plaque."

Reaper stopped walking. "But they all had the same sores. It had to be a disease."

"Vampires can't get sick," Nathan reminded Reaper.

Wasn't that the truth. And not only couldn't we get sick, but any disease the human carried prior to their induction to the fang and heartless society disappeared. Poof, instant cure for whatever ailed you.

"So, if it isn't a disease, what is it?" Reaper started pacing again.

Time for that chat with Eddie. *What do you know?*

They were vampires in the traditional sense, but also more. More power, hunger, anger, than any vampire I have ever witnessed. Once they grow older their blood lust will be out of control. Baby vampires are hungry, but never to this extreme. Someone is amping up the urge to feed. But why?

What could cause such an extreme change?

Then I remembered the needle I had snagged, rushed to my coat and pulled it out of the pocket. I held it up for Reaper and Nathan to see. "A drug?"

Reaper walked over and took the needle from my hand, examining the tiny bit of orange liquid that remained at the bottom. "You got this from the house?"

"They were scattered all over the floor."

"What do you think it's being used for?"

I took the needle back, giving it one last, long look before placing it on my kitchen table. "That's what we have to find out."

Once again we were left with more questions than answers. Things went from bad to really fucking worse, taking this case from frustrating to really irritating and impossible.

Why couldn't some other vampire assassin swoop in and save the day?

Chapter Thirteen

M y first clue that something was off was the ray of
sunshine trying to pry my lids apart and greet my baby
blues with its cheery demeanor. I don't do cheery, and I certainly
don't do the sun. So what the hell was up?

Even though I didn't want to, I forced my eyes open and
shielded them from the blinding white room I found myself in
the middle of. White granite floors. White granite walls. White
granite pillars. All gleaming like a freshly polished fang.

And leaning against a pillar in all his angelic glory—Caleb.

In his designer black suit, coal black wings, and dark hair, he
was a giant smudge against the pearly landscape.

One look at his fuck-it's-you face, and I knew we were
wearing matching expressions. What a shitty way to start
the day.

Caleb and I had a hate-hate relationship. He hated me, and
I hated him even more. Our brief first encounter saddled me
with a fifty-year prison sentence as the Higher Powers personal
executioner. I didn't have high hopes for this conversation.

"Why am I here?"

Caleb pushed off the pillar, adjusted the cuffs of his black
Burberry suit, and ran a hand through his perfectly coiffed hair.
He walked over to stand closer to me, and as he turned he
smacked me in the face with a large black wing. "We need to
have a chat."

I picked a black feather out of my hair. "About?"

Before he answered, the sheer white curtains at the back
of the room parted. A tall man in jeans, and a white button
down shirt with a long sword at his waist walked in. His
shoulder length blond hair framed a handsome face with coal
black eyes and the royal pendant hung in the deep v of his

button-down shirt. Fuck, Kadmus. That meant the queen was close.

Yep. Right behind him walked the queen of the vampire race. Our only living royalty, Divinity.

Eddie sucked in a breath and I felt an unexpected emotion ping the thread of our bond. Love. WTF?

Her red hair fell in a braid across her pale shoulder, and ended by her waist. Her gold silk and beaded gown, a dress that belonged in a royal court or at a fancy ball, swished against the tile floor. Up close she was tiny, maybe three inches shorter than me, with slight features, that made her seem more like a child playing dress-up and less like a woman who controlled the whole vampire race.

I was sure protocol dictated I kneel, but I hadn't voted for her, so I remained standing.

Kadmus stepped forward and placed his hand on my shoulder, forcing me to my knees. "Show some respect."

Caleb chuckled from the sideline.

"Kadmus, allow her to stand." Divinity motioned to two empty chairs in the center of the room. I would have stood, but Kadmus' hand still pressed down. One scathing look from his queen and he let go.

I elbowed him in the gut when I walked past, then took a seat next to her highness. She worked at spreading her long skirt around her feet. I didn't have a long skirt, so I picked at the heel of my boot. Once she was perfectly arranged she turned her attention to me.

"We,"—she waved her hands back and forth to indicate her and Caleb— "need your help."

"You know I kill vampires for a living?"

Caleb groaned. Kadmus's hand tightened on the top of his sword. Eddie remained silent. Divinity laughed. Glad I amused someone.

"It's no secret to me what you do, or why you do it."

"That's good because I'm all about full disclosure." I looked at Caleb. "On that note, why are you working with the vampires?"

He fluffed his wings and took a step closer to Divinity. A sign of unity? "We have common interests and a common enemy."

Divinity spoke up. "Have you ever heard of Delano Melazi?"

"Delano Melazi. One of the Seven Sovereign leaders, most feared vampire on the planet, and the only one to ever escape the VAU's public executions. What vampire hasn't?"

"Then this conversation should be brief." Caleb said the words like that was a good thing.

"You can teleport me back home and it can be non-existent."

Divinity cleared her throat, ignored our bantering and continued on. "Delano Melazi has made it his mission to destroy the Sovereign leaders and me." The hand on Kadmus' sword tightened. Making me believe the rumors that he was more than her bodyguard were true. "We need your help to take down the army he is building and save the Sovereign leaders."

The Sovereign leaders were the vampires form of government. Seven, no six vampires, now that Delano had been impeached, far older, tougher, and stronger than me, who wrote the rules, ruled the lands, and dealt out judgment. No one crossed the leaders and lived to talk about. Almost no one, two vampires still walked the earth after defying the leaders, Kadmus, who stood in front of me, and Delano, who they wanted me to hunt.

"You want me to go after Delano Melazi?" I already knew the answer. Hell. No.

"For now we just want you to locate his general in the Chicago area. The assassins in the other cities will do their part to locate theirs—"

"Other assassins?"

"Yes."

"Others like me?"

His words clogged my ears, and swirled their way into my brain, finally resting in my mind like a brick. Others? Like me? I wasn't the only executioner out there? Holy shit, it felt like someone just dropped a bomb on me. All these years I thought I was the only one. How had I never known this?

"I'm not the only one?" I lasered a stare-down at all of them.

Caleb gave me his best don't-be-stupid look. "Certainly not. Although you are the most frustrating."

I gave him my best you're-an-asshole face. "Are they all vampires?"

"No. We have werewolves, a couple of witches, and the rest are vampires."

Wow, just wow. It was going to take some time to process this, but right now it made me feel a little better about my life.

Divinity stood and stepped closer, her hand now resting on my shoulder. Eddie flared at her touch. Her eyes popped wide, but then she gave a light head shake. Power radiated from the tips of her fingers and seeped into my skin. It flowed through my body. Starting from where her hand sat, an electric bolt that flowed through my shoulder, chest, into my heart, and then moved downward, until my toes tingled. "Will you help us, Alexis?"

I shook my shoulders, hoping to remove the last trace of her energy from my body. "What's in it for me?"

"Isn't being helpful enough of a reward?" Caleb asked, then turned to Divinity and pointed at me. "I told you she could be difficult."

Divinity eyed me. "Not difficult. Smart. Resourceful." She turned her gaze to Caleb. "Isn't that why you picked her?"

Caleb's lips tightened in a thin line. "What's your answer, Alexis?"

"Why are you teaming up with the enemy, Caleb?" I leaned back in my chair and waited for his explanation.

He pulled at his collar, and repositioned his tie. "Delano is creating more vampires and it's my job to remove the threat.

Divinity needs him removed so there isn't a threat against the throne. I control the resources, you and the other assassins, so she came to me for help. For once we have a common goal." He stopped fidgeting with his clothes and let his hands fall to his side. "Now that I've explained, I need your answer."

"I'll do it."

Caleb opened his mouth, but I held up my finger to stop the words about to rush past his lips. "But, I want time off my contract."

"No." Caleb practically spit the word out.

"Then have fun finding someone else." I stood, dusted off my pants and headed to the door.

"Alexis, wait," Divinity called to me. I stopped my exit and turned to face her. "Allow me a moment to speak with Caleb in private."

They went behind the curtains for their little chat, and Kadmus stayed with me, but his eyes never left his queen.

"So, are the stories true?"

"Stories?" he asked, but never met my eyes. His attention stayed focus on the curtain his queen had disappeared behind.

"Poisonous barbs, vampire assassins." I turned my fingers into ugly claws. "Creatures of unspeakable horror?"

The stories of how Kadmus rescued Divinity from an eternal slumber and brought her back to take over her father's throne were a thing of legend in the vampire society. He risked his life to save her, fought creatures that only existed in nightmares, and lived through things that would have killed a weaker soul. All to save his queen and his race.

His lips lifted in a miniscule smile. "Every single one."

"Was it worth it?"

Before he could answer Divinity and Caleb walked back in, but I didn't need him to say the words. The light that lit up his eyes when she entered the room was all the proof I needed. To Kadmus, she was worth it.

"Three years off your contract," Caleb said.

"You're going to have to do better than that, fly boy." Daddy always said to aim high. "Ten."

"Five."

"Eight."

"Six, and that's my final offer."

Six years off would leave me with forty-one years, thirty-eight weeks, and ten days left on my sentence, not much in the grand scheme of things, but far less than what I had when I started out.

"Deal."

Caleb stepped in front of my chair. He reached up and touched the center of my forehead with the tip of his finger. An electric current started at the point he touched, and shot like a guided missile just under the surface of my flesh, and whizzed around my brand.

My ass shot out of the chair like a bullet. "What the hell did you just do to me?"

"I amended your contract." He sat back down, like his little bit of torture was nothing.

I rubbed at the flaring pain on my hip. "There wasn't an easier way to do that?"

"There was, but I chose the fun way."

Ugh. I hated angels. "Thanks for the warning."

Caleb tilted his head and shrugged one shoulder. "Once you locate Delano's right hand man in Chicago you need to find out Delano's location of operation."

"I already know who his general is."

"How did you manage that?"

"Stumbled upon it. I've already taken out one of his nests too."

Caleb slapped his hands on his thighs and stood. "Why didn't you tell us this sooner?"

"If I did I'd still have an extra six years of working for you."

Caleb tossed his hands in the air and ruffled his wings.

"Like I said…resourceful," Divinity spoke up.

"I'd have chosen another word." It didn't take a rocket scientist to figure out what word he would have used.

"We have faith in you, Alexis Black." Divinity nodded her head in my direction before taking Kadmus' hand, standing to leave.

I followed her lead, without the handsome body guard helping me, but before whatever mode of transportation that brought me here could whisk me away, Eddie spoke.

Alexis, please give her a message for me.

Who? The queen?

Yes.

Sure. Whatever.

Tell her she has her mother's eyes. Eyes that I have not seen in a thousand years.

My cold, dead, non-beating heart dropped into my stomach.

How would you know that, Eddie?

Because I'm her father.

My blood iced.

Yes. Caleb bestowed you with the spirit of Vlad the Impaler.

I was going to pluck every feather off that angel's wings.

Please, Alexis. Tell her for me, I need her to know that I am still here.

I cleared my throat, not sure how to even approach this conversation. "Excuse me, your majesty." She looked at me with those haunting eyes. "Umm…Eddie."

He slashed at my insides.

"I mean your father has a message for you." I relayed said message.

Her smile light and happy lit up the room. "I felt him when I touched you, but I wasn't sure you realized whose spirit laid within you."

I let my evil death stare settle on Caleb. "I didn't until two minutes ago."

The queen gave a death stare of her own. "Caleb, how come you never told her the father of all vampires shared her body?"

Caleb fluttered his wings under her scrutiny and a few feathers floated around the room. "It didn't seem important to her mission."

"Unimportant my ass, you winged freak." I stopped myself before I said or did something that would shorten my immortal life span. "For two years I have called the father of all Vampires Eddie."

Kadmus broke his stoic guard protocol and busted out a laugh. "You named Vlad the Impaler Eddie?"

He was lucky he carried a pointy sword.

Divinty broke up the tension, putting her hand on my wrist. I wasn't sure if it was to calm me or feel her father's spirit. "Alexis, my father would want you to fight for our race. What is happening to these vampires is wrong. They are suffering and I wouldn't trust anyone but the soul strong enough to handle my father's spirit to fight this battle." Her Queenship bowed.

Damn.

"I'll do my best, your majesty." Then I pointed at Caleb. "For her. Not you."

Caleb flapped his wings again and flipped me the bird. "Just don't fuck up." Everything went black.

I reappeared in my room, and did a full body pat down for any sign of a new tattoo.

Now you understand the full power at your disposal if you choose to use it. Stop fighting me and you will be stronger than you have ever imagined.

Whatever. I'm still calling you Eddie.

Chapter Fourteen

My unexpected visit with the angel from hell and the
vampire queen left me exhausted. Then Reaper had
shown up at it's-way-too-early-to-deal-with-his-attitude o'clock
and announced that Operation Hunt and Kill Terrance was in
full effect. Terrance needed to be found, but I wished it could
wait until I was dressed, showered and fed.

I sat crisscross applesauce in one of my kitchen chairs. One
hand wrapped around a mug of blood, the other resting on
Nathan's ghostly wrist. I listened as Reaper and he debated the
color code system Reaper was using on the map of the city that
now covered half of the tabletop. Reaper hoped that his little
science experiment would help us locate the center of the
attacks, and therefore Terrance's base of operation.

The other half of the table looked as if a high-end tech
store had a baby on top of it. Computers, phones, walkie-talkies,
and police scanners covered every available inch.

I had planned on telling them about my Royal body
snatcher and visit with the queen, but they had been arguing
since I entered the room, so I left them to their bitching and sat
back and listened.

"You bloody wanker." Nathan tried to pound his fist on the
tabletop, but it just floated through. "Why would you put purple
there, it clearly needs a green dot."

Reaper picked up one sheet out of at least fifteen sheets of
paper and held it in front of Nathan's face. "Look at the
numbers again, ghost-boy, it's purple."

Nathan peaked out from behind the paper. "But a green dot
would make that our center."

"I'm. Not. Done. Yet." Each word got louder than the one
before it, like a teakettle whistle. Reaper put his head back

down and continued to place brightly colored dots on the map.

Nathan floated over Reaper's shoulder and quietly watched him continue to work. The crackle from the police scanner was the only noise left in the room until someone pounded on my downstairs door.

"Expecting someone?" Nathan asked.

"Practically everyone I know is already in this room." I got on the elevator in the wake of my pathetic proclamation.

One deep breath and I knew who waited on the other side of the door. Julian Monroe, back for another visit. I tugged at the bottom of my mid-drift sweatshirt, silently wishing there was more material to cover the top of my brand poking out of my lowrise sweats.

Heavy fists pounded on the door again and I gave up trying to cover my flesh and pulled open the heavy steel.

Standing in front of me was not the perfectly put together doctor I was used to seeing. Instead, Julian looked like a man after a six-day bender of tequila and vodka.

I pulled the door open enough for him to come in. "Did you get hit by a bus on the way over?"

He pushed past me. "I've got a big problem and you're the only one I can trust to help me."

"Your sister?"

"Worse." We walked over to the elevator and pushed the button to take us up. "I need your help."

I had already offered to help him locate his sister, now he wanted something else. We stayed in silence until we stepped off the elevator. Both Reaper and Nathan turned to look at our company.

"Doctor Hottie came for a house call." Nathan floated closer to us.

I grabbed his wrist before he passed by and he solidified. It was time for Julian to meet the third member of our grisly group. "Julian, this is Nathan."

Julian's inspection started at the top of Nathan's head and traveled down. He paused and watched the sparks that shot out from where my hand touched his flesh. "Fascinating." The scientist in him took over and he reached out, touching the purplish-blue electric currents that flowed between us. "He's a ghost?"

"I prefer Spook of Spectacular." Nathan did some sort of fancy bow he must have learned in his old court days.

"He only appears when you touch?"

I let go of Nathan and he faded away. "I seem to be the only one who can see him when we're not in contact." I placed my hand on his shoulder and he reappeared.

Julian stepped closer and put his hand on Nathan's arm. "He's solid."

Nathan shrugged away from his touch. "Enough of the touchy feely. Didn't you come here for a reason?"

Julian gave him a lopsided smile, ran a hand through his beyond-a-finger-combing hair and pulled out one of the kitchen chairs, but didn't sit down; instead, he started pacing the room. I let go of Nathan and settled myself into a chair.

After a few moments I couldn't take it anymore. "You ready to share?"

He stopped in front of me, stuffed his hands into his jean pocket and leaned against the kitchen counter. "Someone broke into my lab last night."

Nathan floated next to me, bobbing up and down like a four-year old who had to pee. I placed my hand on his arm. "Did they steal a body?" He looked hopeful that Julian would have a fun horror story to share of dismembered bodies being stolen from the morgue.

Julian shook his head. "Not that lab. My personal lab, where I do my private research. When I got there last night I found the door pried open and the place trashed."

"Did they take anything?" I asked.

He picked up one of the bright yellow walkie-talkies from

the table and started to switch it on and off. "Yes. A serum I've developed. All of it. Every last drop." He pushed off the counter and started pacing again.

Reaper stopped placing his little dots and looked up at Julian. "What does the serum do?"

Julian's strides got longer. He scrubbed his hands over his face and his heartbeat took off. Whatever this serum did, the good Doctor was worried. He cleared his throat. "When injected into someone with supernatural abilities, let's say a werewolf, it masks the physical characteristics and returns the user's body and functions, such as heart rate, breathing, aggression, and all the senses back to more human levels. It hides those abilities and allows the user to walk around undetected to other supernaturals."

More questions about the mysterious Julian Monroe torpedoed my curiosity. Then I remembered the needle sitting on the counter. I grabbed it and held it up. "Does it look like this?"

Julian snatched the needled from my hand, pushed the plunger and let the leftover liquid fall to his fingertip. He sniffed then tasted it. "Where did you find this?"

"At the nest we destroyed last night. They were all over the place, including sticking out of the vampires' arms."

He tossed the needle across the table. "Fuck."

"That would be a yes?"

His mouth twitched. "That's a yes. But there's something not quite right with it. Like something has been added to the original formula. I can't tell what it is until I get it back to the lab and examine it."

I sat back down and folded my arms over my chest. "Why would you develop something like this?"

This time his smile reached his eyes and, for the first time that evening, I saw the man who I had met two nights ago. He settled in the chair next to me and placed the walkie-talkie back on the table. Reaper put his map aside and Nathan floated over the couch. We all waited for Julian to answer my questions.

"I created the serum to help a friend of mine, a werewolf, who needed to hide from his former pack. It was a matter of life and death and took me six years to find the correct ingredients." Secrets played hide and seek in his eyes. He was keeping something from us, but what and why? His unwillingness to share the whole story scratched at my nerves.

Reaper took the needle from the table and turned it around, watching the liquid coat the inside. "What's in it?"

"A combination of herbs. Some poisonous, some not, but each ingredient serves a very important purpose. The most important part of it is Wolfsbane." He took the needle from Reaper's hand and stared at the tiny bit of liquid, then placed it on the table.

"When used properly it has the ability to slow the racing heartbeat and pulse of the werewolf to mimic the slower human heart rate. Then Valerian Root, a natural mood enhancer. Scorpion Venom to stop the physical change. Skullcap to lower anxiety, which is a trigger for the werewolf to change. Green Cardamom to dull the personality. And finally it is all mixed in liquid mistletoe, which hides the true nature of the wolf."

"And someone drank this willingly?" I let the high pitch of my voice tell him how absurd I thought the idea was.

"Not drank, injected."

I shuddered at the thought of someone sticking the nasty concoction in their veins.

"I'm sorry that someone broke into your lab, and they took your work, but what does this have to do with us?" Reaper nodded his head in agreement.

"I believe whoever took it is trying to hide in plain sight." He sat in the chair next to me and met my eyes. "Hiding from you. From whatever gives you the ability to detect the supernatural with just a sniff."

"About that." I paused for dramatic effect or because I was chicken shit. Who knew? "I found out last night that I share a body with the spirit of Vlad the Impaler..."

Nathan fizzed, fizzled, and faded.

When he returned he so eloquently said, "No f'ing way."

"Yep. Seems my friend the angel thought I would be a fitting host for his most holiness."

"So, your alter ego is actually the father of all vampires?" This from Reaper. "Well, that explains the horrific mood swings."

I flipped him off in the most graceful way as possible. Both fingers held high and straight.

I turned my attention to Julian to continue our conversation. "No supernatural could even begin to escape detection," I said with a smile and a head tilt.

"A werewolf using this serum could be sitting across the table from you right now and you would never know it."

"I doubt it."

He shook his head. "I don't.

Reaper spoke up. "Any idea who stole it?"

"Terrance."

"How did he know about it?" I asked.

"My sister told him. She's the only person, besides me, that knows where my lab is located."

"How many vials are we talking about?"

"Almost fifty." He tapped his lip with his index finger. "Each vial contains ten injections."

I quickly did the math in my head. "So, we're talking about five hundred injections in total."

"Can anything but a werewolf use it?"

"I don't know." He raised and lowered his shoulders. "I've never tested it on anything but a werewolf."

"The vampires I encountered last night were covered in open sores and pus. Could that be a side effect?"

Julian turned his gaze on me. "It sounds like they had a bad reaction, but I won't know for sure until I find out what they added to the serum."

"Would it kill them?"

Nathan bounced around to get my attention, then held out his arm. I touched him and became solid. "Could your serum control Vlad? Make it so she could walk among other vampires undetected?"

I removed my hand, folded my arms over my chest, and let him fade away.

"The original serum might be able to suppress her vampire urges, but I can't be completely sure until I have a live sample or test subject."

"I turned them all to ash." Then I quickly added, "And I am not volunteering."

Nathan moved closer and brushed against me, turning solid again. "Think about it, Alexis. A fail-safe in case you get in a jam. A way to help Reaper if he is buggered up. Possibly a chance to walk among the undead again without having to stake them."

Injecting an unknown substance didn't sound like the best idea, but having a couple doses around if I needed them couldn't hurt. No one said I had to use it. "Is it possible to leave a couple vials with me? You know, just in case." Eddie/Vlad started playing slice and dice with my insides.

"Sure, but I can't guarantee it won't have some side effects."

I started to smile but let it fall into a frown. "Can't be any worse than what I deal with every single day."

Reaper went back to his maps and paper, but before he started placing any more dots he looked up at us. "We need to work faster."

We all sat and watched him. He flipped through the papers, placed more dots, then stepped back and looked at his handy work. "Here." He pointed to an area on the map surrounded by multiple colored dots, except at the center. The center was empty.

"Gear up," he said. "It's time to find Terrance."

Chapter Fifteen

I t took us twenty minutes to convince Julian to go home and give up his plea to join our hunting party. I already had one human in the group to protect and didn't need another. After an argument, and no chance at winning, he stormed off with the proclamation he was off to brew some more of his wonder drug.

We piled in the car and headed through the suburbs in search of Terrance. My Chemical Romance drowned out Nathan's non-stop commentary from the back of the car. The section of road we traveled wasn't lined with the typical forests and green belts of the suburbs. These roads were lined with industrial buildings and factories.

According to Reaper's early evening of research, we were headed to the center of the attacks. According to his reasoning this is where we would find our guy. According to my vampire intuition things were going to get ugly. Again.

After nearly getting Reaper killed at the farm house I didn't want to take any more chances, but I had to think of a good excuse to keep him in the car and out of harm's way.

An impossible task I most likely wouldn't accomplish.

Reaper parked in a centrally located lot and stopped the engine. "I think we should separate and take a look around." He opened his car door and headed to the trunk.

I quickly got out and raced after him. "After what happened last time I think that is a horrible idea. We don't know what we're walking into."

"This place is huge. We'll never be able to cover all the ground with just the two of us." He protested with a wave of an arm and his signature sneer.

"Make that three of us." Nathan came up behind us.

I turned and looked at Nathan. "You can help me search." Then I swiveled to look at Reaper. "How about you drive around and see if you can find anything."

It wasn't the best plan, you could hear the Chevelle coming from ten miles away, but it would keep Reaper safe behind two tons of metal and glass.

His mouth opened, closed, and then opened again, but the retort never passed his vocal cords. He walked back to the car, slammed the door, and cranked the engine.

Nathan and I walked through the abandoned warehouses and factories with foreclosure notices pasted to the doors. The only thing we came across were a few rats, and stray cats. If there was any vampire activity in this area it wasn't where I was standing.

"It's quiet around here," Nathan pointed out.

I stopped and listened. The usual background noise of bugs and birds was missing. The only sounds in the area were the rustle of leaves being blown across the asphalt by the fall breeze, and the grumble of the Chevelle in the background.

But the lack of noise wasn't the only problem. Where was the homeless population that usually frequented these areas? Had they moved on or been recruited?

The Chevelle rumbled in our direction, Reaper waved his arm from the window. The car stopped next to us, and he kicked the passenger side open. "I need your nose."

"Just what a girl desires to be wanted for," I said on my way to the car.

After I closed my door, Reaper said, "I think I found something about a quarter of a mile north of here, but I can't be sure."

We drove north, but not far, just a few buildings between where Reaper was sure he found something and where Nathan and I had been. Even with the windows rolled up the smell of blood and death permeated the inside of the car.

The car hadn't even stopped when I opened my door and

stepped out. I gestured for Reaper to stay behind. There was no indication what we were up against, but I wasn't taking any chances this time. He cussed me out from inside the car, but I didn't care if he was upset that I had just regulated him to the kiddie table.

He let out a string of profanities, but didn't make a move to get out of the car. Had the other night scared him more than he wanted to admit? I put my Glock in my hand and unclicked the safety.

Nathan floated next to me. "Want me to go in first?"

With a shake of my head I turned in the direction of a grey stone building with three large smoke stacks sticking out of the top. There was blood in the building I was sure of it, but whether it was coming from a single creature or a mass murder I couldn't tell. The wind kicked up the back of my duster and sent the smell of blood straight into my nostrils.

Eddie woke, stretched, and came alive.

Time to play?

We'll see. Be ready.

The door sat slightly ajar so I nudged it the rest of the way with the toe of my boot. I took a look and stopped. Frozen. Horrified.

"Bloody hell." Nathan's eloquent words were exactly what I was thinking.

The walls looked as if Jackson Pollack was going through his red period. Crimson covered every single surface in the small room. Body parts and hunks of flesh laid in large clumps on the floor.

The sight of gore caused bile to rise up the back of my throat and settle on my tongue. I swallowed it down and rushed out of the room for some fresh air and back up. There was no way I could face that room again without someone at my side. I leaned against the building and allowed the clean air to flow through my lungs and out through my mouth.

Reaper came up behind me. "What did you find?"

"Blood. Death. A fucking mess." I took another gulp of air and then stood straight. My sonar wasn't going off, so it seemed I was the only supernatural in the vicinity.

Reaper followed me into the empty room of death, but after his first glance he ran back outside and threw up. He came back in wiping his mouth with the edge of his sleeve and walked deeper into the carnage, avoiding messing with the crime scene. "This was a slaughter."

"A bloody massacre if you ask me," Nathan said.

The wind kicked up again and the smell of fresh blood was accompanied by the stench of vampire. Eddie roared, scratched, clawed, and bit to get free. Forcing my feet toward the direction of the smell, through a maze of concrete, metal, and glass. I stopped in front of a large square building. It was nothing special on the outside, just one small door and no windows. But inside something dark and evil and horrible lurked.

"Be prepared," I whispered to Reaper. He pulled out his gun, and we opened the door.

Tremors quaked through my body. The scene hit too close to home.

Large meat hooks hung from the ceiling, only the typical pigs and cows you expected to see hanging from them were replaced with human bodies. Humans who hung by their feet, useless arms dangled, blood dripped from deep gashes across their throats. The red drops landed in bottles positioned on a conveyer belt underneath the unwilling donors.

Eddie vaulted to life seconds before the vampire walked in. Shotgun aimed at my chest.

"You don't belong here." His finger stroked the trigger.

One single vampire left to guard the room, and judging by his appearance and the way his arms shook, a newly turned one.

"I've got this." Placing one foot in front of the other I approached our little friend.

"Stop walking." His words trembled like a kid who was afraid of the dark.

For once I listened. Instead of walking I ran to where he stood. I wrenched the gun out of his hand, turned it around, pulled the trigger, and gave him a second mouth, this one located in his throat. He fell to the ground, clutching at the wound, gagging on his own blood. I leaned down and rammed my stake through his heart. His body convulsed, and then burst into flames.

With my head held high, I listened for anyone coming through the door. Nothing. We seemed to be alone, except for the dead humans hanging from the ceiling.

"What the hell are they doing here?" Reaper couldn't even begin to hide the disgust in his voice.

"It's a blood bank," I answered. "I've never actually seen one, but I've heard about them." I stepped closer to the row of dead bodies and bile rose in my throat. "When the vampires were forced back underground they started places like this. They provide food and income. Too bad it requires torture and death to run one." I turned in a circle and stared at the carnage surrounding us. "The Sovereign body had them outlawed years ago though."

Seeing the fear frozen on the faces of the innocent bums and beggars hanging from the hooks brought a rage to the surface I didn't even know I was capable of. My blood boiled, heating my body from the inside out, taking my rage to a whole new level of pissed off. The anger pushed long buried memories to the surface, forcing tears from my eyes and panic in my steps.

I ran over and hopped up on the conveyer belt and tried to lift the closest person off the hook. But the hook went through the anklebone and without help I couldn't get him off.

"Reaper, help me." Panic coated my words.

He came over, but instead of climbing up he placed his hand on my foot. "We need to contact the authorities."

"No. We have to get them down." I tried lifting again but only managed to make it worse.

Nathan floated close. "Alexis, you can't help them anymore,

they're dead. Let Reaper contact the VAU. They know what needs to be done, how to contact their loved ones."

Listen to your allies. Eddie sounded as sad as I felt.

They didn't understand, could never understand what memories these hanging lifeless bodies brought back. My mother and father hanging in the barn, allowed just enough air to keep them alive, to keep their blood flowing. Four vampires below feasting from their calves, and inner thighs. Xavier holding my head, forcing me to watch the life leave their eyes as the blood left their bodies. The horse's reins around my sister Lysette's neck while they prepared her for the same fate. Xavier forcing me to choose, my life for hers. But it wasn't death he offered me. How I wish it would have been.

"No. I can save them. I can help them. Just help me get them down. I've got to try."

"They're not your family," Nathan said.

For the briefest moment, my gaze locked on his, and then my hands fell to my side in defeat. I climbed down. Sank to the ground. And gave up.

Nathan followed. "The only way to help them is to find Terrance and shove that dagger of yours up his arse."

I ran my fingers through my hair, composed myself, and finally forced myself up off the ground. "Call Coleman." I headed to the door. "I don't want to be here when he arrives."

"Give me a moment and I'll meet you at the car."

"You stay. I'm going to walk." I opened the door and stepped out into the cool night.

Nathan popped up beside me, but didn't talk—he knew me. Knew my need to be alone. My need to drown in the memories. My need to work through the demons of the past.

So I walked. When I got tired of walking I jogged. When I got tired of jogging I ran. And it felt good.

But it didn't erase the demons.

Chapter Sixteen

The Underground. Sixty-two miles of tunnels buried forty feet below the city of Chicago. When they were in use, between 1906 and 1959, they were delivery tunnels that took goods to the surface. Today they housed a supernatural den of illicit activities. A den of illicit activities that Reaper, Nathan, and I were about to enter.

"Do you even remember where the entrance is?" Reaper asked in his ever so doubtful tone.

After the Eradication, the remaining vampires fled back into the shadows to survive. The Underground seemed like the best place to stay out of the public eye, so the local coven helped spell the front doors to keep the unwanted out. It may have been five years and one angelic contract since I entered the Underground, but the green mage magic, that marked its location, still lit up the night sky like a homing beacon.

I continued to follow the glowing green path, hoping my lack of response was enough of an answer.

"The VAU would make me Chief of Police if I helped them find this place."

You can't let him lead the VAU here. Eddie poked, prodded, and pleaded.

I stopped walking and turned on him. "Promise me you will never lead them here?" My hands on my hips, feet spread wide and narrowed eyes were enough of a hint that we were not moving forward until he made that promise.

After a pregnant pause that made me wonder if he would ever speak the word, he mumbled, "Promise. Not that it should matter to you."

True, it was my job to hunt and kill the supernatural population, but the Underground represented a place of safety, security, sanctuary and I wasn't going to be responsible for the massacre that would take place if the VAU ever stepped through the doors.

We stepped closer to the entrance and magic zipped through my body.

I stopped in front of a non-descript metal door, placed my hand on the beat up knob and waited for the tiny pinprick that would test my blood. I'd never tried to get in since I accepted Caleb's offer and a part of me worried that my tainted blood would trigger the alarms. Four nail biting seconds later and the knob glowed green, right before the door clicked and opened.

Only a select group of humans—who wanted to mingle with danger—went in the Underground. They paid for admittance with money, sex, blood and sworn loyalty to the vamps, weres and witches who ran the show.

And because my partner threatened to end my 'blood-sucking life', his words, not mine, if I refused to let him help, tonight Reaper was my guest. A guest I hoped wouldn't get eaten.

I pulled the door wide for my partners and stepped aside. "Ready for this?" Reaper brushed past me, followed by Nathan.

We entered a large room with two staircases and walls made out of corrugated metal that smelled of a mixture of piss, beer, and blood. Eddie stirred, but stayed deep in the abyss. Competing bass rhythms snuck out from under each of the doors that guarded the tunnels. The staircase on the right led to the human side of the club. The staircase to the left led to the freak side.

I took a step to the right, due to my need to kill anything of the non-human variety; I would be hanging with the humans. "This is where we split up. Nathan, go with Reaper and come find me if there are any problems." I wasn't comfortable with sending Reaper into the Underground without back up, but I had lost the argument back at my place.

I started walking to the staircase on the right, but before I got halfway there Nathan stopped me. "Wait, before you go I want to try something."

Nathan stepped close. Too close. His hand touched mine, his feet touched mine, his chest touched mine. Purple and blue sparks filled the air around us. He took another step forward and disappeared right into my body.

I heard his thoughts, he hoped this would work. Sensed his emotions, worry, fear, and elation. Felt the beat of his ghostly heart, just like my own that stopped beating so long ago. It was like we were one. It was also creepy and a complete violation of my personal space. I needed him out. Wanted him out. Had to get him out.

I started to bounce up and down, and flapped my arms like some epileptic chicken. "Ugh. Ick. Ick. Ick. Get out."

PWOP. When we separated it sounded like a bubble burst. Nathan stood in front of us, but he wasn't transparent anymore. He looked solid, corporeal, human.

"What did you just do?" Reaper walked around Nathan poking him in various places, his fingers landing on flesh instead of going straight through. "I can see you without Alexis touching you."

"I leached some of her energy." Nathan's shit eating grin said he was proud.

"Shouldn't you have asked first?" My grumpy tone outlined I was pissed.

He shushed me with a wave of his hand. "Before you get brassed off, I have a theory."

"Better be a good one for that invasion of the body snatcher routine."

He hit me with a steely glare before he continued. "For some reason, Alexis and I are able to do remarkable things when we touch and tickle. I wanted to see what would happen if I jumped into her being. Possessed her if you will. Could I bring some of her energy with me so I could manipulate objects in the outside world?" He gave Reaper a shove in the shoulder knocking him off balance. "And it seems my bloody theory was correct."

"So, what was the purpose of this little science experiment?" I asked, still not convinced it was necessary.

"That was just the first part, to see how useful I can be." He walked over and picked up a soda can off the ground. "Next we have to see if I can leave your side." He turned and walked out the door and didn't come poofing back. Instead he walked through again with a Cheshire cat grin on his face. "I'm useful now. Although, I'm not sure Papa Vlad was happy to share his portion of your body with me."

Nathan had a point; even if I wasn't happy about the way he proved it. When we got home we were going to have a long talk about personal space and ick factors, but for tonight having a ghost who could now touch things with Reaper would alleviate some of my worries.

I tossed him a stake and he caught it. "Looks like you're going into the vampire den of debauchery with Reaper." I put my hand on Nathan's shoulder. "Good plan. Next time ask."

I turned and walked into the stairwell. The door slammed behind me and the loud bass of the techno music vibrated the rickety metal stairs. Multi-colored lights flickered on and off. The stench of cigarettes, pot, and various kinds of alcohol wafted up from below, not a pleasant odor, but at least it wasn't the smell of blood, death, and decay. My foot hit the concrete at the bottom of the steps and I walked into the first tunnel.

Bodies writhed in time with the music, blocking my way to the bar. I wound in and out, hoping they didn't brush their sweat on my leather, and headed to the back of the room. Plopping down in the nearest bar stool, I watched.

"What can I get you?" the bartender asked.

"A beer." He left to fetch my drink and I laid a twenty on the bar top.

I needed to continue on through the tunnels and look for

Terrance, but a few moments spent pretending to be human wouldn't kill anyone.

The bottle clicked on the fake marble counter when the bartender returned. I picked it up and held it up to my nose, took a big whiff of barley and wished I could actually drink it. But the ability to enjoy anything other than plasma was stolen from me when I became a vampire.

Why do you pine for a human life of weakness?

I wouldn't expect you to understand. You chose to become a monster. I was forced to become one.

What you call monster, I call superior.

That's one reason we don't see fang to fang.

Fifteen minutes of observing the human world was all I would allow myself, and I continued on deeper into the labyrinth. Instead of stopping in each tunnel and looking for Terrance, I wandered through the halls and let my nose do the searching.

When I hit the entrance to the fourth tunnel Nathan popped in. He looked like he had seen a ghost, which was ironic considering.

"You've got to get in there." He pointed to the exit.

"Trouble?"

"That's a bloody understatement." Nathan snorted. "We were searching for Terrance, when out of nowhere, that bloody partner of yours takes off like a bloomin' duffer, yelling, "I'll kill you.""

Without another word, Nathan and I ran towards the exit, back up the stairs and toward the Supernatural entrance. My hand closed around the door handle, and I practically wrenched it off the hinges when it clicked open. I took the stairs two at a time as I flew into the deep carnivorous blackness, not caring what would happen to me once I encountered a full room of non-humans.

My body started bumping to a beat, but not the one that blared over the speakers. The brand flared to life, the beast woke up, and my blood thumped, burned, and pulsed like nothing I've ever felt before. I staggered to the nearest wall and leaned against it.

Four deep breaths in. Four deep breaths out. Again. And again. And again. Until they calmed me, controlled me, centered me. Just enough to stop the mini earthquake causing my legs to shake.

I felt around in my pocket for the needle Julian had dropped off, and pulled it out. The orange liquid glowed in the black light. I didn't want to stick myself, but if I entered the room without some way to control Eddie, Reaper would die. Along with any other vampire, werewolf, fairy, or witch I came across. Time to find out if Julian's wonder drug worked on me.

I removed the protective tip with my teeth, spat it to the floor, and slammed the needle into my thigh. The liquid flowed under my flesh, and entered my blood stream like a steaming hot bullet. Minutes passed and nothing else happened.

Then I heard Eddie, far off in the distance, muffled and murky. *You'll need my strength.*

Then silence.

The thumping in my chest dissipated, and the urge to tear out some vampire throats disappeared.

For the first time in two years I felt like a normal non-hijacked-by-the-king vampire.

I pulled out my stake and followed Nathan, who had waited, through the crowd of gyrating bodies. Everything seemed to be going well until someone bumped into me and my control nose-dived out the window.

Flesh upon flesh shot an electric current through my body. My hand shot out and drove my stake through an old leather bomber jacket and straight into someone's chest.

Damn. Things were about to get ugly.

"What the fuck?" A very pissed off biker-looking dude wrapped his hand around mine and pulled the stake out, leaving a gaping bloody hole in his chest.

The hand holding mine began to morph. The hair elongated, the claws extended and dug into my flesh. I fought against the half-man and half-wolf that now stood in front of me, but he held on tight. I looked up and his toothy grin said it all. He was going to eat me alive.

He yanked me to the floor, holding on tight. The bones in his body popping and rearranging themselves, hair sprouted over every exposed bit of skin, and his nose turned into a muzzle. His transformation complete, the werewolf put his two front paws on my shoulders and pushed me lower. Drool dripped onto my face when he licked his lips, and a growl ruffled the fur at his throat.

"Hey, fido," Nathan yelled, but the werewolf just flicked his ears in the direction of Nathan's voice. He wasn't about to let his meal out of his sight.

Eddie had been right. I needed him.

Right when I was about to make my move that would send the werewolf flying across the room, a flash of pale blonde marine crew cut flew through the crowd in hot pursuit of a tall, lanky vampire.

"There's Reaper," Nathan yelled.

Reaper ran across the crowded dance floor and through a beaded curtain that led to another tunnel.

"Nathan, follow him," I yelled.

I didn't have time to tumble around with a lump of fur when I had a partner to save.

Wiggling my stake out of his claws, one hand grabbed the wolf by his scruff and the other slammed the pointy tip into one of the paws that straddled my shoulders. The sharp wood stuck into the floor, holding his paw down with it.

The wolf howled. A howl loud enough to alert any buddy nearby that he was in trouble. I shoved his massive fury body off me and kicked him while he was down. Picking myself up off the ground, I left the mutt lying on the floor.

There was no time to look back and see if he had dislodged

the stake. I followed Nathan around the dance floor, past the bar, and into the back room where Reaper had disappeared.

The light was dim, just a few sconces with drippy candles, that hung on the walls. Small alcoves, carved out of the walls of the tunnel were filled with vampires and their hopefully willing donors. Moans, groans, and cries of ecstasy flowed out into the hall. I checked each and everyone for Reaper.

A burly looking blood sucker, straight out of The Godfather, stood in the middle of the hall, arms crossed over his chest, blocking my forward motion. I moved to the left, to try and pass him, but he stepped into my path.

"Private feeding, no one's allowed."

Nathan managed to sneak past the guard so easily, I wondered if some of his borrowed energy was fading. "Reaper's down here," he yelled.

This time the growl that left my throat had nothing to do with the beast, it was all me. "Move or die."

He put his hand on my shoulder and tried to turn me around. I reached up and grabbed his wrist and bent it back. The bones snapped. The vampire screamed. And while he nursed his broken arm, I grabbed the backup stake hidden in the inner pocket of my duster, slammed into his heart, and walked through his ash.

Who needed the beast?

A third of the way down, in one of the larger alcoves, Reaper stood, pinned against the wall, his arms trying to push off the vampire who was ready to tear his throat out.

Not on my watch.

I needed to distract the vampire enough to get Reaper out of here. I pointed to me, to the vampire, to Reaper and to the exit, hoping that Nathan would get the hint and lead Reaper out of the club when I got the vampire off of him. Nathan nodded his head, in what I hoped was agreement.

I raised one side of my upper lip, hoping it made me look menacing, and tapped the vampire on the shoulder. He turned, but seemed very unimpressed by what stood behind him, then he turned back to Reaper.

Screw being subtle. I wrenched him away from Reaper and punched him in the face.

Instead of running, Reaper got between the vampire and I, trying to wrestle him to the ground. Now, I'll admit Reaper is a big man, but nothing against the unnatural strength of a vampire. The vampire tossed Reaper to the side, took one look at me, and then ran out of the tunnel.

Reaper stood up and took off after him. I took off after both of them. The vampire went up the stairs. Reaper followed. The vampire went out the front door. Reaper followed. I made it outside just in time to see the vampire leap to the roof of a building and take off into the night.

Reaper fell to his knees, head in his hand, an anguished scream parted his lips as it was torn from his throat.

I rushed to his side, and laid my hand on his shoulder. The warmth of his body leached into my cold skin. When he didn't pull away from my touch, I lowered myself to the ground next to him. "Reaper?"

The eyes that met mine were filled with anguish. "He killed my wife."

Chapter Seventeen

He killed my wife.

Those four words echoed off the concrete walls and assaulted me over and over again. Those four words told me more about Reaper than anything he'd said in the past two years. Those four words made me look at the man who knelt on the ground with his head buried in his hands in a whole different light.

As long as I've known him, I've never seen a hint of emotion, unless you counted pissed off. He was stoic, straight-faced, serious. But not at this moment. At this moment he was broken.

He fell farther to the ground, as if his legs couldn't support the weight his past piled on his shoulders. I reached down and wrapped my hand around his thick bicep intending to help him up. Reaper's hand closed over mine and he squeezed. At first I thought it was out of kindness, but his fingers squeezed harder, then he pried my fingers off his shoulder and shoved my hand away.

"Don't touch me." His words filled with hatred. His eyes radiated with it too.

Hatred for me. Hatred for vampires. Hatred for anything that didn't fit his idea of normal.

It didn't intimidate me. I had hatred in spades.

I put both hands up in the air and backed up one step.

I'm not sure who Reaper saw at the moment, but it wasn't his partner of the past two years. Right now I was the cause of all his misery, loneliness, and despair.

I was the enemy.

Speaking of enemies, we also had an angry pack of were-wolves on our tail, so staying out in the open wasn't the wisest idea. I needed to get Reaper to follow me farther into the shelter of the abandoned buildings that surrounded us.

The steps I took were slow and deliberate, coaxing him to follow me, come and get me, anything to get him out of the way of the real danger that was surely stalking us.

We entered the shadows and Reaper closed the distance between us. He grabbed the front of my shirt and pulled me close. The other hand wrapped around my hair and wrenched my head back, exposing my neck. Vulnerable.

A growl escaped my throat, a warning Reaper wouldn't heed.

"There's who I was looking for. The part of you that can't pretend to be human." He pushed me away and I stumbled.

"Alexis?" Nathan called from the sideline.

I held up one finger to stop him before he came over. If Reaper wanted to play, heaven help him. All I could promise is I'd do whatever it took to make sure he came out of the fight alive.

A roll of my shoulders, a crack of my knuckles, a toss of my long braid over my shoulder, and I was ready. I winked at my opponent.

A war cry was the only warning of his imminent attack. Reaper rushed forward. Full speed. I stood my ground and waited. Anticipated. Looked forward to it. We met head on and collided in a flurry of fists, flesh, and frustration.

He kicked at my stomach, I blocked it with my hand, not paying attention to the fist aimed at my face.

Damn, it was like being hit by a cement brick.

The impact knocked me back. I ran at him with my own kicks, my own fist flying, and I didn't hold back. I caught him in the chest, the hip, the leg, the side. I punched, he punched. I bled, he bled. The anger was pouring off him, out of him, and I was the perfect punching bag. The face of his enemy who was here and now, plus, I could take a beating. And I let him. I let him get the upper hand. I let him use me. I let him take advantage. Why?

Because that's what friends do. And even if Reaper didn't, I considered him a friend.

I let Reaper have his pound of flesh.

We kept at it until he went down…hard. Once he was on the ground, nursing his left knee I climbed up on his chest and pushed his arms over his head, locking them in place.

"Are you done?"

He bucked his pelvis trying to knock me to the ground. "Off. Now."

"Not until you calm down."

"Fuck you, vampire." The word vampire hurled as an insult.

"But not the one you want?"

"Because you let him get away." And there it was. The reason he attacked. I hadn't moved fast enough to keep the source of his anger from escaping. I'd failed him.

But if Reaper wanted to play the blame game I was up for it. "It's not my fault you're weak."

His head snapped up and his mouth dropped open. He stared at me, his eyes telling me how much he wanted to get back up and shut my mouth…permanently.

He wiggled his hands out of my grasp and his fist connected with my jaw. He leaned to the side and got off me. His hands covered his face to hide the tears I spied before he could hide them.

There he sat, on his knees, head in his hands. No words could express the pain that radiated from him. He was falling apart, reliving the worst thing to happen in his life, he was going to lose it, and soon if I didn't step in and help.

I said the one thing I knew would sink into his thick scull. "I'm not the enemy and you'd see that if you stopped hiding behind your prejudice."

Nathan came over and helped me up. While Reaper composed himself, I brushed the dirt off my clothes, and tried to fix my hair. Walking to an open area of grass and trees, I sat down on the leaf-covered ground and waited. Wondering if Reaper could come back from whatever twisted memory had him in its clutches.

After several minutes he walked to where I was and sat on the ground across from me. His hands shook when he folded them in his lap. Nathan came up behind us, and I kept my hand on his ankle to keep him visible. Reaper looked between us, his eyes wide, sad, dead.

"Feel better?" I asked.

"No," his voice was haunted, lost in a memory of the past.

"Want to talk about it"." He shook his head. I wasn't giving up. "Tell me about your wife?"

His eyes flared, his fist clenched, his mouth moved into a snarl. Good. Pissed off Reaper I could deal with. Pissed off Reaper was familiar.

"I…I can't." His words skipped like a rock over water.

"Can't or won't?"

"I haven't talked about her in three years."

"Why not?"

He stood, walked a few feet away and leaned against the rough bark of a tree. He wrapped his arms around his stomach. "I can't," he repeated.

"Listen, Reaper, I know I'm the last person you want to talk to, but I'm who you've got at the moment. I can't help you unless you tell me what's going on."

Silence. Nothing but silence. Reaper stood lost in thought, lost in the past, lost in his pain. Just so very, very lost.

Do I keep pushing him or let him talk to me on his own? How do I get him to understand that no matter what I was, I was still human in my heart?

"What was her name?"

At first I didn't think he would answer me, but then in the quietest voice he said, "Loralie."

"That's a beautiful name."

He came back to where I sat and lowered onto the ground, his palms running over the green blades of grass.

"How old were you when you got married?"

"I was twenty-eight, she was twenty-six." He paused and scrubbed his hand over his face. "We got married when I got back from basic training."

"Army?"

"Marines."

"That explains a lot." That comment earned me a sneer.

"Kids?"

"She was six months pregnant when she died."

"How did it happen?"

His face fell into his hands, his head shook slowly. Then he started telling me his story. A story I thought I would never hear. A story I would never forget. "I was a detective for the VAU, Coleman was my partner. We had just brought in a huge mover in the vampire Underground. Things were going so well. I was up for a big promotion because of the bust; the love of my life was pregnant with our first child. Life was good." He stopped talking and stared into the night. I wanted to prompt him to keep going, but held my tongue.

"It was a Friday night and we were coming out of a movie. It was busy, people all around, I never expected the vampire." He choked on the word. "He came out of nowhere. Grabbed her. Held her. Told me he had a message from Antonio. Said, you kill one of mine, I kill one of yours. It all happened so fast. He sank his fangs into her neck and drank. He tossed her to the ground, but not before he tore out her throat. I had to make a choice, run after the vampire or take care of my wife. I ran to Loralie and held her head in my lap. Someone called 911, and I held her and watched her fade away until they came."

I let the silence stretch until it was see-through-thin. "They couldn't save her?"

"They tried, they really did. They rushed her to the closest hospital and performed an emergency C-section." Reaper broke down, he sobbed, quiet body shaking sobs. I placed my hand on his back, hoping to offer him some comfort. Surprised when he didn't move away from my touch.

"Loralie died during the surgery. They told me the baby only had moments to live, lack of oxygen had done its damage. They handed her to me, and I held my daughter for the ten minutes that she lived." He wiped his eyes with the back of his hand. "Looked into her eyes, touched her fingers, her toes, smelled her, loved her. Then she died in my arms." His voice trailed off on the last word.

The man next to me was usually so calm, so composed, so serious, but right now he was open and raw.

I let him sob. I let him have the time he needed. We sat on the grass together in silence. That was the best support I could offer him.

"How did Caleb find you?"

"I was a mess. Drunk, contemplating suicide." He hung his head low. "I'd gotten put on suspension from the VAU for attacking a fellow officer. I'd lost everything. My job, my family, my sanity. I was standing at a cross road, and both directions looked pretty grim. Caleb came to me. Gave me a choice, an option to make the world a better place. To save other women and children and families."

"Did you know you would be working with a vampire?"

"Yes."

"What did he tell you about me?"

"That you were different than the others. That like me, you wanted revenge against one of the monsters. That you were more human than vampire." He looked back at the ground. "I tried to get past what you were, believe Caleb, but once I saw you, it didn't matter. I couldn't see past the pale skin, the fangs, the monster that lived inside of you. No matter what you felt on the inside you were still a vampire on the outside."

"Why didn't you quit?"

"You were my only chance at revenge, my best weapon to

take out the vampire population. Better than the VAU. Better than going out on my own, risking my own life."

"So you used the tools Caleb gave you? Me."

"I used you." He paused. "And I don't regret it. What if tonight was my last chance at revenge and I blew it?"

Being used seemed to be a major theme in my life. First by my sire. By Caleb. James Coleman and the VAU. Reaper. The list just keeps getting longer and longer. It should bother me. If I searched deep down in my soul it probably did, but on the surface, where I lived most days, I understood.

I didn't have the adequate skills to bandage Reaper's raw and bleeding heart. But I did have one thing to offer him. Something only someone with my particular skill set could provide. Something I didn't offer lightly.

Revenge. Hatred. Pain. Those were the things Reaper and I had in common. It made me understand him. Want to help him.

"I'll help you find the vampire who killed your wife and child." It was a promise and I took my promises very seriously. One day I would offer up the monster who had hurt the man sitting in front of me. The man I considered more than a partner. Whose tragic life drove him to do what he could to keep others from the pain and hurt that he carried with him every day. A man who I had more in common with than I originally thought.

Just another thing added to my ever-growing to-do list. Find and kill Terrance. Locate Julian's missing twin. Help Reaper with revenge against a murderous bloodsucker. Save humanity.

Damn, I'm a busy girl.

Chapter Eighteen

J ulian's sister worked at a BSDM club. A tiny detail he failed to mention when he gave me the address, but became apparent the moment the cab pulled up in front of the repurposed warehouse with a neon orange and pink sign flashing the name "Cuff's".

Nathan bobbed up and down in the seat next to me, clapping his hands together like an excited seal waiting for a fish. "This is going to be fun," he half yipped and half barked.

This was the backup plan since our visit to the Underground turned out to be a complete and utter failure. Nathan and I deposited a battered Reaper back at his place and headed out to search for Julia. So far she was our only connection, which made her our only lead.

I paid the driver, hopped out, made my way to the entrance and stopped when I spied Julian waiting in line for admittance.

"Think he's here for business or pleasure?" Nathan asked.

I really hoped the answer was business. "Guess we'll find out."

I walked over to him, and tapped him on the shoulder. When he turned and looked at me, my heart did an odd little two-step because of the oh-so-sexy smile that lifted his lips.

"Out for a night on the town?"

To my relief he shook his head. "Trying to find Julia. This is my first stop."

"Thought you were banned?" I nudged his shoulder with mine.

"I was hoping to play up the missing sister, concerned brother routine and plead for mercy."

"I told you I'd help you find her."

"I know, but I just can't sit and wait."

I understood what he was saying. I wasn't the sit around and wait type either. I slipped my arm through his and pulled him out of line.

"They'll never let you through without waiting in line. Only VIP's get to move to the front."

"Trust me."

I put a little extra sway into my hips, a little lick of the lips, a little pushing out of my breasts. Then I topped it all off with some vampire mojo. The bouncer looked me up and down, well more like down then up. He started at my legs, up to my hips, stomach, breasts, and then finally my face.

He pushed open the doors. "Evening," he said with a lift of his chin.

I walked past him, giving him a little finger wave, and a wink. His heart rate picked up and the blood rushed through his body, most likely heading south for a nice long rest.

The door closed behind us and cut off the protests from the people still waiting in line.

"He didn't even notice me," Julian said. "That must come in handy."

"The vampire pheromones or the girl parts?"

He looked at the aforementioned girl parts. "Both."

"They have their advantages."

We walked through a set of swinging doors and my arm slipped from Julian's.

Cuff's was the perfect name for the club. If you were a psychopath.

Julian, Nathan, and I were surrounded by a sea of whips, chains, and leather. From the wide-eyed looks of lust from my two companions, I was the only one who felt uncomfortable.

Around me, men and women were engaged in all sorts of sexual acts. Some handcuffed to the walls. Others led around by leashes. Large cages hung from the ceiling with fully naked women bumping and grinding to the body-thumping beat. A large stage took up the center of the room, and men shoved bills into the barely-there panties of the women shaking it on the glitter-covered floor for their entertainment.

"There are some randy blokes in this place." Nathan gawked like a kid at Disneyland. "This is my kind of club."

"I'm so happy you approve."

Julian looked over my shoulder. "Nathan?"

I nodded and made my way through the crowd, passing several naked couples getting hot and heavy on the bright pink velvet couches. Privacy was so overrated.

Nathan's constant commentary faded into the background. When I looked back he hovered close to one of the cages, his hands wrapped around the bar, watching an Asian girl get down and dirty with herself. Calling him would only draw attention to myself, so I opted to let him enjoy his time out, and continued to follow Julian.

He led us through the rest of the crowd and to the bar. I tried to blend in, but I was over dressed.

We settled into a couple of bar stools and waited for the bartender to notice us. The girl who approached us had more metal in her face than the city iron works. Her hair was dyed turquoise, and she must have used a paintball gun to apply her eye makeup.

"What can I get you?" she shouted over the music's deep base.

"Information. I'm looking for Julia Monroe. I heard she worked here." I took control of the investigation.

"You a cop?"

"I'm her brother." Julian spoke up.

She turned and looked at him. "So, you're Julian. She talked about you all the time."

"When's the last time you saw her?" I asked.

"It's been a few weeks."

"Any idea where she is?"

"No idea, but Ivy might." She looked at the watch. "She's due on stage in twenty minutes. Puts on a really good show, worth the wait."

"I guess we'll wait." Julian and I ordered a couple of beers and settled into a pair of bar stools to wait for Ivy to appear.

The music changed to Nine Inch Nails Closer and Julian grabbed my hand and yanked me onto the dance floor. He pulled me tight, the warmth from his body seeping through my leather, warming me to the core.

His hands slid from the center of back and came to rest at the edge of my low-rise pants. His fingers crept under my t-shirt, igniting tiny fires of lust up and down my spine.

He pulled me closer, letting me know the attraction I felt for him was mutual. He buried his face in my neck, breath coming out slow and warm, body grinding against mine. It was all enough to make me forget about searching for his missing twin and murderous vampire, and start searching for the nearest dark corner.

The DJ announced that Ivy was up next and the spell broke. Damn my stupid sense of responsibility.

I put enough distance between us to calm my raging hormones. "We should head over and wait for her set to end."

He looked at me, the words are-you-sure written all over his face. I shrugged my shoulders and gave him a half smile, half frown.

We settled into one of the tables that surrounded the dance floor and waited for Ivy to make her grand entrance.

"I used your serum tonight."

He leaned forward and touched my skin, looked deep into my eyes, and then tested my pulse. "How do you feel?"

"Normal." I sighed. "Like a normal vampire, not a blood thirsty monster programmed to eat every other creature of the night that I come across. It seems to have controlled the angrier parts of my personality."

Those angrier parts would give me hell when they came back from being comfortably numb.

"I don't know how long the effects will last."

"That's okay. I can enjoy the feeling while it's here."

"You're not like the rest of the vampires, are you?" His words surprised me.

"A blood thirsty killer?" I couldn't keep the humor from entering my voice. He shrugged his shoulders and nodded his head. "I fight the urge every day."

"So you didn't choose the fanged lifestyle?"

My past wasn't something I shared willingly and certainly not with someone I just met. Although I had just contemplated doing naughty things with him, but that didn't give him an open ticket to my soul. Only one person knew the story of how I was turned and right now he was front and center waiting for some T and A.

"No." I hoped the music would start and save me from any more questions.

"How did it happen?" He leaned his elbows on the sticky spilled-drink covered table and waited for my answer.

It surprised me how much I wanted to open up to Julian. Something in the way he looked at me, like he really cared and wasn't just trying to fill up the time with inane chitchat made me want to share my story.

"The village I grew up in was raided by a very old, very powerful vampire." I stopped talking and picked at a hole in the vinyl chair. Even though all of this happened so long ago it still brought up painful memories of the people I couldn't save. Of the lives lost. Of my humanity erased at the hand of a sadistic bastard.

Julian placed his hand on mine and squeezed. The small touch gave me enough courage to go on.

"My twin brother, Andre, and I were on our way back home from town when it all started. We rushed to help our family, but when we got there it was too late." I skipped the gruesome details, not for Julian's sake, but for mine. "The vampire gave Andre and I a choice. Leave with him, and our parents and little sister, Lysette, lived. Refuse him and they died."

"Why did he choose the two of you?"

I shook my head before I answered. "Xavier, my sire, liked to collect rare items. Something about Andre and I intrigued him. Maybe it was the matching black hair and deep blue eyes, the already pale skin, the fact that we looked like real life Dresden dolls."

"So, he collected you?"

I nodded. "Yep. Just another rare item to him."

"And your family? Did he let them live?"

"No." I picked the bottle of beer up off the bar to give me something to focus on. "After we agreed his goons grabbed us. As we were being led out of the barn he had our parents' throats slit. When we struggled to get free he used Lysette as a bargaining chip. Our cooperation for her life. He took her with us to ensure we did what he asked."

The slow, sensual lyrics of Sex (I am) cut off his next question. It was for the best because the story I had to tell only got worse from that point on. Pain. Betrayal. Torture. The start of my vampire life wasn't pretty or magical or whatever the goth kids thought when they played pretend. It was vicious.

Ivy strolled sensually up to the pole in the center of the floor. The multi-colored lights reflected off her short black hair, adding a rainbow of colors to it.

She wore a hot pink bejeweled bra and panty combo, and plenty of body glitter. Her breasts were round, solid, large, and fake, but her taut skin, and tight ass showed that she took care of herself.

She completed her striptease to a round of catcalls and whistles and collected the bills scattered all over the stage, tucking them in her G-string. Julian raised a twenty over his head and she wound her way to our table.

She looked at both of us like we were dessert and licked her lips. "Who gets the lap dance?"

"Neither." My voice came out a lot higher than I intended. But the tips of her nipples were right in the line of my sight making it hard to focus on anything else but the silver glitter that covered them.

Julian laid the twenty on the table and pushed out the chair between us. "We're looking for information about Julia Monroe. I'm her brother, Julian."

Ivy leaned close and whispered, "I've got to keep up a show for management, or they'll make me move on." She turned the chair around and straddled it, slipped the twenty off the table and put it with the rest of her collection, making sure to pull the silky fabric out and give Julian a peek. "You haven't found her yet?"

He pulled his gaze away from her crotch. "When was the last time you heard from her?"

"About a week." She placed the tip of her finger between her teeth like she was thinking and then drew it down her breast. "When she started dating Terrance she became more and more withdrawn from me."

The flirting was getting to be a little much for me. "Can you tell me anything about Terrance? Where he hangs out. How to get a hold of him?"

She turned her attention from Julian and onto me. She licked her lips and reached out and touched my hair. "You two into threesomes?" Maybe I should have let Julian handle her.

"Not tonight." Julian answered for us. "Anything you can tell us about Terrance would be extremely helpful. He pulled another twenty out of his wallet. Ivy thrust her hips closer to Julian and waited for him to tuck it into place.

"He used to brag that he was the most powerful vampire in the city. That he had plans to be the leader of the vampire race. No one was allowed near him unless they wanted to join in his little army."

"Do you know how to get a hold of him?" Julian asked.

"He left a number with a few of us in case we ever met anyone interested in being part of his merry band of psychos. I've got to make the rounds, but when I get a chance I'll run back to my dressing room and get it for you. I'll leave it with the bouncer."

"How long?" I was anxious to leave.

"Give me ten minutes." She got off the chair and sauntered off to the next table willing to pay for her services.

"Looks like we might have our first break in the case," I said.

We sat back in our chairs and waited out the ten minutes with light conversation and front row seats to our own private strip show.

A little bit later Ivy wandered to the back and then headed to the front door. "Looks like it's time to go." I stood and waited for Julian to join me.

We got to the front door, asked for the number and left the building.

I expected to part ways with Julian, but he pushed me against the brick wall and leaned close. He touched underneath my chin with his index finger, and gently tilted my head until our lips were millimeters apart. "I'm really glad I met you, Alexis," he said with a wicked smile.

He closed the distance between us. Tentatively, gently, questioning. His lips touched mine. I leaned in and we kissed.

A spine melting kiss. A toe curling kiss. A kiss that made me forget about vampires and naked women and morals.

I opened my mouth and our tongues met and danced. His hands started at my shoulders, traveled down to my arms and then one cupped my breast. The other grabbed my ass and lifted me until I was straddling his hips. He pushed me into the wall, the brick cutting into my flesh only adding to the excitement of the moment.

"I want you," he whispered. "Here. Your place. I don't care where, just tell me you want me too."

I wasn't sure if he was hot and horny because of the visit to the strip club or the attraction I had felt since the day I met him in the morgue, and right now I didn't care.

"Let's go to my place."

Chapter Nineteen

W e burst through the elevator door. A trail of shoes in our wake, lips pressed together, my legs wrapped around his hips, his hands grabbing my ass.

Raja pinned her ears, growled, hissed, and then took refuge on her cat tree in the corner. She'd just have to get used to having Julian around, because if I had my choice he'd be here more often.

I tossed my keys in the general vicinity of the kitchen table, not caring where they landed. Right now the only thing on my mind was getting Julian naked. Well, that and not eating him during sex, hopefully the serum continued to work, because having Eddie come roaring back to life during sex would be a major cock block.

He carried me over to the couch, and slowly laid me down, his mouth never leaving mine. The heat between us could melt metal. His hands roamed over my body and then caressed my breasts through the thin fabric of my t-shirt.

A small tremor shook my apartment.

Nathan poofed in. "Rude vampire. Couldn't even wait for the burlesque show to…" His mumbling stopped. "Damn fine specimen." The last words I heard before he disappeared.

But even Nathan's presence couldn't extinguish the lust riding me hard.

Julian removed his lips from mine, and I instantly missed their warmth. "Did the room just shake?"

"Nathan's back."

"Do you want to stop?"

"Not a chance." I pulled him close and kissed him, hoping to show him how much I really didn't want to stop.

His mouth clamped down on mine again and he kissed me back, long and slow.

His tongue slipped between my lips, playfully touching mine.

Hands that knew what they were doing crept under my shirt, and followed an invisible trail up my stomach to the underside of my breast. I silently begged that he wouldn't stop and he didn't. He undid the clasp of my bra, and pulled my t-shirt up over my head. He bent down and licked my nipples, teased them, nipped them between his teeth, until the mixture of pleasure and pain drew a groan from my mouth. It was intoxicating, and I never wanted it to end.

His mouth moved to my belly button then to the edge of my leathers. He undid the button and crept just below the waist-band of my panties. Leaving feather light touches. "Oh god." The breathless words left my mouth when he replaced his finger with his lips.

"I've wanted to do this all night. Hell, I've wanted to do this since the first moment I saw you." He slid my pants down my hips, removing the one layer of clothing that kept us from being skin to skin. Then hooked his fingers in the edge of my polka dot silk panties and ripped them off.

He stared at my naked body, taking in all my curves as though memorizing them for later. His eyes darkened with lust, and for a moment I imagined they went from blue to amber. "Perfect," he said before lowering his mouth back to mine.

His hand stopped between my thighs and his fingers dove deep, working me, teasing me to the point of orgasm, then stop-ping, causing me to cry out in frustration. He looked at me, something savage glinted in his gaze, and a half smile curled his lips. Lowering his head, he separated my fold with his tongue, licking deeper and deeper. Entering me with his fingers, driving me to orgasm. I ran my hands through his hair, forcing more pressure on my sex, forcing his mouth to move deeper. His tongue moved faster, so did his fingers. The orgasm ripped through me, tearing a trembling cry from my throat, leaving me panting and breathless.

Eddie stirred, woken by the flutters that ran through my body. I took a deep breath and waited for him to settle again. Refusing to allow that part of my life to enter into this part of my life. The beast had a specific time and place and during sex was not it.

And as much as I enjoyed what Julian had just done, it was my turn to be in control.

I sat up, meeting Julian's mouth on the way, tasting the salt of my pleasure on his lips. His head dipped back down to my breasts, but I tilted it up to meet my lips again.

"Your turn," I whispered in his ear with a tiny nip on the lobe.

I stood, taking Julian with me, pulled his shirt over his head, fumbled with the buckle of his belt. When his jeans were undone, I knelt in front of him and slowly pulled them down his body, leaving him standing in a pair of black boxer briefs. A puffed up scar ran along his hip bone just above the edge of the fabric, leaning over, I ran my tongue up the rough edges. He moaned. A moan that sent me into a frenzy of must-have-him-now. Removing his boxers, releasing his large, rigid, hardness springing from its cloth prison, I reached up and took his penis in my hand, and rubbed my thumb across the tip. His head arched back and he sighed. I did it again, smearing the evidence of his arousal on his skin. Licking the tip with a flick of my tongue, removing the remaining liquid off his shaft, tasting how much he enjoyed my attention, knowing that for this very second I controlled him.

He stared down at me, and then I took him in my mouth. Sucking, nipping, licking. He gasped when I took his balls in my hand and massaged them. His fingers ran through my hair, over my back, along my arms. I licked across the surface of his balls. Sucking at the soft skin.

"Alexis, I need you, all of you," he groaned, his hands running through my hair, getting tangled in the curls.

But I wasn't ready to give him all of me, not until he came, not until I tasted his pleasure.

I pushed him onto the couch, sucked harder, stroked more, and teased until his legs trembled. When he came, he grasped the back of my head, forcing me to swallow every last bit.

Grasping Julian's hand, I guided him back to my bedroom. I pushed him onto the bed and straddled him. His head fell back and he groaned when my hand wrapped around his limp sex and began stroking. Long slow strokes guaranteed to make him hard and ready for what was about to come.

When he was at full attention, I placed his dick at the crux of my thighs and rubbed, building the friction between us. Letting him have an earth-shattering taste to entice him.

He cupped my breasts and moved his fingers in small circles around the nipples, building an intensity of his own. I bent over and kissed his lips, tugging at them with my teeth. Then I moved to his neck, his ear, his chest.

In a spur of a second, he flipped us over, pinning me underneath him, obviously wanting to be in control for a while. Rubbing his penis against my slit, bringing me back to a frenzied orgasm that rocked me.

My fist wrapped around him again and began to stroke hot and fast, causing his eyes to roll back in his head. He crawled back up my body and kissed me long and hard.

"No more teasing." He practically growled and separated my legs with his own. He bumped himself against my core, and pushed, but not enough to enter, just enough to hurtle me past sanity.

"Fuck me, Julian," I begged, needing him to fill me, erase the throbbing with his cock.

And he did, with a determined push. His thickness rubbed against me, his length filling my core. I tilted my hips and took him in as far as I could. Wanting all of him, deep inside of me. Wanting the connection sex would bring.

He started out slow, pulling almost all the way out, then forcing his way back in. Lifting my hips, I forced him to bury his penis into my flesh. My gaze never leaving his. Julian's rhythm picked up, rough and fast and I matched it with my own. He plunged into my body over and over. Stabbing me hard and deep. Our flesh pounding in a united rhythm. The bed knocked against the wall, pillows and blankets hit the floor, and he took me to a level of ecstasy I had never known before.

When my orgasm hit, the aftershocks rendered my limbs useless. Julian pumped away on top of me, continuing to slam me into the bed, faster and faster, harder and harder, more intense. Something savage flickered across his features, then he grunted and released his seed deep into my body.

He fell to the side and wrapped his arms around me. His hand caressed the side of my face, tender and sweet. "I don't know what it is about you, Alexis Black, but I've never wanted anyone like I want you."

His words made my heart do a dance. Boy, was I twitterpated.

Then he started the foreplay all over again and we continued to explore each other again until just before the sun came up.

When it came time to part ways, I walked him to the elevator.

He tweaked the tip of my nose and kissed the corner of my mouth. "Regrets?" He asked.

"No. You?"

He leaned forward and pulled me in for a deep kiss. "Never. Not with you." He let me go. "I'd like to see you tonight."

I wanted the same thing, to forget about everything else and get lost in bed with Julian, but real life had a way of sneaking in and throwing a bucket of cold water on any plans until

Terrance was caught and life was safe again. "I'd like that, but I have to see how things go with the case."

"Fair enough. Call me later. Let me know if you've got any news about Julia." He leaned in and whispered in my ear, "Good night, Alexis Black." He pulled back the elevator cage and stepped on.

I watched him disappear, wishing that he didn't have to leave, then I turned around and walked into the kitchen to warm my dinner.

"Is he as good in the sack as he sounds?" Nathan's voice reminded me that I should be embarrassed by last night's sex-a-thon.

"Good girls don't kiss and tell."

"Luv, your were anything but a good girl last night."

I removed my blood from the microwave and settled on the couch next to Nathan. "I think I'm entering dangerous territory with him."

"Nothing wrong with a good old bang in the hay."

"That's the problem. I'm not sure I want it to be just the occasional..." I stopped, not sure if I wanted to use the British slang. "Bang in the hay."

"Alexis, neither does he."

"If I were human this would be so much easier. I wouldn't have to worry about vamping out and eating him during sex. Or while we were cuddling on the couch." I grabbed a pillow and wrapped my arms around it, as if I couldn't protect myself from the hurt that would eventually come when Julian realized I was a monster.

"He already knows what you are and he hasn't scampered away yet. Hell, he keeps getting in deeper and deeper." He nudged me with his shoulder. "Get it deeper and deeper."

I threw my pillow at him and it floated right through him. Nathan had a way of making everything seem better. Always had. I could have a lot worst ghosts for a roommate.

I got up from the couch, stretched and yawned. "Time for me to get some sleep."

I was halfway down the hallway when Nathan called my name. "I only watched for a little bit." He broke out in a fit of laughter. "Just teasing you. There're some things I don't need to see."

I slammed my door and settled into my bed. The smell of Julian's cologne coated my pillows and sheets. I wrapped them around me, comforted by the aroma.

BASKING in the afterglow of last night's sex session was not going to happen. Not when Reaper marched into my room first thing the next evening and pulled back my blankets.

"We've got a problem." He stood and stared at me as if waiting for me to snap to attention like a good little soldier.

I pointed to the door. "Ten minutes."

He walked out. And just like that real life reared its ugly head and reminded me of my obligations.

I searched for any signs of Eddie, and found him sulking.

You dulled me.

It had to be done.

Never again.

That's not your choice.

We'll see.

I'm not sure I liked being threatened from my own self-conscious, but that was a problem for another day.

I got up and slipped on my clothes from the night before, tried to comb the snarls out of my hair, and then went out to face the night. I stopped in front of my bed and imagined Julian still wrapped up in the sheets, his arms draped over me.

Then I cleared my head and walked out.

Reaper was hunched over his maps, placing colored dots once again. Nathan floated next to him, silently supervising.

I walked over and sat next to them and placed my hand on Nathan's wrist. "What's the problem?"

Reaper placed one last dot on his map before he turned and faced me. "Coleman called. They found five bodies last night. All drained of their blood. Covered in fang marks. Just like the girl at the park."

"There's another nest out there."

"How many people is this bloke turning?" Nathan asked.

"More than the VAU can handle." Reaper returned to his dots. "Coleman's lost. Out of his element. He needs us. Told me he'd do anything to catch this monster."

"Including working with the enemy?"

"Including asking a vampire for help." He put the sheet down on the table and sat next to me. "He needs your help. We all do. The VAU can't catch this guy. They can't even find him. But you, you know how they think, how they move. You can get close. And I think you are the only one out there that can go head to head with Terrance and survive." He stood up and placed his hand on my shoulder. "You're all we've got."

Reaper didn't realize it, but he just placed a ten-ton cement brick on my shoulders and asked me to run a marathon. I hated being a vampire. Didn't want to know how they thought, how they moved. I never asked for any of this. And I certainly didn't want to be the only one who could kill this monster.

But sometimes the only way to catch a monster is with a monster.

"He's got a point, Alexis," Nathan added. "You grew up in one of the toughest Nests. Xavier is revered and feared in the vampire world for the way he treats his protégées. Plus, you have the soul of Vlad the Impaler. If anyone can go fang to fang with a monster like Terrance, it's you."

Nice of them to just keep piling on the guilt. "How long until you find the center?"

He didn't say anything at first, just kept placing dot after dot after dot. He laid a green one on top of a whole group of other green ones and then pointed to the section. "It's here."

The universe was obviously trying to tell me to get off my ass and hunt this creep down.

"Give me a few minutes to get cleaned up." I ran my hands through my sex- tousled hair. "The sooner we catch Terrance, the safer the streets will be."

And I guess I'm just the girl for the job.

Chapter Twenty

Nathan, Reaper, and I stood in front of a structure that used the term building loosely. It was even worse than the farmhouse where we found the first nest. I guess since I destroyed their first base of operations they had to move on to smaller and seedier surroundings.

Eddie practically tossed Reaper from one end of the gym to the other when we sparred, guess he was holding a grudge. It had felt glorious to be normal again, but I knew that the side effects of taking the serum for a long period of time were more than I wanted to deal with. One time was enough for this vampire.

I could almost taste the blood in the air. Thick and metallic with a tinge of something else, something pungent, I couldn't quite place. If they were on Julian's wonder drug it could be any number of a dozen mysterious herbs and chemicals.

So far the only side effect of the serum was a faint itch under the surface of my skin, an itch way too deep to scratch. I was just thankful there were no boils and pus.

I wrapped my hand around Reva and rolled my shoulders. "Ready for this?"

Reaper clicked off the safety on his gun. "Let's do it."

I took the first step, my foot slipping on a pile of ooze that coated the rotted wood. Reaper caught my arm and kept my butt from hitting the ground. "You all right?"

Bending down, I ran my finger through the substance, lifted it to my nose and smelled it. Then I ran my other fingers over it. "Not sure what this shit is, but it smells like urine and peppermint and feels like Silly Puddy." I wiped the foreign substance on my pant leg and continued on.

Reaper pushed open the door and stepped back. I waited

ten seconds in case anyone decided to charge us. When nothing more exciting than a stiff breeze happened I walked in.

And stepped into a room full of already dead half-vampires, half-humans. No piles of ash. No bloody messes on the floor. No living creatures.

Just body after body after body piled on each other in various corners of the gore infested room. Along with at least two dozen empty hypodermic needles strewn across the floor.

Ever see anything like this before, Eddie?

Not in all my years.

There went my hope that having the Vampire father stuffed into my body would prove to be helpful.

Reaper stepped in. "Jesus."

Kneeling next to one of the human piles, I examined the remains. The same bloody pockets of pus covered their bodies. I opened the mouth of a teenage boy, the closest to me. He didn't have any fangs. In fact, they all still looked human. None of the tell tale oddities that newly turned vampires have.

"They died before they could completely change over."

"But what killed them?" Reaper knelt next to me.

Nathan grabbed my arm. "There aren't any puncture wounds or bullet wounds or fang marks."

I twisted the head of the man in front of me, it rolled to the side with an eerie ease. "Broken neck."

Reaper stood up and attempted to wipe the grime off his jeans. "But why kill a room full of people he wanted to turn?"

"Let's look around. Maybe we can find something that will give us an inside analysis of Terrance's sick thought process."

We all went our separate ways. Nathan floated off to the kitchen, I picked the upstairs, and Reaper walked the room we had entered. When I stepped onto the landing it was obvious something was wrong. The bloody body hanging from the ceiling was a dead giveaway.

I walked closer. The man had been homeless judging by the dirty ripped clothing that hung off his skinny frame. The beard that covered the lower half of his face was full of grey hair, matching the salt and pepper routine on the top of his head. His once brown eyes stared across the room at the stained wallpaper. The rope around his neck left deep, red gashes in the flesh of his neck. A large blade sticking out of his chest held an envelope to his body, the words "Evil's Assassin" written in scrawled writing. I pulled out the blade and grabbed the paper before it hit the ground.

The envelope was heavy in my hands, the thick linen paper, not something you found in your local office supply store. I turned it over and ran my hand over the black wax seal with a fancy filigree "D" engraved in it.

Taking the stairs two at a time, I called for Reaper and Nathan. Once they were present I showed them the envelope. "Looks like he was expecting me." I broke the seal and pulled out the matching paper.

I've tried to ignore your presence, as I don't relish in killing my own kind, unlike you, but you continue to make it difficult when you show up where you are not wanted.

I'll let this stand as my first, last, and only warning.

Walk away. Leave me to my plight and I will leave you to yours. But if you persist on following this path you are currently on, then I shall make it personal.

I will snatch those you care about, those you hold dear, and make them pay for your actions. As I've proved by the bodies of those I was hoping would join my army, I have no problem with killing those who step in my way. You would be smart to remember that in the future.

There wasn't a signature to mark who it had come from, but judging by the wax marking and the old world look to the hand writing, it was obvious Delano had left it. I folded the paper back up and stuffed it into the envelope. "Looks like I've been warned." I considered tossing the whole thing on the pile of dead bodies, but reconsidered and stuffed the note in my pocket. "Too bad I'm horrible at following directions."

"And it seems I have found something that might help us."

Reaper held up two tickets in his hand. "They're for a place called "Wet Dreams", think it's worth checking out?"

"Sounds like a date to me."

Reaper started to walk away, but I put my hand on his shoulder to stop him. "Should we take one of the bodies to Julian? See if he can analyze it? Give us any new information?"

"It couldn't hurt." He walked over to the pile of bodies and lifted the carcass of an older woman off the top.

I called Julian from the car and informed him that we were delivering a sample from the nest to the morgue and to meet us there. He sounded giddy at the thought of dissecting and analyzing the dead body. Almost as giddy as I felt about seeing him again.

After depositing the body, one of the needles, and leaving Julian bent over her sore covered flesh, Reaper, Nathan, and I headed out to Wet Dream's.

WE WALKED UP to the entrance to "Wet Dream's." Having discussed the plan in the car, Reaper was going to check out the perimeter, since Terrance obviously knew I was hunting for him, and I would hang back in the shadows. Any sign of Terrance or Julia and he'd send Nathan for me.

The club was higher class than "Cuff's", but still kinkier than I would have preferred. I think this one would be considered more of a gentleman's club than a sex club, but what did I know.

I leaned against a charcoal grey wall, closest to the rest room, and tried to blend in. A hand wrapped around my waist, pulled me close, and ground what I hoped was something other than his penis into my backside. "Hey, gorgeous, wanna dance?" I didn't but Eddie was ready, but I'm pretty sure Eddie's idea of dancing wasn't what he was looking for.

I grabbed the idiot's wrist and applied just enough pressure to hurt, but not too much I might accidentally break the fragile bones. He let out a scared squeak, and his hands fell away from me. I turned around and faced the Danny DeVito look-alike who was now rubbing his wrist. "I'm not the girl for you. Go find someone who is interested in the short and hairy type."

But lover boy didn't seem to get the hint. He grabbed my hand and pulled me off to the side in an alcove between the men's room and the ladies room. "You've got a real attitude. Maybe someone should spank the sass out of you."

"It's not an attitude. I just don't like drunk, persistent, fucks."

"What did you just say?"

"Do you really need me to repeat it?"

"Someone needs to teach you a lesson." He looked me up and down. "Take you down a few pegs."

"Take your best shot."

He grabbed my arm and started pulling me close, and I let him. Nothing wrong with letting him think he had me right where he wanted me. His hand wrapped itself through my hair and then pulled my head back. His body pressed close to mine, and once again he rubbed his pudgy crotch against my hip.

Nathan snickered in the background. "Poor sod. Going to get more than he bargained for tonight."

The guy's hand started to slide up my shirt, getting dangerously close to no-no land. I grabbed his elbow and whispered, "You better remove your hand before I bite it off."

"Now we're talking," he said, but then he looked at my face. My fangs. My eyes. The beast who now stared at him from the depths of my soul.

He took off and never looked back.

Nathan floated closer. "You scared the piss out of him. Poor sod might never pick up another girl in a bar."

"Then I just did the female species a favor."

I settled back into my corner. "Why aren't you with Reaper?"

"He stopped to take a piss. I don't need to see what he's packing in his camos."

Nathan settled in next to me, a bored expression on his ghostly features. "I liked the other club better." He grumped. "Can we go back?"

"No." I tracked the crowd, looking for Reaper.

"The old Alexis would have gone with me."

"Maybe. Once upon a time." I looked over at Nathan and his my-puppy-just-died expression and remembered that he was forever doomed to go where I went and do what I did. What a boring existence. "Tell you what, when this case is over I'll take you back."

"I'm holding you to that." His frown turned upside down. Nathan nudged my arm. "Hey, is that Julian's missing twin?

I followed his arm. A girl at the bar matched the picture from Julian's wallet. From a distance, she shared her brother's dark hair and intense blue eyes, but that's where the similarities ended. Her outfit left little to the imagination, her breasts spilled out of her bustier top, and her ass cheeks hung out of a pair of way-too-small black tuxedo shorts. She clicked her hot pink nails on the bar as she waited for her order. Her head tilted when she laughed at the bartender and her neck sported some serious fang marks. Guess the clientele didn't care if the help helped feed the local vampire serial killer as long as their tits were hanging out of their uniform.

"That's our girl. Go get Reaper. Tell him we found her."

I held my ground even though I wanted to rush out, grab her by the hair and drag her back to her brother. She stood at the bar, not caring that her twin spent every waking minute searching for her. Not caring that she was bumping uglies with a crazed killer.

She filled her tray with some glasses and went on her way. Reaper turned the corner and bumped right into her, the tray toppling over, covering the two of them in ice and liquor. Normally, no matter how far away I was I could hear their conversation, but the music rattled the walls, making it impossible for me to hear. Thank god for the eagles eye view of what was going on.

Reaper and Julia bent over to pick up the broken glass. He grabbed a napkin off the ground and started to wipe the mess off her chest. She pushed his hand away and took over the duty. He leaned in and I watched his lips move. She nodded and smiled and then reached into the pocket of her booty shorts and pulled out a card. She slipped it into Reaper's palm and continued to pick up the glass.

They parted ways and Reaper headed out the front door. I followed behind, feeling bad that I wasn't dragging Julia with me, but at least I now knew where she was and could tell Julian.

Reaper waited for me inside the Chevelle. I climbed in beside him. "Tell me she gave you a number to reach Terrance."

"I got the golden ticket." He held up a cream colored, rectangle business card, the writing in small black letters, nothing but a name and phone number.

"Time to set up that meeting and put an end to Terrance's reign of terror." Things were starting to go our way. And I hoped that in less than twenty-four hours Terrance would be dead. Julia would be back with her twin. And the VAU would be out of my life for good.

It felt good to be optimistic.

Chapter Twenty-One

Wat does one pack when getting ready to meet a sadistic vampire hell bent on wiping out the human race? That was what Reaper and I were trying to figure out at the moment. I wanted him to pack his whole arsenal, but he thought it might be overkill.

Over kill or get killed, seemed like a no brainer to me.

Reaper called the number Julia had given him when we got back to my place. He hung up with a date, time, destination and a newfound determination to kick Terrance's butt.

Reaper's plan had me waiting on the outside, ready to rush in and save the night, while he walked in and presented himself as a hopeful new recruit. As plans went it seemed like a good one, except for the part where I let Reaper stroll into a room full of sick vampires.

One day. That's how long we had before Reaper walked into Terrance's den of death. One day to wait. One day to prepare. One day to hope that Terrance didn't go on a killing spree.

A large aerial photo of the house where Terrance was holding up shop was sprawled across my kitchen table. The area was desolate and surrounded by forest. The closest neighbors at least five miles away. The perfect place to house a secret vampire society.

I pointed to a circle of trees. "Nathan and I could hide here. I'd be close enough to get to you if things go bad."

"Too close. They'll smell you immediately." He moved my finger along the picture and placed it on top of another set of trees farther away than I was comfortable with. "Here."

"Too far. I wouldn't be there in time if they attack you."

He let go of his side of the map and it rolled up. "I'm going to be fine. This is the best chance we have to get to him. If they sense you around they'll spook, possibly kill me. It's better if you're far away."

"But—"

He slapped his hand over my mouth and I smelled the ink from the map on his fingers. "I know you're worried, but this isn't the first time I've confronted a vampire. Ex-VAU agent, remember?" His words carried that and-it's-not-up-for-discussion tone to it. I really hated that tone.

"I remember," I mumbled from underneath his fingers, but my agreement didn't erase the worry that coated my nerves. I decided to let it drop and let him think I was okay with a plan that might get him killed or even worse, turned into a vampire.

"Good. Then this is where you'll be waiting for me."

And because I was part of a team, I agreed to wait in a place that was much farther than I liked. Yea for team spirit.

Reaper and I spent the next hour going over possible escape routes and worse case scenarios. By the time he left I had snapped at Nathan for annoying me and was pacing the floor.

That's about the time I decided to call Julian.

My excuse to call—I wanted to tell him that we found Julia, but that was just a cover up for wanting him near. Doctor Julian Monroe had sliced his way into my heart as if he had a set of claws and the wound was deep. It's a shame that one night of hot sex turned this tough vampire into a simpering lovesick fool.

Julian showed up with a loud bang on the downstairs door. I went down to greet him and my breath caught when I saw him. Memories of his tongue licking my body up and down, his fingers guiding me to orgasm, and the feeling of him pumping inside of me, brought a blush to my cheeks, nose, ears. The fact that I would love to be in the same position soon raised my lips in a very wicked smile.

Julian stepped forward and wiped that smile away with his lips. "I'm so glad you called." He tugged at the strap of my tank top, lowering it so it exposed the top of my breast. He bent his head and licked along the soft flesh and the reason I invited him over got drowned out by desire and a throbbing from my sex.

We kissed our way back to the elevator and on the ride up. I opened the cage and we continued on over to the couch. I pulled my lips from his. "Nathan, out."

"If this is going to continue to be a thing we need to figure out a code for horny vampire in the house. A pair of knickers on the door?" he said, but left the room.

Julian and I headed to the couch and he continued to explore my body with his hands, mouth, and tongue. Things were progressing rather quickly, but it didn't matter, everything else in the world could wait. Tonight I needed this. Call it stress relief with the added bonus of a climax.

We disappeared into my room and it was easy to close the door on the maps and plans and possibility of death of the next night. I let Julian be a distraction and it felt good. Damn good.

But no matter how good I felt when we walked through the thin piece of plywood an hour later, the fear, urgency and uncertainty of the real world came back with a vengeance.

Now that my first reason for inviting Julian was done it was time to move on to the second one. I grabbed his hand and led him over to our makeshift control center.

He surveyed the photo. "What's this?"

"It's where Terrance is holding up."

"You found him?"

"We found Julia too."

He forgot all the stuff on the table and looked up at me. "Is she here?" The eagerness in his voice made my next words stumble out.

"No. I left her at the club."

Betrayal. Disappointment. Anger. Those were the emotions that marred his handsome face, and then anger settled on his down-turned lips and lowered brows.

"You found her and then left her?"

"We need her to get to Terrance, she's our only connection

to him." The pleading tone in my voice irritated me, made me feel weak. "If I would have snatched her out of the club, then Terrance would know that something was up." I pulled the note from the nest out from under a pile of papers on the table and handed it to him. "And obviously he already knows I'm coming for him."

Julian grabbed the paper from my hand, read it, and then handed it back. "It's my sister's life on the line."

I held up my hand to stop him. "No, it's more than your sister's life. It's the life of a lot of innocent people who didn't choose to become the target of a nasty vampire." I stepped close, but kept my hands to myself. "The girls in the morgue. They were his doing."

He took two large steps away from me. "All the more reason to yank her out of there. He's dangerous." His hand sliced through the air punctuating his thought.

I refused to let him distance himself from me, so I moved closer and laid my hand on his shoulder. "She's not in any danger."

"How can you say that?" His tone wasn't full of anger anymore, it was filled with worry.

"I saw her. She's happy. Content. Laughing. If she wanted to leave she had the opportunity. She doesn't want to. Just give us twenty-four hours and this will all be over and we'll get her out."

Julian flopped down on the couch. He scrubbed his hand over his face and let out a disgusted sigh.

I sat next to him and folded my feet under my butt. "I know it's hard—".

"It's not just hard, it's impossible. I'm all she has left, and she's turned her back on me." His words held a hint of regret.

"When are you going after Terrance?"

"Reaper's meeting is tomorrow night at eight."

"Tell me where and I'll meet you there."

"No."

"No?" Not anger, more like how dare you tell me what to do.

"That's not my choice to make. I work with Reaper, he has a say too." It was true. It wasn't my call to make. Reaper's life was on the line tomorrow, not mine. Inviting Julian to come with us could potentially get him killed.

He pulled his cell phone out of his pocket and held it out. "Then ask him."

I looked at the phone in his hand. There was no way I wanted Julian to come with. I didn't want to lose him if things went sideways. To risk his life like I was risking Reaper's. But telling him to sit and wait for me to rescue his twin sister wasn't the answer either. And by the look in his eyes, even if I told him to sit tight he would hunt me down. The man sitting on my couch was a man determined to find his missing twin and if I stood in his way, it would be the end of our new relationship.

I took the phone from his hand, but instead of dialing Reaper, I placed it on the coffee table. "Calling Reaper won't get us the answer you want."

"What will?"

"Be here tomorrow night at seven-thirty. If he sees that you are willing to help and won't take no for an answer, you may have a chance at being included." His scowl quickly switched to a smile. I held up my hand. "But I can't promise he will allow you to come with."

"He'll agree."

"How can you be so certain?"

"I've got a plan and it won't fail." He slipped his shoes on his feet and stood.

When we reached the elevator, I waited for him to pull back the cage, but instead he turned and wrapped me in his arms.

Close to my ear he whispered, "I know you worry about me, about having another person to protect, to save, and I love that you care so much, but I'm tougher than you know. I can handle whatever we walk into tomorrow."

I opened my mouth to interrupt but he covered my lips with his and kissed me long and deep and with a lot of tongue. Whatever argument I had blew away on a stiff breeze of feelings long buried.

His lips left mine. "Good night, Alexis." Then he got on the elevator and I watched him leave.

"Reaper is going to kick your skinny vampire butt when Doctor Hottie shows up tomorrow night," said Nathan, the ghostly buzz kill.

"I didn't have a choice."

"That's a crock. You had a choice, you just don't want him to stop offering you rides on his Wee Willy Winkle."

And once again Mr. Blunt And Obvious spoke the words out loud that we both knew were true.

Laughter burst out of me. Crazy, insane, bubbling from the pit of my belly laughter. I couldn't stop and I didn't want to, because tonight might be the last night that I had something to laugh about.

Chapter Twenty-Two

F ive minutes ago my cell phone rang. A very pissed off Reaper yelled, "Get your blood-sucking ass down here this instant."

I made the decision to make him wait and let the last three calls go straight to voice mail. When the pounding on the downstairs door got to the steel denting range I grabbed my leather duster, an extra stake, and headed down.

Nathan hovered next to me. "Think he's simmered down?"

"No. And I was happier when I had three inches of metal between us."

Even before I opened the outside door, Julian and Reaper's heated disagreement seeped into my small foyer.

I opened the door and two sets of eyes turned in my direction. Julian backed away and leaned against the hood of the Chevelle, his hands shoved in the pockets of his jeans. Reaper came rushing forward, one finger pointed at me, the other hand gripping the side arm on his hip.

"You invited him to come with us?"

"No."

"Then why is he here?"

I nudged my chin toward Julian. "Why don't you ask him?"

I crossed my arms over my chest and took the empty spot next to Julian by the car. This wasn't my battle. If I had my choice, Julian would be safely tucked away in my bed waiting for me to come home and help me release the tension of a stressful night. If he wanted to be included tonight, he was going to have to battle Reaper for a place on the team.

"You're pretending to be the neutral party?" Nathan came up next to me.

"More like acting as the referee and controlling the bloodshed."

Julian pushed away from the car and met Reaper face to face. "My sister is with that monster and if there is a chance that I can get her out, I'm taking it."

Reaper stepped closer, bumping Julian in the chest. "You'll get me killed and I don't know you well enough to die for you."

"You won't even know I'm there," Julian countered.

"Are you going to pull a Nathan and turn invisible, because that is the only way this group of vampires will not notice your pulsing vein walking through the doors."

"I'll worry about my veins and you worry about yours."

Reaper's face turned a lovely shade of purple. "You're. Not. Coming." He turned on me. "He's not coming." Nothing like being forced into participation.

"He'll just follow us," I answered, hoping to stay neutral, but point out the obvious.

"Not if I break both his legs."

"Oh good, we just entered the bodily damage part of the discussion," Nathan snickered from the sideline.

Julian clenched his fists at his side. "Are you threatening me?"

"Yes." Spit flew from Reaper's mouth and landed on Julian's face. "This is the only chance we have of catching this monster. You and your white knight routine are going to mess it up and then we may never get him again. Do you want the blood of the hundreds of humans who will die by him on your hands?"

"I only care about the blood of one person with that bastard and it's my sister's." Julian pulled a pack of tissue out of the pocket of his jeans and wiped Reaper's spit from his face. "I can either be invited or I'll follow you."

It was time to stop this fight and start thinking about the dangers that lie ahead. I stepped forward and wedged myself between the two heated males, placed my hands on two chests and used my enhanced strength to separate them.

I looked at Julian first, but didn't remove my hand. "Reaper has a point. You could get him hurt or killed looking for Julia."

"You said you'd help me." His words formed a knife of guilt and stabbed my heart.

"And I am." I let my hand fall from Reaper's chest and faced Julian. "I told you I'd get her out and I will, but not until after we have Terrance."

"Not good enough."

My anger rose. "What do you want me to do? Let you walk in and get yourself killed, or even worse, turned into a vampire?" And with just a few words I ended up emasculating him.

"I'm not fragile, something you need to protect." He ran his hands through his hair. "I'm tougher than you know and I'm going with you. If anyone has a problem with that, they can take it up with me afterwards."

He turned around, opened the door of the Chevelle and slid into the back seat.

The door closed with a bang.

Reaper turned his fury on me. "I'm not going to be responsible for his well-being."

"I'll keep him with me and try to convince him that running into a den of vampires is dangerous for his health." I walked to the car, but before I opened the door I added, "Let's just continue on with the plan, so we can catch this guy."

Reaper and I got in the car. He glanced back at Julian. "You're her problem." Then he started the car and pulled out of my parking lot.

To say that anger filled the air was an understatement. It wrapped around every living person in the small-enclosed space and squeezed the air out of the car. Nathan and I were safe from dying from suffocation due to male stubbornness, but Reaper and Julian would be the first to succumb.

Someone had to fill Julian in on the plans or he would be in the way and that would just cause another fight, something we didn't need in the middle of our mission. Since Reaper wasn't talking, and Nathan turned everything into a joke, I guess that left me.

"Julian, Reaper is going in under the pretense of joining up with Terrance."

"What will you be doing?"

"Acting as backup in case things go sour."

He shot a nasty look at the back of Reaper's head. "He doesn't want you involved either."

"I'd keep each one of you out of this if I could walk into that house and do this myself, but the moment I show up, someone is dying, and with the amount of vampires he has created in the past few weeks, I'm afraid I'd be out numbered and out fanged."

"I trust you to help me get Julia out, but him." He pointed his thumb in Reaper's direction. "He doesn't give a shit if my sister lives or dies."

Nathan, who had been sitting back and enjoying the show, spoke up. "Grab my arm, China Doll."

The sparks flew and Nathan solidified. "I've got an idea. Why don't I go in with Reaper and see if I can't locate Julia."

"The vampires can see you." Reaper piped up from the driver's seat. The only words he had muttered since I started explaining the plan to Julian.

"It's either Doctor Hottie here, or the ghost that can float through walls." He paused and seemed to be contemplating his next words. "I was planning on following you anyway. This will just give me something to do."

"I'd rather have the spook, than your boyfriend."

I started to open my mouth and tell Reaper that Julian wasn't my boyfriend, but decided it wasn't worth the debate. Priorities.

"Then it's settled. Julian, you stay with me and Nathan will go poke around to find Julia. When he locates her he can come tell us if it's safe for you to snatch her."

Julian sat for a few moments, his face in silent contemplation. "That works."

Nathan turned in my direction, a look that I couldn't interpret on his ghostly face. "I'm going to need to borrow some of your energy."

"Of course you will." I sat back and began to mentally prepare myself for Nathan invading my personal space.

After a few minutes of silence, Julian said, "I analyzed the sample you brought me."

"Was it your serum?"

"Not exactly. It looks like they've been trying to recreate it. Possibly change the composition to get rid of some of the more damaging side effects."

"Like bloody, pus filled sores?"

"That's one of them. But the serum does seem to be masking their supernatural scent, it's doing what it was made to do, so whoever is working on tweaking it is good at what they do."

"So, as you suggested, they are hiding in plain sight." Julian nodded. "Hiding from you."

Terrance had found a loophole, a way to get around the Assassins in the cities. A way to build his army right under our noses. And tonight I would put an end to his plans, his army and most importantly…him.

We drove the rest of the way listening to Nathan's vast array of dirty limericks and filthy jokes, just his way to lighten the mood and relieve the tension. And it worked.

We pulled into the clearing and Reaper cut the engine. We all sat in silence. I couldn't be sure what was running through everyone else's thoughts, but I knew mine.

Get everyone out alive. Kill Terrance. Put an end to this nightmare.

I stopped praying after two years of captivity in Xavier's house of horrors, but tonight might be a good night to resume my relationship with the big man upstairs. Reaper went to the trunk and popped open his secret compartment of weapons.

He pulled out a small handgun, almost smaller than the palm of his hand, and two knives. The gun went into the waist-band of his pants, and the knives slipped into the sheaths hidden in his army boots.

"You know they'll search you, right?"

He grabbed another gun from the trunk of the car and put it in the pocket of his zip up sweatshirt. "I'm hoping they'll find the guns and stop looking." He bent down and pulled his pants down over the tops of his boots. "The knives are located on the interior of the boots, so even if they do a pat down, they'll probably miss them."

Nathan cleared his throat. "Ready for me?"

An uncontrollable shiver shook my body. I steeled my spine and tried to act like the bad ass my reputation boasted.

Nathan stepped forward and into my body, even with the warning it sent shivers through me. I threw up my mental shields, hoping to hide any details I wanted to keep private from nosey ghosts. Sharing my body wasn't as bad the second time around, but I was still grateful when Nathan vaulted out.

"Let's see if it worked." He walked over to Reaper and slapped him in the ass. "Like a bloody charm."

Reaper grabbed his wrist before Nathan got away. "Better watch it, spook, or I'll find an exorcist."

Nathan yanked his hand free from Reaper's grasp and raised his eyebrows in his best Fozzie the Bear impersonation. "Waka, Waka."

Reaper ignored the ghostly instigator and tossed me his keys. "See you soon," he said.

Ex-marine, former VAU agent, and all around bad ass, those were all the titles that Reaper held, but he was also my friend and I couldn't let him walk down the road, to meet up with a monster without letting him know that I cared.

I stepped forward and placed my hand on his shoulder. "You

come back to me, in one piece, without any fang marks or bullet holes. Please."

The corner of his mouth lifted. "You won't get rid of me that easy. Someone has to be around to police your fangs."

Nathan walked over. "If anything goes wrong in there, I'll come get you." I nodded my head in confirmation.

Then I watched Nathan and Reaper head down the narrow road through the dense forest that would lead them to Terrance and hopefully the end of this nightmare.

Julian came up behind me and rubbed his hands up and down my arms. "He'll be fine. The man's too stubborn to die."

"There are far worse things than death." I was walking proof.

"He's strong and he has Nathan with him. If anything goes wrong you'll be able to help."

"I just wish I was with him."

He turned me to face him and kissed the tip of my nose. "Sometimes you have to sit and wait. You can't handle every problem on your own—you have to learn to allow others to help."

I entwined my fingers into his, settled against his chest and allowed the words to sink in. Since the day I escaped from Xavier, I've been on my own. Andre and I had separated so we couldn't be found and used against the other. I didn't know where he went and he had no clue where I was. Separated for our safety. On that very day I vowed never to feel responsible for another living soul.

Fast forward fifty years. Now I have two humans and one ghost I've allowed to worm their ways into my heart and feel responsible for their well-being. As much as I appreciated Julian's words, I couldn't relax and sit and wait.

I needed to be next to Reaper. Helping. Fighting. Protecting.

And just when I was going to explain my thoughts to Julian, Nathan came back.

"Your sister's in a place where you can nab her. All the

vampires are preoccupied with Reaper. If you want your chance, this is the only one you're going to get. Better make it fast."

Julian turned me around and kissed me full on the lips. "Everything's going to be fine."

He left me sitting in the dark and followed Nathan back down the asphalt. Leaving me wondering when I stopped being in charge and turned into the sidekick.

Chapter Twenty-Three

Pacing, pacing, pacing. That's all I did while waiting for Nathan, Reaper, or Julian to return. I worked hard to keep my mind off of what was happening in the house a mere football field away, but thoughts of blood and death and dead friends kept creeping in, but I had made a promise to let Reaper do this on his own, and if I broke it now, he'd never trust me again.

Twenty minutes of waiting and I contemplated leaving my post and moving closer to see what I was missing. Then I thought about the danger my close proximity could cause, and decided that I would do more harm than good.

I was relieved when two sets of footsteps crunched the fallen leaves on the ground. Peeking around the trees I spied Julian. His expression was grim, determined and, slightly pissed off. The girl being pushed in front of him was just as pissed off. Julian had one hand wrapped around her upper arm, the other covered her mouth. Tears streamed down her face and smeared her mascara. She struggled under his hold and a flurry of semi-muted curse words filled the silence.

"I see you found her," I said, stating the obvious.

Julian gave her a shove toward the car, but the moment he released her she attempted to run back down the path. He stepped forward and blocked her getaway. "Stay."

"Fuck you, Julian." She emphasized her words with her middle finger high in the air.

Julian stepped forward and grabbed her arm again, she was kicking at his shin, but it didn't seem like it bothered him. "I tried to be nice, but you obviously need time to cool off." He dragged her to the car, opened the door, and shoved her inside.

The slamming of the door cut off her objection to her

imprisonment. "Would you block the other door in case she tries to get away?"

I walked to the other side and leaned against the door just as she was pulling on the handle. She stopped when I glared at her and slumped in the seat.

Then she decided to take her anger out on the front car seat and continued to punch and kick the vinyl. She better watch it. If she did any damage to Reaper's car a pissed off brother would be the least of her worries.

"Now what?"

"I'm going to give her a few minutes to cool off. When she's done with her tantrum, I'll pull her out and talk some sense into her."

I leaned down and looked through the window, which was steaming up from the heat pouring off her severely pissed off body. "She might need a little longer than a few minutes."

"It's for the best."

"Did you see Reaper when you were up there?" I glanced in the direction of the house.

"No, but Nathan gave me a message for you. His words. I'm watching the wanker, no need to worry."

That small bit of information brought me the tiniest bit of relief.

Julia continued to yell from inside the car. I didn't have the energy to waste trying to yell over her to continue my conversation with Julian, so I leaned against the cool metal and waited. We'd have time to talk when all this was done and over. Fifteen minutes after Julian had forced her into the car, Julia rolled down her window and started spewing venom at her brother. "Julian, you piece of shit. You can't do this to me. Let me out immediately,"

Julian stuck his face in front of the window. "I can, and I will. At least until you understand how much danger you're putting yourself in."

"Go to hell. I don't need you to protect me anymore. I've got Terrance."

I'd seen the way Terrance treated those around him. If Julia thought she was safe, she was fooling herself. Maybe love was so blind she couldn't see the sick and twisted monster she worshipped.

Julian opened the car door, and pulled her out. "That piece of shit vampire is nothing more than a murderer."

I tried not to take the piece of shit vampire comment to heart. Telling myself that Terrance and I were nothing alike, but the words still clung to my useless ticker with little poisonous barbs of doubt that infiltrated the walls.

He shook her once, and then pulled her close. "I'm the only one you have left to protect you, or did you forget?"

"I shouldn't need protection, and I wouldn't if you hadn't made us run and hide like cowards." Julia got in his face and snarled. "We should have fought for our rightful place."

"If we had fought, we would both be lying next to mom and dad in the graveyard."

I stood looking at the twins, their words confusing me. I felt like there was something I was missing. Something wedged between the lines so tightly that I'd completely miss it without careful inspection.

"I can't save your skin if you keep doing stupid shit." Julian's deep voice carried a bit of growl.

"I don't want you to save me. I want you to leave me alone."

"So the pack can find you. Hurt you. Kill you?"

Little bells started to tinkle at the word pack. Only wild animals and supernatural beings had packs.

Has your new lover been hiding something from you? I guess Eddie had been listening too.

I ignored my inner tag along and focused on what the twins were saying.

"They don't want me, they want you." She pushed against her brother's chest. "I'm a female, and of no use to them, but you, you're next in line. Terrance says I'm safer if I'm away from you."

"He can't keep you safe. And if they catch you they'll use you to get to me. Just like they used Mom to get to Dad."

My Eddie sense detected some deep secrets in Julian's fucked up family tree.

"They wouldn't hurt me." Her doubt carried through her words.

Julian grabbed her arm, shaking her slightly. "Being hurt would be the least of your worries. In fact, being dead would be better than what they would do to you." She grimaced when he squeezed her arms tighter. "They'd capture you. Torture you for my whereabouts. Then they'd rape you, one after another until you were pregnant. All so they could have a royal heir to control. Once you gave birth, you'd be expendable and then you'd be dead. "

"You don't know that."

The twins faced off, both staring at each other, one with a look of concern, the other with a look of hatred. What had Julian done to earn his sister's loathing?

Julian grabbed two fistfuls of his hair. After a few minutes, his hands fell to his side. "Julia, listen, I'm trying to do the right thing here."

"No, you're not. You're not doing what's best for me. Only what's best for you."

"Kolb. Can't. Find. You." Each word more controlled than the other. The only sign of his true rage were the tight fists at his side.

"He already has," she hurled at him.

Julian grabbed her arms again, his hands shaking. "How? When?"

"He works with Terrance now. I ran into him a week ago and he told me I was safe from him. That the pack only wants you. You're the alpha wolf, not me."

Alpha wolf.

My head jerked to look at Julian, but he wasn't focusing on me, he was too intent on what his sister was saying.

It wasn't possible. Julian couldn't be a werewolf. I would have known, Eddie would have known. Smelled him. Felt his otherworldliness. Tried to eat him.

How had he escaped the beast's notice?

Then I remembered his words the night he told us about his serum being stolen. *"A werewolf on the serum could be sitting across the table from you right now and you would never know it."* Damn, he had come right out and told me, but I never even suspected.

There were other hints too: the flash of amber in his eyes during sex, how he beat Reaper and me to my home that night after the morgue.

The serum. It wasn't for a friend. It was for Julian. For his sister. A way to hide from whatever problems surrounded them.

He had lied. Lied to get close to me. To use me.

What did that mean for our relationship? I obviously couldn't trust him. And what did he really feel for me? Those poisonous bards of doubt sank their teeth deeper into my heart. So deep it would take more than a pair of tweezers to remove them; it would take open-heart surgery.

We haven't killed a werewolf in a while.

And we're not starting tonight.

Only a matter of time until his miracle juice wears off and we'll be forced to. Remember Nathan?

I won't let it happen.

Julian owed me answers and an explanation, and I was about to step forward and demand them when gunshots erupted from the direction of the house.

Ten shots from a small caliber pistol, like the one Reaper tucked into his pocket before he left. Then more from something larger and far tougher than Reaper's side-arm.

Shit. I knew this was a bad idea.

More and more gunfire peppered the silence of the surrounding area. I glanced at Julian and the look he gave me broke my heart. A look filled with regret, unhappiness and the words I'm sorry. But right now I couldn't worry about my shattered love life, I had to get to Reaper and fast because the smell of fresh blood overpowered the smell of the late August breeze and burning leaves.

Eddie sprang to life. I could always count on him when it came to a good fisticuffs.

I turned my back on Julian and raced down the sidewalk. Raced to save Reaper. Raced to save the day.

I just hoped I didn't fail my partner like I failed my parents.

Chapter Twenty-Four

The bushes lining the sidewalk waved in the breeze, their pungent juniper smell over powering, but not strong enough to cover the stench of the supernatural. Eighty-five feet into my rescue mission Eddie slashed my insides for release.

Give me control.

No.

Only I can save your human.

You can only have control when I have no hope.

I meant it. Eddie would never control my body as long as I was still alive to keep him on a tight leash.

I pulled in a deep breath and slowed down to a jog. My eyes searched through the darkness for anything lurking in the bushes. The more vampires I killed getting to the house, the less I had to worry about once I was inside.

Plus, if I let anything get past me, I put Julian and Julia in danger. Although I was pretty sure he could take care of himself, now that I knew what truly lurked under the handsome exterior, and smart guy persona.

Now if only Nathan would make an appearance and help me with some recon work. It would be nice to know what dimension of hell I was walking into.

Where the heck was our ghostly partner anyway?

I spotted the enemy before I found Nathan. Three vampires up ahead, all a shade of white that doesn't exist on the color spectrum, meaning they weren't new vampires. They blocked my path. Waiting for me.

Time to play. Eddie's excitement surged through our bond.

I didn't want to close the distance between us too quickly, making them feel nice and comfortable confronting a five-foot-six female vampire worked well with my plans. They were carrying guns on their hips, but didn't pull them out and try to fill me with lead. For that I was thankful.

When I got an arm's length away I launched myself into a flip over their head and landed behind them. They spun to face me, but when they got around my dagger was in my hand. I sliced and one head fell to the ground and rolled into the bushes that lined the sidewalk. The last two charged. The first in line bent over, wrapped his arms around my waist, and took me down. My head hit the ground hard, but not hard enough to render me useless.

The second vampire thought it would be a good idea to try and wrestle Reva out of my hands. He tried to pry my fingers off the hilt, but I just held on tight and used the momentum of his actions to my advantage. He pulled. I pushed. The dagger sliced through his neck and his head rolled to the ground, joining his buddies on the perfectly manicured lawn.

"They never told us you were that strong or fast." The last vampire's tone was a mix of awe and fear. Mostly fear.

That's the problem with my particular skill set—the rumors never make it to the general population because no one is alive long enough to spread them.

I pushed his buddies headless body off of my chest and stood up. The last vampire looked at his fallen comrades, back at me, then backed away, his hands held high. It wouldn't help, he was in my sights and there was no way I was letting him walk out of here alive.

Three fast steps brought me closer to my target. I pulled my stake out of the loop on my pants and took two more steps. Grabbing him by the shirt, I was ready to plunge my stake into his heart and end him. Wanted to end him. Then a deep masculine scream came from the house and broke through the quiet night. Made my breath catch and I forgot about the vampire in my clutches. He raised his hand and buried his knife in my chest up to the hilt. The silver stung like a scorpion bite, but it wouldn't render me dead.

Bastard! I removed the blade. Blood dribbled down my shirt for a moment before my body began to heal itself. What he didn't anticipate was death by his own weapon. I gripped the hilt and sliced a large gaping line over his heart. Then I buried my stake into his now visible blood pumper. His body burst into flame, but I didn't stick around to see him dissolve to ash.

Nathan appeared at my side. "One more coming your way."

As much as I wanted to take a moment to ask Nathan what was going on, I didn't have the time to waste. Hopefully he would stay by my side and guide me along.

I nodded and ran off the concrete and into the bushes, a sneak attack to throw him off. I pushed through the branches and leaves until I was behind the vampire laying in wait. Once settled behind them, I popped out, quiet as a bat.

I stabbed the vampire through the back, but the stake didn't go in far enough to kill him. He turned around with it stuck in his bone, pulling it out of my hand. Snapping into action, I snatched Reva from her sheath and went for his throat. My dagger sank deep, and while he fought to remove it, I reached around and shoved the stake all the way through, finishing the job. He burst into ash.

"Four coming through the trees," Nathan advised. "Terrance sent every sodding vampire in the house out to hunt you down when he found out Reaper's true identity."

My stomach flip-flopped at the thought of Reaper in the hands of Terrance. The large trunks hid me as I made my way through the oak trees and roots until I came upon the first of the four vampires out hunting for me. No surprise attack this time.

He held his 9mm gun in his hand high, and pulled the trigger. Leaving me just seconds to dodge the Super Man speeding bullet aimed at my heart. It whizzed past my ear and stuck in the tree behind me. Too close, and judging by the look of his gun there were six others waiting to follow their friend.

I let Eddie have a bit more freedom.

Ready?

Always.

The sound of the gun called his friends from out of their hiding places and they all decided to use me as target practice. Bullets flew by and most missed their mark. Most, but not all.

One bullet lodged in my hip, stuck in the bone. The second went straight through my thigh. The pain dulled my vision, causing me to see nothing but black. The ground coming fast at my face.

Eddie pushed past the pain. Forced me to my feet. He bull-dozed me forward and made me front and center in a vampire killing frenzy. Tearing off limbs and twisting off heads with my bare hands. Tearing out throats with my fangs. Fighting to survive. Fighting to rescue Reaper.

With the last vampire sent back to hell, I stepped back on the path, determined to get to my partner. The silver bullet lodged in my bone felt like it dug in a little deeper with every step I took. The hole in my leg seeped blood. I was a fucking mess, but Eddie kept me upright.

Nathan floated close, examining my wound. "Alexis, you've got to get to Doctor Hottie. I don't think my healing power is strong enough to remove a bullet, but he can."

"Later." I gritted my teeth to move past the pain. "Need to find Reaper first."

"He's not there. Terrance threw him in a car and took off."

I continued on my route to the house, hoping there was something there that would lead me to Reaper. But the only thing I found was a wide open front door and the smell of blood.

I inhaled deeply. Human blood. Damn.

I stepped over the threshold, using the doorjamb for support. I knew before I entered the room that it would be empty, but I still had to check.

Blood splattered the couch, and easy chairs set up in the living room. Three piles of ash decorated the expensive Oriental rug. At least Reaper had managed to take a few out before they took him.

"Do you know where they took him?"

"No idea. They piled him in a dark blue car. I tried to follow, but then zapped back to you when they got too far away."

Worry for Reaper crept through my mind and trampled my heart. I couldn't leave him in the clutches of the vampires, especially this vampire. Not after everything I had learned about his family. Reaper would rather die than be turned.

There was one person who knew where they might go and I'd beat the information out of her if I had to.

I limped back to the car, losing more blood by the minute. Julian saw me coming back and rushed to my side, leaving his sister fuming against the white striped hood of the car.

He pushed my hand out of the way. "Alexis, let me see."

My hand fell away and the pain almost rendered me unconscious. Julian inspected the wound. "Why aren't you healing?"

"Silver bullet." I stopped and took a deep breath. "Stuck in the hole. Stopping me from healing." I slipped to the ground, unable to hold my weight up for another second.

"Julia, get your ass over here," Julian demanded.

"I'm not helping you save her."

Nathan marched over, grabbed her by the arm and marched her to her brother. At that point I was thankful for his energy stealing power. He pushed her toward Julian. "Help him or I'll figure out a way to posses you and jump your body in front of an oncoming train."

Julia didn't argue, and knelt next to me. "What do you want me to do?" Her voice sullen and pissed off.

"Hold her shoulders down. I'm going to have to dig the bullet out and all I have is a pocket knife." He leaned forward so I could see his face. "This is going to hurt."

Nodding, I braced for the pain. He touched the bullet lodged in my bone with the tip of a knife and I immediately cursed the darkness in my life. Cursed Caleb and his deal. Cursed everything hammering its ugliness directly in my path.

Cursed Terrance, promising that once I could stand I'd hunt his bitch ass down and kill him.

Eddie tore at my shields, my control. My fingers wrapped around Julian's neck, squeezing until the pain stopped.

He used a strength I would never have guessed he possessed, reminding me that he wasn't human either, and unpeeled my fingers from his skin.

"Sit on her hand. I've almost got it."

He started back at the bullet. I resisted the urge to kill him and allowed him to do his job. *Plink.* The bullet hit the ground and the pain faded.

My skin tingled as it started to knit back together and I pushed myself into a sitting position.

Julian turned to his sister. "Does your boyfriend have you so messed up that you hesitated to help keep someone alive?"

"With her dead, Terrance's plan will succeed."

Her brother opened his mouth for another verbal slap down, but I was feeling better and had had enough with their sibling bickering.

I reached up and grabbed Julia around the upper arm… hard. To her credit she didn't flinch, and she didn't pull away, she met my eyes head on. "I've got a very limited amount of time to save my partner. Where are they taking him?" I demanded, giving her arm a little shake for emphasis.

"I'm not telling you."

"You will or you won't live through the night."

Julian stepped forward, his eyes focused on the girl in my hands and not on me. "Alexis, let me talk to her."

I should have been upset with him for his lies by omission, but he'd just saved my life so I owed him some courtesy. I didn't owe his sister jack shit.

I turned to him and let all my anger seep into my voice. "No. She doesn't respect you enough to answer you." I knew I was shooting low, but at the moment bruising his ego was the least of my worries.

"What makes you think I respect you? You're an abomination, a joke among the Underground." She spat. "A vampire who is too cowardly to be a true vampire. Too afraid to take the power she was given. Your Sire wasted his blood turning you. You're a monster. Killing your own kind. That's what Terrance says."

"Oh, the opinion of a serial killer. That holds a lot of weight."

"At least he is honest about who he is." She tried to pull out of my grip.

"Julia, I'm going to let you get away with what you just said because I am friends with your brother, but know this. If anyone else dared utter those words to me, they would be missing a few vital organs to survive."

"That's right, you just kill those who don't agree with you."

"I kill those who deserve to die." I squeezed her arm tighter. "And right now you're not doing anything to make me feel like you deserve to live."

I pulled her close. Let my eyes flare red. Watched hers get huge. I unleashed Eddie just enough to scare the piss out of her. I was more honest about who I was, and what I had become than anyone she would ever meet. If who I truly was didn't scare the information out of her, she was truly gone. Nothing I could do or say would get her back for her brother.

"Tell me where they are taking Reaper," I demanded.

She turned her head so she didn't have to look at me. "I won't."

Julian reached up and touched my shoulder. To his credit he didn't even flinch when I looked at him. "Let me."

I gave up, let my hand fall away, and stepped to the side. Now that the pain was gone, my features returned to their normal non-monster looks, but I turned my back on the twins anyways.

"Julia, this is a human's life we are talking about. Not another Undergrounder."

"Who cares about the humans? We're stronger. We deserve to be in control."

Her words let me know just how truly brainwashed she was. Poor Julian, he might never get his sister back.

"You don't mean that." His voice couldn't mask his disappointment in her. "What's happened to you?"

"I learned the truth."

I couldn't hold my tongue. Not with Reaper's life on the line. "The truth according to the vampire you so obviously worship?"

"I love him. I don't worship him."

I grabbed the keys to the Chevelle out of my pocket, and marched to the car. After opening the trunk, I searched through Reaper's papers for the pictures that James had given him of the crime scene and the victims. Slamming the trunk, I walked back to where Julia stood with her arms crossed over her chest, and her chin jutted in the air. Stupid, stubborn girl didn't have a clue how much of a monster the man she loved really was.

I held up the first picture, the one of the first two girls Reaper and I rescued. The one of a young girl, close to Julia's age, her throat torn out, blood surrounding her. The other of the girl I didn't save, the one who ended up in Julian's morgue, her dead eyes staring at the camera. "This is the monster you are protecting, and this is just two of his victims."

"He didn't hurt those girls." She tried to avert her eyes. I grabbed her chin and forced her to look at what her lover had done.

"He created the monsters that did," I spat. "It may not have been by his own two hands, but it was by his actions they are dead."

Julian stepped forward and pointed to the girl he had on his slab just days before. "She was nineteen years old. I stitched up the holes the vampires that fed from her left behind. Hundreds of puncture wounds from fangs. I made her presentable so her parents could have an open casket when they buried their child." He pushed the pictures into her hands and stepped back.

She studied the photos then handed them back to Julian. "They took him to the Blood Bank."

I sucked in my breath, hoping to hold the fear inside. If Reaper was headed to a blood bank, I may not be fast enough to save him before they drained him dry.

I pushed her into the car, cranked the engine, and pulled out of the parking lot with a squeal of wheels. "For your sake, he better be alive when we get there."

Chapter Twenty-Five

At first, Julia refused to give me the address, insisting she would guide me. Then I reminded her that the option to rip out her throat and drink her dry was still on the table. She finally came clean with the information. I plugged the information into the GPS and followed the twists and turns that got me closer to Reaper.

Her shitty attitude only made me want to replenish my lost blood with hers. Then I remembered that she wasn't human, but a werewolf. I'd never ingested werewolf blood. Would it have the same effect on me as human blood or would it make me sick? That thought then reminded me that Julian had lied to me. Betrayed me.

Now I understood the fear he felt the day I walked into the morgue. He wasn't sure if his serum could hold up when confronted with Evil's Assassin. He'd told me a lie about why he made the serum in the first place. What else had he lied about? I wanted answers, but now wasn't the time and our current audience didn't need to be privy to our sexual history.

Instead, I focused my attention on the conversation between brother and sister. "How can you be around her?" I gritted my teeth at Julia's whiney tone and forced my hand firmly on the steering wheel to keep from reaching back and strangling her.

"Alexis is just doing her job." Julian defended me. I was still pissed at him, but it brought a smile to my face.

"Told you he understood your true nature." Nathan piped up from the passenger seat.

"Her job involves killing our kind for a living. For her own selfish purpose."

"She is no different than Kolb. Remember him, the man who murdered our parents for his own agenda," he shot back.

I took offence at being compared to Kolb, not that I knew him, but I didn't kill for joy or agenda, I killed to survive. One more problem for another day.

"Kolb had his reasons for killing our parents." She turned in her seat and faced her brother. "She kills because she wants to."

"You don't know why she does what she does."

"Terrance told me she does it so she can become human again. Is that true?" Her voice rose and I assumed she was addressing me.

"Yes." I didn't offer an explanation, she didn't deserve one.

"But why? Why give up all your power. Why turn yourself into something so weak?"

Such a shame that one twisted vampire turned this girl into a human hating bigot with low morals and poor judgment. "You're young, a baby compared to me. Someday you will learn that happiness can't be bought with the power and control you have over other people."

"Control keeps you from being weak, from being used."

"If you're hanging around the right people, then you won't have to worry about being used." I turned my head and glanced at her brother from the corner of my eye. "You need to find a better class of people to surround yourself with."

"Who? Someone like you?" She sat back in her seat and crossed her arms over her chest. "No thanks."

Because a homicidal maniac was better than the vampire sitting next to her. "Julian, I hate to say it, but your sister might be a lost cause."

Nathan harrumphed from the back. "Bloody sodding waste of flesh if you ask me."

The GPS told me to turn left in one mile. I turned off the road before I hit the mile mark and cut the engine.

Before I stepped out of the car Julia grabbed my arm. "Please don't kill Terrance."

I removed her hand from my flesh. "If I have my way, he

will be the first one I stake." I slid out of the car and slammed the door.

"Nathan, head over and tell me what I'm about to walk into." Nathan gave me an aye-aye captain salute and left.

For once I was thankful for Reaper's trunk full of firepower. I rifled through the arsenal and slipped stakes and guns in all the appropriate places. There was nothing wrong with going in covered with enough weapons to take down a whole city.

Nathan's voice preceded his ghostly form. "It's bloody awful in there."

"What's going on?"

"The wankers have him hung up like a slab of beef. He's still alive, but not for long if you don't get in there and do something."

I slid Reva into her sheath. "How many vamps?"

"Twelve vampires, four wolves guarding the front entrance and two at the rear."

"I've seen worse," the false bravado strong in my words. I started to the warehouse.

There was a commotion behind me. A scuffle, a scream, and a growl. I turned just in time to see a large wolf with soft pearl grey fur, flecked with black and brown, bust through the car door. Fur still damp from the change, ears pinned, fangs bared, anger radiating from its deep brown eyes. It charged at my throat.

Only two werewolves in the car and Julian stood there in shock. That left Julia. I held up my arm to block the attack, and she clamped down on my forearm, closing her teeth around it, with enough force to break the bone. I kicked her in the chest, and she yelped, tumbling backwards. Four large puncture wounds wrapped around my wrist, all oozing blood.

I pulled my dagger out of its sheath and waited for her to come at me again. She did, this time going for my ankles and legs. I dodged her teeth and claws and punched her in the head.

She fell to the ground, and I placed my boot on her flanks, the tip of my blade at her throat.

Julian ran over, but he didn't say anything. He just waited to see what my next move would be.

Blood dripped from my arm and fell to the ground. I wiped it on my jeans. "You're lucky I have a complicated relationship with your brother."

The wolf beneath my feet whined but didn't try to move.

I looked at Julian. "Get her out of here." I lifted my boot, and the wolf crawled on her belly, her head down low, over to her brother.

He reached down and grabbed her by the scruff, then looked at me. "I'm sorry," he said. "For everything." Then he dragged his sister along with him back to the car.

I called out to him. "You owe me an explanation when this is all over."

He nodded. "I know, and I promise you'll get it."

"Were-bitch thought she would give you a toss?" Nathan asked with a smile in his voice.

I raised my arm and examined the already healing bite marks. "Stupid love-sick fool." I let my arm drop back to my side. "If they know who Reaper is, they'll be expecting me." I nodded to the building. "What do you suggest?"

"Hike up your brass balls and walk right through the front door. Like you're the Prime Minister and this is 10 Downing Street."

Sometimes Nathan's obscure English references were lost on me, but I got the idea.

He had a point, but I needed to tread carefully. I had Reaper to worry about. Barging through the front would give Terrance plenty of time to rip out his throat, and then I would fail my rescue mission. But then again, tearing four werewolves from tip to tail would show him exactly the kind of badass he was dealing with.

Decision made.

Give me control.

All I need is your normal boost of power. I can take on a pack of werewolves.

We'll see.

The walk through the old warehouses with their broken windows and gratified bricks gave me the time I needed to come up with a plan. A good plan? Maybe not, but a plan.

The closer I got to the Blood Bank, the more intense the fire that traced my brand became. The redder the world looked. The longer my fangs grew. Eddie stirred just under the surface. Waiting. Anticipating the upcoming confrontation. For once I didn't fight his presence.

I soaked in all the power Eddie had to offer.

There was a stack of empty crates under the window. I climbed up and hooked my hand over the edge of the window frame and peered inside.

Reaper hung upside down, fingers barely touching the filthy ground. A large cut on his forehead oozed blood, and two large fang marks marred his neck. Shit, they had fed from him.

Five humans, ranging in age and gender, hung next to him, all in the same predicament.

I sucked back the growl that wanted to escape. The anger that seeped in at seeing Reaper dangling. The urge to run through those doors and kick ass. But being rash and unprepared wouldn't help me.

Instead, I assessed the situation.

Vampire guards stood with large rifles in their arms. Probably filled with silver bullets. Four fuzzy werewolves guarded the rear and paced back and forth in front of steel door. Ears perked, nails clicking on the pavement, and nostrils flared.

I spared one last glance into the window. A vampire stepped out from an office to the left, dragging another vampire covered in gaping cuts and dripping blood along with him. He threw the vamp across the room, and walked back to the row of humans hanging from the meat hooks.

"Five humans are all you could bring me?" His voice boomed through the nearly empty room. "Pathetic haul, and will in no way feed the fledglings."

The vampire cringed in the corner, his voice as shaky as his legs. "I'm sorry, Terrance."

My enemy.

From where I stood, he didn't look like much. Six feet tall, thin, slicked back dark hair, and dark eyes to match. I'd met a thousand other vampires like him in my undead years. Although he did possess something the others hadn't. Confidence. You could see it in the way he held his head with regal superiority. His pushed back shoulders. Chin tilted up. The curl to his lips, not a smile, not a smirk. Standing before me was a man who did not expect to lose this battle.

Terrance walked by the row of humans. He stopped in front of Reaper, bent down, and grabbed his chin between his fingers. "And you. What should I do with you?"

Reaper struggled under his touch, but Terrance didn't let go.

"A slow death of blood loss is too good for you." Terrance's hand squeezed and Reaper cried out. "No. I need to find your weakness. Exploit it. Like you tried to exploit mine."

Shit.

Ten feet separated me from the front door and my rescue mission. I jumped from the crate, ready to barge in and help my partner. Took one silent step after another that would take me onto the battlefield, and stood next to the corner of the building, ready to take on the werewolf guards.

Out of nowhere, Julia rushed through the doors, screaming, "She's here. Evil's Assassin is here."

Double shit.

Well, there went my entrance, my element of surprise, and my plan.

I crept back to my crates to see how Terrance reacted to Julia's news.

Terrance released his hold on Reaper and walked over to the distraught Julia.

He wrapped her up in his arms. "You played your part perfectly, my tiny wolf."

She melted into his arms, and soaked up his affections before she said, "My brother was with her. I had to fight him to get away. I came as soon as I could. She plans on killing you."

His grip fell away from Julia and he walked back over to Reaper. He kneed him on the side of the head. "I wouldn't expect anything less from a traitor of her kind. That's why I have her partner. He's my insurance policy." He walked back to Julia and wrapped his arms back around her. "He's human. She'll do anything in her power to save him." He stroked Julia's face with the back of his hand. "And I'll do everything in mine to make sure I see her dead before the night is out."

Challenge accepted.

Chapter Twenty-Six

The hand that once caressed Julia's cheek reeled back and slapped her. A slap so unexpected, she flew across the room and landed in a pile of old bloody rags. Her body lay limp for several seconds before she reached up and covered the already developing red marks with her hand. Tears rolled down her cheeks, highlighting the betrayal and hurt swimming in her eyes.

"Why?" I couldn't tell what was shaking more, her hands or her voice.

Terrance turned on her, but didn't go near her, instead he bellowed, "You're not needed anymore. I've got the serum, the only thing you were good for."

"But...but...you said you loved me." She crawled on her knees like some sort of pathetic submissive creature. "You love me." Her voice slow and low.

He marched across the room and snatched her by the arms, giving her a fang-rattling shake. "Stupid mongrel." He released her and she crumpled to the ground at his feet. "I have about as much love for you as your own kind does."

I'll admit that Julia was not high on my list of people I wanted to sit across the table from at Thanksgiving dinner, but no one deserved to be treated like dirt. Used and discarded when they're not wanted anymore.

Terrance gestured to one of his lackeys. "Bind and hang her." Two vampires stepped forward and yanked her off her knees. They dragged her next to Reaper and tied her ankles and wrists. Once she was secure, Terrance turned his back on her.

Julia fought against the ties. "No, please don't."

The vampires flipped her over and hung her on the empty

hook next to Reaper. She struggled, moving the chain, bumping into him.

"Terrance, Terrance." Her screams and pleas fell on uninterested ears.

Terrance turned, walked over and knelt down next to her. His hand cupped her chin. "Maybe just one last taste. I love the kick your werewolf blood delivers. The power that flows from your body to mine." He licked his lips and plunged his fangs into her neck. There was nothing sweet or kind about the way he tore into her throat. The bite was savage and brutal.

Julia wailed and then passed out. Terrance lifted his head from her neck, her blood dripping down his chin. Pulling a handkerchief from his pocket, he wiped away the dribbles, then stepped close to Reaper. "You and I are going to have a little chat."

Reaper spit at Terrance, a glob of mucus mixed with blood hung off the vampire's shirtfront. Terrance's hand reached out and smacked Reaper across the face, sending him swinging from side to side.

"Human filth," Terrance spat.

"Vampire vermin," Reaper retorted.

"I'll not be the vermin for much longer. Soon, your kind will bow to me. Right after I slaughter the Sovereign Body."

"It'll never happen," Reaper said.

"Oh?" Terrance raised one eyebrow in question.

"Alexis will stop you."

Terrance stopped Reaper's still swaying body, and forced him to meet his eyes. "No. Evil's Assassin won't be alive long enough to stop me."

"You're not strong enough to kill her."

"It doesn't matter if I am strong enough. I have you. I have it under great authority she is willing to sacrifice herself for those she cares for. Does she care enough about you to lay her life on the line?"

Reaper's laughter started out silent and slow, but soon

turned into a great big gafaw. "Alexis won't sacrifice herself for me. We don't have that kind of relationship."

The words rolled so effortlessly from Reaper's lips, I wondered if he actually believed them to be true. We've had our differences, but no matter how badly he treated me I would never leave him to this fate.

"Someone get me a knife." Terrance looked around the room until one of the waiting vampires brought him over a serrated blade. "Time to gather some information about your co-worker."

"Alexis, do something," Nathan prompted from beside me.

From inside I heard Reaper growl, "I won't tell you anything, even if you cut off my balls."

"Well, that's an interesting suggestion." Terrance moved to unbuckle Reaper's belt.

Lucifer's hairy balls. Things just got serious.

I jumped off the crates and crept along the wall, careful to stay in the shadows. through the four angry werewolves covering the front door. I just hoped the noise distracted Terrance enough that he left Reaper alone until I made it inside.

"Nathan, keep an eye on Reaper. Tell me if Terrance does anything to him."

"What are you going to do?"

"Train a few dogs, then come in and save the day."

Nathan walked through the wall and disappeared.

Let's go protect your partner's manhood. Eddie pushed more power between our bond. I felt energized. Unstoppable. Invincible.

I stepped out of the shadows and stood in front of the first set of doors. The wolves were standing in the foyer, just beyond them. I stuck my fingers in my mouth and let out a loud whistle, guaranteed to get the dogs attention. I pulled Reva out of her sheath and placed her firmly in my right hand. Then I braced myself for an onslaught of fur and fangs.

Four large wolves burst through the doors and growled. They split up and circled around me, inching closer, chests low to the ground, stalking me. Trying to intimidate me. I had to admit it was working.

The pale beige werewolf off to my left moved fast, clasping his jaws over my forearm with such force I half expected it to be hanging by nothing but muscle. I jabbed my finger into his crystal blue eye. He yelped and let go. I took a second to glance and make sure my arm was still intact. It was, but now it looked like a Rottweiler's chew toy. The wolf charged, but this time I was prepared and drew my blade across its neck sending an arc of blood into the sky. His body fell to the ground. One dead dog.

The second and third wolves, one a reddish brown, the other a salt and pepper grey, decided to attack at the same time. The red wolf went for my legs, trying to knock me off my feet. Too many years of sparring with Reaper prepared me for that move, so I sidestepped and watched him slide past me, his nails digging into the ground, kicking up tiny cyclones of dirt.

The grey wolf leapt four feet off the ground, front paws landing on my chest, knocking me to my back. Reva slipped out of my hand and skidded out of reach.

Mr. Fuzzy-and-Furious pinned me. His rotted yellow teeth just centimeters away from my jugular, and the putrid drool dropping onto my neck. His breath was rank, like death. The other two wolves moved close, the one holding me down bared his teeth and growled. They both backed off, but circled close by.

My hands were pinned between my thighs and the wolf's feet. I bent my leg and brought the top of my boot close to my hands. My fingers brushed the top of the stake and slid it out of the sheath.

Slowly, ever so slowly, my arm inched toward my target and finally I jammed the stake up into the soft off-white fur that covered his belly. Pushing hard, driving it through the flesh, and sent him howling, with my stake stuck in his skin. I pulled a silver blade out of my pants and threw it. Watched it arch in the air and landed in the wolf's chest up to the hilt. He fell over. Dead.

Walking over, I nudged the furry carcass with the tip of my boot before removing my stake. The two remaining wolves sat back on their hunches and howled. A deep, long song to honor the dead.

Their song finished and the largest grey wolf looked at me, something almost human glittered in his eyes. Quickly replaced with anger so severe I knew he was contemplating all the ways he would make me suffer.

The last two wolves pounced. I grabbed the grey one around the head and twisted. His spine cracked, and his head flopped to the side without the bone to help hold it up.

The final, tawny colored wolf circled me, smarter than his friends, looking for an opening, or waiting for me to make a mistake. I was too smart for that. I stood up. Faced him. Gave him a come and get it gesture.

He ran past my left side, and I reached out and grabbed him by the back leg, and pulled him close. He howled and kicked. His nails digging into my flesh, forcing me to let go or lose my hand. He ran across the empty yard, turned and stared me down. I couldn't read the emotion in his eyes or the look on his face. I wasn't Doctor Doolittle, but I knew pissed off when I saw it. That wolf was pissed. In one fluid motion he ran the distance between us, ears pinned, teeth showing.

He got closer and closer, then pushed off the ground into the air. I moved before his feet could connect with my chest, and he landed behind me. I turned as he started to rush forward. Held my blade out, point straight at his heart, and sank it deep into his chest. For an added bonus I twisted the blade before I yanked it out.

The life left his eyes and he fell to the ground. Nathan waited at the entrance. "Very impressive."

"Reaper?" The word rushed past my lips.

"Still alive." He gestured toward his twigs and berries."And intact. Terrance heard the commotion and started rallying the troops."

I dusted the dog hair off my clothes. "What's waiting for me?"

"At least fifteen vampires, three more wolves, and a very pissed off enemy."

I'm strong, old, and fast, but what was waiting for me on the other side of those doors was more than I could handle. Vlad however was older, stronger, and far more dangerous than anything that waited in that room.

I might owe Caleb an apology after tonight.

I loosened Eddie's leash. Giving him more control, more freedom, more power over my physical being than I have ever done before. I had to hope for two things. One. That the father of all vampires could defeat the sadistic fuck in the warehouse. Two. That I could shove the genie back in the bottle when the battle was over.

Not bothering to remove the blood of Terrance's werewolf guards from my clothes, face, and hair, I stepped forward. Pushed through the doors and introduced Terrance to the vampire they called Evil's Assassin.

Chapter Twenty-Seven

I love to make an entrance and tonight was one of my best. Covered in werewolf remains, stake in one hand, Reva in the other, and one angry lip curl, showed Terrance that I meant business.

By my estimation, fifteen vampires, three werewolves, and one sick twisted fuck stood between me and any chance I had of saving Reaper's life.

Reaper, Julia, and five other humans, all of the unclean variety hung from meat hooks over a conveyer belt. Bottles sat below their heads, a few held an ounce or two of blood, others still empty.

I slashed Reva in the air in front of me. "You ready to die, Terrance?"

The vampires, arranged in a firing squad line-up, raised their weapons, aimed at my heart, fingers tugging slightly on the triggers, just waiting for a command to shoot. Terrance parted his troops and held up one finger. "Don't kill her just yet."

"Big mistake. You should take the shot when you have it."

Terrance stepped next to Reaper, pulled out a knife and held it to my partner's throat. "But then you would miss his death."

There were two ways I could play this. I just hoped I chose wisely. "What's one human in the grand scheme of things?" Here's to hoping my lie wasn't too obvious.

Terrance's brow lifted when he smirked. "You expect me to believe you care nothing for this man?"

"He's a pain in my ass." I shrugged. "Life would be way less complicated without him."

Maybe my lack of interest in Reaper would keep him safe, but Terrance was crazy and you could never be sure of a crazy person's true intention. I was gambling with Reaper's life and hopefully the vampire in front of me didn't call my bluff.

"I don't believe you," he pushed his blade deeper into the soft skin of Reaper's throat. Reaper pulled air between his clenched teeth. The blade didn't go deep, but a trickle of blood escaped, taking my confidence with it. But I started down this path, no backing down now.

I walked forward, hand out, palm flat. "Here, let me."

Terrance smiled. A smile that made the Wicked Queen from Snow White seem sweet and demure. "Tricky, aren't you?"

I fluttered my eyelashes. "Don't trust me?" My tone full of sarcasm.

Relief warmed my insides when he walked away from Reaper and returned to stand in front of his guards.

"How could anyone trust an abomination like you?"

"Better an abomination than a psycho."

"There's a purpose to my madness. A great purpose."

"To be the lackey of a ruined vampire. A vampire so bent on revenge he can't see that his plan will fail?"

"Delano is a great man, a great vampire. He will propel the vampire race to the dominant status it deserves."

"Didn't they already try that?"

Terrance shook his head. "No, they tried to coexist with the humans. This time vampires will control the humans."

One thing Nathan and I always discussed when we watched movies, is all bad guys suffered from too-much-information-syndrome. Instead of walking in and shooting their enemy, they talked and talked and talked. It always got them killed. But in this case, I needed Terrance and his diarrhea of the mouth.

"This is Delano's plan?" I motioned to the hanging bodies. "Wipe the humans off the planet so the food chain is gone?"

"He's not wiping them off the planet. He's building an army. An army of undead. Once the army is built, the remaining humans will have no choice but to bow down and worship us."

"You mean the army I have spent the past few days turning to ash? How's that working for you?"

Terrance charged me, his blade high above his head, but stopped short, a hair's breadth away from my face. His hand wrapped around my throat, cutting off my air.

"A human-loving-whore like yourself would never understand."

"I'm a vampire too. This would be my society as well," I reminded him.

"You ceased being a vampire the day you let an angel manipulate you into turning your back on your race. The day you chose your love for the weak and pathetic humans over your own kind. The day you signed a contract to kill every vampire you came across." His fingers squeezed tighter and tighter with every accusation he spoke.

"Wrong." I gripped his hand and pried it away from my flesh. "I ceased being a human when one of your kind killed everyone I loved, stole me away, and forced me into a lifestyle I never wanted." I shoved him away and he stumbled into his back up. "I'm trying to get back the life I never wanted to give up. Killing assholes like you is the cherry on top."

"I don't have time for you and your silly reasoning," he said. "Release the wolves."

The vampires behind him separated and three large wolves took center stage. They stopped next to Terrance. He ran his fingers over the ears of the two closest wolves, and then settled his hands in their scruff. He bent close and smiled at me before he whispered just loud enough for me to hear. "She killed your friends. Avenge them."

The wolves rushed me. The vampires cocked their guns, bullets loaded in the chamber. Looked like I had my choice. Death by a hundred holes or mauling.

I only had seconds to choose.

Eddie chose for me and we ran toward the firing squad. When the first bullet left the gun, I was over their heads and on the ground behind them. There was only enough time to grab one head and twist before they all turned.

I swung Reva and swiped at the four vampires in front of me. The blade slashed through their stomachs, spilling internal organs all over the floor. Still not enough to kill them, but it gave me a chance to stick a stake in their hearts and finish them off. But, I wasn't ready to put them down. No, I wanted their writhing bodies to be a warning to the rest.

Eddie let out a whoop I would be certain to tease him about when we walked out of here alive.

Terrance screamed at the wolves to attack, but the werewolves were hidden behind the vampires, using them as an undead shield. I guess they didn't want revenge as badly as they thought.

Guns discharged, bullets flew, most missing their target, except for two bullets. One tore through my stomach, the other through my upper arm, sending Reva flying from my grasp. It fell between the line of vampires and my feet. One of the vampires lunged for it, but he wasn't fast enough to avoid my size seven boot in his face. I scooped down, grabbed the hilt, and slashed the blade through his throat. Stake through his chest. Another one turned to ash.

One brave wolf stepped through the crowd, he charged, but didn't stand a chance because my stake ended up in his skull. The rest of the werewolves flattened their ears, turned tail and ran out through the doors I had entered earlier.

With the werewolves gone, that left ten vampires and Terrance.

My hip hurt, my arm hurt, and I was sure Reaper was sick of hanging around. Time to move things along.

"Shoot her. Damn you. Shoot her." Terrance bellowed from his hiding place behind the conveyer belt.

"You've got guns and a butt load of bullets, but you've already seen what I can do with my little dagger." I pointed to the pile of stomachs and intestines on the floor.

The remaining vamps exchanged glances with each other. They lowered their guns and held up their hands in surrender. Then they cleared the path that would lead to my target.

Terrance pulled a shotgun out from under the conveyer belt. "If they're too cowardly to pull the trigger, I'll do it for them. For the vampire race."

Bam. Bam. The double barrels shot out tiny pellets across the room, I ducked, but a few still managed to embed themselves into my chest, lungs, and plenty of other vital organs. Had I been human the lead would have killed me.

One thing that my supernatural ability gave me was super speed, not just fast, but blink of the eye fast, and I didn't use it very often. Right about now seemed like the perfect time to show the world what this tiny pissed off vampire was made of.

I ran as fast as I could at Terrance and grabbed him by the throat. My stake raised. Eager to plunge it into his Grinch-sized grizzly heart.

Then the front door blew off its hinges and the largest coal black wolf I had ever seen stood in the center of the room. Its amber eyes practically glowed as he searched the room, and settled on me. It looked like the wolves ran off to get reinforcements. The wolf's eyes didn't leave mine, and I knew just by looking at him that he was going to be hard to kill.

The black beast took off at a full run in my direction, his nails scraping on the floor, his lips pulled back in a snarl, and a vibrating growl coming from deep in his throat. I had a choice to make, protect my throat from the hairy bullet train, or continue ending Terrance's life.

I released my grip on Terrance, pushing him away, and braced for impact.

The wolf changed its course and ran past me, snapping at the vampire on the floor, his teeth closed around his neck.

"Julian, no." Julia's voice stopped time.

I turned and looked at the wolf with the vampire chew toy. Julian was a big motherfucker.

As much as I wanted to admire the beautiful specimen of wolf standing in the middle of the room gnawing on my enemy, I was slightly pissed off that he just ruined my chance of getting rid of Terrance once and for all.

Damn men always had to go and complicate the situation.

Chapter Twenty-Eight

The wolf version of Julian held Terrance down, his canine jaw snapping over and over again, trying to find a way to rip out the enemy's throat.

His twin sister cried and begged for her vampire lover's life from next to Reaper. The poor girl was going to need a girl's night out in a major way when this was all over.

Eddie fought for the chance to step into the fight, upset he lost the chance to make the kill. For once I totally agreed with my soul intruder.

Terrance growled, a menacing, deep growl and flipped Julian off his chest. Julian landed in a heap on the floor and scrambled to get back to his feet. But before he could right himself, Terrance took the upper hand and pinned the wolf to the ground. He wrapped his hand through Julian's heavy coat and around his throat. Terrance lowered his fangs, a smile curling his lips. He moved fast, teeth parting Julian's fur and finding his flesh.

The wolf whined, his paws kicking trying to remove Terrance, head thrashing, looking for a way to dislodge the vampire feeding from him, but only causing Terrance to clamp down harder. Blood leaked out of Terrance's mouth and soon Julian's struggling eased.

I stepped forward, dagger raised, hoping to save Julian from being drained completely. I snuck behind Terrance, swung my dagger over my head and braced for when it would slice through his neck.

Terrance ducked and his hand shot out, hitting me in the calf, distracting me enough to miss the gun he pulled out of his pocket until the cool metal butted against my chest.

"Drop the sword and back away or your furry lover will

die." He lifted Julian by the scruff and held his head, while the rest of his body lay limp on the floor.

Blood matted Julian's fur and his eyes drooped. Fear for his life was the only reason I followed Terrance's directions. My hand shook when I dropped Reva at my feet and took two large steps back on equally shaky legs.

Terrance walked closer, took the toe of his shoe and kicked Reva across the room, far out of my reach. He shook Julian, tearing a snarl from the nearly unconscious wolf. "It's not a surprise that the two of you fell for one another. After all, you're both traitors to your race. Too afraid to embrace the power you possess." He threw Julian's struggling body across the room. The wolf hit the wall with a bone-crunching thud, and slid to the floor, where he laid in a pile of fur, blood, and drool.

I wanted to rush to Julian, to see that he was okay, but I needed to worry about the vampire in front of me, and not the unconscious werewolf behind me. Out of the corner of my eye I saw Nathan float over to Julian's still body. He lowered his head to Julian's chest and after what seemed like an eternity he nodded.

Relief filled my bones.

If I had been closer, Nathan could grab my foot and heal Julian right away, but I was stuck across the room being held at gunpoint by a maniac.

Terrance stood with the gun still pointed at my chest. "Only one of us will be leaving this warehouse tonight."

Then he pulled the trigger until every last silver bullet left the chamber. Ten to be exact. Ten bullets that knocked me back into the nearest wall and burrowed their way through flesh and bone and heart, coming out the other side, but leaving a gaping hole in their wake. A hole the size of a soda can, leaving my heart exposed.

My strength faltered and I slid to the ground. Flesh burning from the silver. Blood pumping from my chest in spurts. And I

knew in my hole-filled-heart that without some divine interven-
tion I was going to die.

The tip of Terrance's super polished dress shoes appeared in
my line of sight. He knelt down, so I could see the triumph that
danced in his eyes. The glee that lifted his lips. And my dagger
that filled his hand.

He turned Reva from side to side, the light catching the
blade, reflecting small dots on the walls. "You've done a lot of
damage with this little toy of yours. Killed many of our kind."
He gestured over to Julian with the tip of the blade. "Plenty of
his kind too."

I attempted a witty comeback, but blood had puddled in my
throat, and the words came out garbled.

"I'll keep your sword and collect your ash in a jar. Proof to
the world that you really are dead and that I killed you."

That's when I learned who started the rumors about my
death. Only now he'd have his proof.

He cocked his arm back and then drove Reva's tip into my
flesh, just below my collarbone and straight into the wall,
pinning me like an insect he collected and placed on display.

"Why?" One word is all I managed to push out.

"Why what?"

"Lie about killing me." I coughed up some blood, clearing
my throat for the rest of my question. "Before you actually did?"

"Quite simple. Control. If I showed the vampire race I was
strong enough to defeat the most feared vampire, then by
default I become the most feared. Then they bow to me. Fear
me. Follow my every order."

"Manipulation."

"Yes. Lies, manipulation, and deceit. In the end, however,
death will come to you by my hand, but not until you've
watched your partner join my army and your lover die." He
placed his hand on the hilt of the dagger and used it to help him
stand, the pressure forcing the blade farther down. A scream of
fury tore from my mouth. From my soul.

He stopped in front of Reaper. "Someone with his knowledge of the inner workings of the VAU and years of working side-by-side with Evil's Assassin should prove to be a very valuable asset." He sank his fangs into Reaper's neck and drew out large gulps of blood.

Eddie raged inside my useless body, trying to force my immobile limbs to move, but my inner monster was as trapped by my wounds as I was.

When Terrance finished, he wiped the blood from his chin and faced me. "I'll start with your wolf." Terrance walked over to Julia and knelt down to meet her eyes. "It's time to watch your brother die."

Julia struggled against her bonds. "You can't kill him, you still need the serum."

"I have everything I need from him. The serum has been analyzed by my own people and right now they are working to remove some of its less than desirable side effects."

Julia called Terrance the same names she had spat at for her own kin just an hour before.

Terrance picked up the discarded shotgun, but instead of aiming it at Julian's head he turned it on his still waiting soldiers, and pulled the trigger, taking out each and every vampire that had refused to do his bidding. They fell to the ground, still alive, but like me, completely useless until their wounds healed.

He turned to face me. "I kill my kind for the greater good. Those who stand in my way once, will not live to stand in my way again." Then he walked through the row of vampires, stake in hand, and started stabbing them to their final death.

A door in the rear opened wide and a vampire stuck his head through the crack.

"Sir, we have an issue that needs your attention."

Terrance turned, annoyance written all over his face. "Can't it wait?"

The vampire cleared his throat and tugged at his collar. "I'm afraid not. Someone has gotten into the storage room and dumped out every last bit of the serum. It's gone."

"Mother fucker." Terrance stormed across the room, stopping at my side. He bent down and caressed my cheek. "It seems you've all been given a ten-minute stay of execution while I attend to some business." On the tail of his words he walked out of the room.

Nathan, who had disappeared, reappeared in the center of the room, floated close and hovered over my lap. He placed his hand on mine. "I knew dumping his precious serum would get rid of Mr. Evil Man. Let's get you healed."

I had never been more grateful for my ghostly partner than at that very moment.

It took my last bit of strength to wrap my fingers around his hand and squeeze, wanting him to know how much I appreciated his presence in my life. Because without him, I wouldn't be around much longer. The sparks flew, and Nathan solidified.

"Bloody huge hole you're sporting here, China Doll." His hand touched the edges. His touch tingled, almost tickled. A warmth I hadn't felt for years spread through my limbs and settled over the wound.

I couldn't tell if the wound was healing, but Nathan's lowered brow gave me the impression that he was concentrating awfully hard. He sucked his bottom lip between his teeth, winced, causing his eyebrow ring to bob up and down.

"The blood stopped. Not sure if it is because you are running out, or I healed most of the damage." His comforting touch left my flesh. "Still got a nasty wound, but you should heal the rest on your own." Nathan sat back on his heels. "Feeling better?"

I tried lifting my hand to touch my wound, but it felt like there were invisible binds tying it to the ground, I couldn't raise it higher than two inches off the floor. The fog hadn't lifted from my brain and I still couldn't manage a full sentence. Something was wrong. My vampire healing should be kicking in, but instead it seemed to be fading farther into the abyss.

The world around me grew fuzzy. My thoughts incoherent. My eyelids grew heavy. Consciousness blinked on and off.

Give me control. I don't want to force it from you. I want you to trust me.

Never.

I'm sorry.

An unnatural howl left my throat. A howl that was full of all my vampire rage, and held no hint of the human I strived to be.

Chapter Twenty-Nine

M y brain roared to life. My mouth suctioned over human flesh. My throat worked to fill my mouth with the metallic tang of blood. My gaze dropped to the struggling bundle in my lap.

My mind reeled at what was happening.

I quickly released my hold on the scared human. He scrambled away. I spit out the blood in my mouth and attempted to back away, wanting to put more distance between my victim and myself. I couldn't move. A passenger in a body I had no control over, while Eddie fought for our survival.

Stop. I screamed through our bond.

Feed or die.

DIE.

You will live.

Eddie forced me forward, my hand wrapped around the man's ankle. I pulled him back in my direction, my nails digging into his flesh. My fangs sank into the soft flesh of his neck. My mind screamed, "no", but the beast hit the mute button and continued to feed.

The man in my arms struggled to push me off, shoved at me with his blood-lost-weakened hands.

"Stop, stop, stop," the man folded on my lap begged, but the beast ignored him too.

How I wished I could.

The blood started as a trickle over my tongue. A bitter warmth that pooled in my mouth, heavy and thick before sliding down my throat, rushing to fill my empty stomach. My lips tightened around the open holes, my tongue pushed at the openings, causing the fluid to flow faster, and my sucking became more urgent, stronger.

Eddie rejoiced at the warmth that filled my mouth, filled my stomach. But emptied my morals. My hopes. My dreams.

The weaker the man in my arms became, the stronger my own body became. The leftover silver bullets Terrance pumped into my body, landed with a quiet *tink* on the dirty floor. The knife wound on my shoulder knit together and closed. My body may have healed all my physical wounds, but my heart hemorrhaged an emotional firestorm.

With the return of my strength, I managed to pull my mouth from the man's neck, force Eddie to stop his drinking, but only for a moment. He fought against me. Fought against my will and bit the man a second time. Fangs clamped onto his neck, a chunk of his skin came loose in my mouth, mixing with the blood, and sliding down my throat.

My arms tightened around the body in my arms, his heart beat slowing to dangerous levels, limbs going limp, head rolling back with the strength to hold it up.

I was losing the battle I fought my whole life to win. I was taking a human life and too weak to stop myself.

If the man in my arms died by my hands, I'd let Terrance stake me and end it all.

I tried once again to remove my mouth from his neck, to unclench my arms and let him fall free. This nameless man in my arms, that was giving me his life. A life I didn't want or deserve. A sacrifice that wasn't mine to ask for. A violation of everything I believed in. A violation that would kill me.

My mouth nursed one last long suck, the blood, slowing to just a few drops again, the last remaining drops he had to offer. His heart beat, then stuttered.

Beat. Stutter. Beat. Stutter.

Then it never beat again.

Eddie killed him. We killed him. I killed him.

Fully satiated, Eddie retreated, ready to give me back control, now that the damage was done. But I didn't want control anymore. Didn't want to open my eyes and see the man, whose name I didn't even know, laying on the ground, his body cooling. I didn't want to look at the life I'd taken. Didn't want to face my weakness. Couldn't face the monster I had fully become.

I pushed the man off my lap, and crawled to the nearest wall, my eyes pinched shut the entire time. I settled my back against the plaster and paint. Curled my legs into my chest. Wrapped my arms around my knees and rocked back and forth. I gave up.

Gave up any hope that I would ever find my humanity. Malicious, murderous, monsters like me didn't deserve to realize their dreams. The contract was broken, I'd killed a human, Caleb would end me, and I'd willing accept the stake through the heart.

"Alexis." Nathan's cool hand wrapped around my upper arm. "Alexis, they need your help. Reaper needs your help."

"Leave me." I pushed his hand away.

"You've got to get up. You're healed. Help them."

Listen to your ghost. Eddie's voice seemed stronger, louder.

Fuck you, Vlad. I slammed the door on the connection between us, something I had never been able to do before, not without Julian's serum.

I opened my eyes, the tears I'd been holding back slowly rolled down my cheeks. "I can't help anyone anymore." My gaze drifted to the man lying at my feet, his blank stare accusing me of horrible acts. He was older, probably a grandfather. The collar of his light blue golf shirt edged with the blood that had leaked from my mouth. "Especially him."

Nathan floated in front of me, trying to block my view of my victim, but I could still make out the way his body lay slumped on the floor through his hazy form.

"You've got to get up. Forget about what just happened. Terrance is coming back, and when he does, Reaper will be turned into his sodding worst fear, Julian will die. Four other innocent humans will die. You. Will. Die."

Anger rose, rushing through my veins, exploding out of my mouth. "I'm already dead. I have been for over one hundred and fifty years. It's time I accept that the only thing keeping me alive, walking, talking, animated is the blood I steal from the living. This isn't a life, it's a lie." I sucked back my sobs.

Nathan settled his hand over mine and for once his usual comforting touch just irritated me. "If you give up. If you let this one accident, this one slip up take you down a dark path, you won't be the only one who suffers. The innocents that you swore to protect, they will suffer. Can you live with that?"

I lifted my shaky hand and pointed at the dead body at my feet. "I can't live with his death on my soul."

"His death served a *purpose*." I flinched at his words, pulling my hand from his. "Without the strength his blood gave you, many more will die. Not just the people in this room." He pointed to everyone I had grown to care for and the few that I didn't even know. "But more innocents, more women, children, families, torn apart because of Terrance." Nathan grabbed my chin, twisted my head and forced me to look at the room full of destruction and carnage. "I didn't sacrifice my own life so you could give up and die"

I looked at Julian lying on the floor, breathing shallow, slow. At Reaper hanging from the hook, blood dripping from the wounds on his neck into a bottle at his feet. At the four remaining humans hanging next to him. At the pain, and horror that Terrance continued to bring to the world, to those I swore to protect, to those I loved.

Forcing my head out of Nathan's grasp, I focused on the dead man again. The man I killed. Not Eddie. Or the vampire I pretended wasn't the real me. It was me. I killed him. Me. Alexis Black. I'd taken my first human life. And that knowledge marred my soul. A betrayal I could never forgive myself for. A blanket of black covered my heart.

But did others deserve to suffer because I was selfish, weak?

I only had to forget long enough to get everyone else in this room out alive. Just a few minutes, a small amount of time, to push past my pain and revulsion and do the right thing. I could still save the others. Not myself. I was beyond saving, but the others who deserved to live. To see the sunrise. Raise their families. Find happiness. Those were the people who deserved to be saved.

And I would. Then I'd let Caleb send me to hell, a place I should have gone long ago.

"Nathan." My voice wobbled. "Find Terrance. Tell me what he's doing."

Nathan placed his hand on my face, cradled my chin, a soft caress. "That's my China Doll." His words soft, full of respect I hadn't earned and didn't deserve.

I didn't move from the wall, but I stretched out my legs, let my arms fall to my side, prayed that my blood on my shirt covered my healed wounds. I needed Terrance to think I was still weak, close to death. I needed the element of surprise on my side.

Terrance may have taken my sword, my stake. Left me with gaping silver filled holes. But he didn't take away my determination. Determination to kick his revenge-seeking ass back to whatever coffin he crawled out of.

"China doll, we have a problem." Nathan's tone full of fear and disbelief.

"Is he gone?" I pushed off the floor, forgetting I was playing possum.

"Terrance, was never Terrance." Nathan floated closer. "The man in that room is Delano Melazi."

"That's not possible. I would have known if it was Delano. His face is scarred."

"Your ghost is very correct." The deep voice of my enemy spoke from behind me and cold chills filled my already aching bones with dread.

"But witches make such wonderful glamour spells. Spells that can erase even the most evil imperfections."

I turned on my heel, forcing myself to face the monster.

Delano stood behind me. Gone were the good old boy looks, the perfect skin, and slicked back hair. What stood in front of me was a nightmare created by his own kind.

Deep furrows of ruined flesh ran across half of his once handsome face. Rivers of scars started at the base of his skull, through his hair, leaving bald patches in the wake of their destruction. The damage traveled down his forehead and over his eye, taking with them his eyelid, leaving only a cloudy orb. His once succulent red lips were gone on one side. In the sections that had the worst damage the flesh was so thin the bone was visible. The flesh was ruined from the top of his head to the hand that clutched an ancient looking amulet. "This is what the face of betrayal looks like. I've kept it hidden while I set my plan in motion." He dropped the amulet to the ground and stepped on it, smashing it beneath his boot. Tendrils of green smoke floated in the air. "But now it's time for the world to know who they are truly dealing with. It's time for me to be in charge of the future of the vampire race."

"You forget that I'm still standing in your way."

That's a good vampire. I ignored the sarcasm in Eddie's tone.

"Even with the extra strength and speed the angels gave you, you don't have what it takes to defeat someone as powerful as me."

He let go of the leash that held his power. It spread through the room, circled around me and squeezed. His power called to mine, taunted and teased, showed me what an almost six-hundred year old vampire felt like. All those years of knowledge, strength, and hatred, housed in one man with his eye on destroying the very people who turned him into the creature who stood in front of me. A creature bent on murder and revenge.

For once I agreed with the vampire in front of me. I wasn't powerful enough to defeat Delano Melazi.

No one was getting out of this room alive.

Chapter Thirty

T here have been very few moments in my life that I've felt intimidated. Speechless. Totally and utterly scared shitless. This moment topped that very short list.

Standing in front of me was the most feared. Most vicious. Most hated vampire in the world. The only vampire in existence who had escaped his public execution at the hands of the VAU. Once a revered leader of the vampire race and a member of the Sovereign Seven. Now a mad man bent on destroying those who stood in his way of world domination.

He wanted to see me dead.

Honestly, if there weren't other lives at stake, I'd gladly lend him my pointy-wooden-vampire-ender.

Every vampire had heard the rumors. How the Sovereign Seven had betrayed Delano. Used him in their attempt to stop the total annihilation of the vampire race at the hands of the very upset humans. They needed a scapegoat and Delano had never been considered a team player. Two bats. One stake. Problem solved.

Until Delano surprised the world with a Houdini act and disappeared in the middle of his comeuppance. I guess no one figured he'd be back and with a very large chip on his horribly scarred shoulders. Can't say I blame him, but that didn't mean I was going to let him end my friends.

Over six hundred years against my measly one hundred and fifty. The odds were not in my favor.

Eddie, do we stand a chance.

Not if you keep me on mute.

Last time you took control you betrayed me.

Last time I took control I saved you.

Another drop of human blood and I will find a way to end you.

Agreed.

"Still think you have a chance against me?" Delano's sarcastic tone told me what his thoughts on the subject were.

"No. But it's better to go down trying, knowing that I did what I could, than to run away like a coward and live with the guilt. Plus, I have a secret weapon."

"Brave little girl, aren't you?" He tilted his head, squinted his one remaining eye and sized me up. "Such a shame your bravery will only get you killed."

"Depends on how you look at it?" I spread my legs and put my hands on my hips. "Now are we going to fight or do you want to continue to try and mind-fuck me?"

Nathan came up next to me. "Alexis, you're stepping onto a killing field with a known crazy man."

I looked at Nathan and smiled. I hoped he could read all the emotions I tried to convey in that one little tilt of my lips. Love. Respect. Friendship. The knowledge that I was going to miss him when I was gone. "There's no one else more qualified for the job."

Nathan placed a kiss on my forehead. "I love you, China Doll." Then he floated over to Reva and kicked her with his toe. The blade slid across the floor and stopped at my feet. At that moment I was thankful I had let him leach my energy.

"By all means, let's make this a fair fight." Delano dropped the gun in his hand and produced a dagger from the waist of his pants.

Eddie sucked in a breath. *That's my dagger.*

Then let's go get your property back.

Be careful, there is a secret compartment filled with liquid silver.

Thanks for the warning.

I picked up Reva, took one last look at those I wanted to save, then shut down the thoughts of, "this is crazy" and "you're going to die."

I didn't wait for Delano to make the first move. That was just prolonging the inevitable. Instead, I held my dagger high above my head and charged. He met me halfway, Vlad's dagger in hand. I thought I had the advantage until he threw his blade. It hit my thigh and stuck.

A pop, a hiss, and then pain sliced through my leg. Liquid silver being injected into my system. Hopefully not into an artery. I reached down and removed the blade, tossed it to the ground behind me, and continued forward. My leg growing numb. Weak.

Delano didn't back down.

When we met in the middle. I had my blade. He had his overly confident smile.

Something wasn't right.

I realized what it was when it was too late. Delano was a lying and cheating bastard.

The stake he pulled from his pocket and launched in my direction just missed its intended deathblow to my heart by millimeters. The wood stuck out of my chest, the liquid silver on its tip entered my system and caused me to stagger back a few steps.

Delano advanced, but I swung Reva wildly in front of me, fending him off until I could manage to remove the stake. I continued to lash out with the dagger and heard a satisfied hiss when it connected with flesh.

The pain was going to be excruciating when I removed the wood, but that knowledge didn't stop me from wrapping my fingers around the base and yanking it out of my chest. Blood that an innocent man had sacrificed to keep me alive pumped from the wound. His death would count.

I called to my beast, begged him to come play, help me take out the monster in front of me, so we could fight another day.

The beast complied. For the first time ever we worked together, as a team.

We sliced Reva through Delano's arms, chest, and legs. Opened up wound after wound. Kept him on the defense instead of the offence. Backed him away from his victims.

I had his stake in one hand and a whole lot of pissed off in my gut. This was one battle I wouldn't lose. We backed Delano into a corner. Stuck between the wall and the pointy hunk of wood poking him in the chest.

He reached out and stuck his fingers in the deep hole in my chest. Forcing me to cry out in pain, and even though my brain fritzed and the lights dimmed, I refused to pass out. The beast surged, giving me the extra bit of energy I needed to shove the stake into his murderous vampire ticker.

The hard wood drilled through his flesh, bone and went on a one-way journey straight into his heart. I expected flames, ash, and satisfaction. But instead the stake bounced off the wall in front of me.

Delano was gone.

The stake hit home, of that I was sure. Was it possible that the man had escaped death twice in one lifetime? If so, he was one lucky bastard.

The liquid silver was still in my system and now that Eddie had retreated, my eyes crossed, and my feet wobbled.

Nathan placed his hand inside my chest and tiny beads of silver fell to the floor. Then he started working on the new gaping hole. I hadn't lost as much blood as the first time, so my natural healing powers helped him heal all my wounds.

Then he reached out, wrapped his arms around me and pulled me tight. "I would have missed you."

Tears of pain, relief, frustration and self-loathing rolled down my cheeks. And I allowed myself just a few moments to bask in my own pity before rescuing everyone else.

Nathan stopped hugging me and floated over to Reaper. "He's alive, but unconscious."

I followed him over, hopped up on the conveyer belt, and gently lifted Reaper off the meat hook. I cradled him in my arms and laid him on the floor. "Nathan, lend me a hand."

I grasped Nathan's hand and we worked to heal Reaper's

wounds. His eyes fluttered open. I held back the new set of tears that filled my eyes.

Reaper rolled to his side and coughed up a glob of blood. "Is he dead?"

"I don't know. But he's gone."

Reaper sat up. "Good enough for me." He surveyed the room, gaze falling on the dead man. "Terrance?"

I lowered my head. "Me." The word low and shaky. One battle was over, but another was about to begin.

Nathan grasped my hand, solidified, and spoke up. "I will not allow you to blame her, to harm her, over something that saved your bloody ass from being turned into vampire. Saved everyone in this room from death."

Reaper's brow crinkled. "Relax spook." He looked at me. "Accident?"

"I blacked out. When I woke up he was in my arms and I was feeding from him. I tried to stop. I really did. But the hunger was too strong. I couldn't stop and before I knew it his heart stopped beating."

Reaper stood and dusted off the back of his pants. He didn't say another word, just hopped up on the conveyer belt and began to lift the first woman off the hook. I stood below him and helped her to the floor.

She was conscious and when I released her, she wrapped her arms around me and hugged me tight. Her sobs filled my ears and her tears wet my shoulder.

She backed away. "You saved us. All of us."

I hid my embarrassment by stepping up to help with the rest of the victims. We left Julia hanging. She was her brother's problem.

I wandered over to where Julian still lay. "Nathan."

We performed an emergency triage on the hurt werewolf and watched while his body shifted back into his human form. The small cuts and bruises that covered his flesh faded into nothingness before he even opened his eyes. His lashes fluttered, then his lids opened. He smiled at me; it was small and weak, but there.

His lies still didn't sit well with me, but that was a problem for another time. My pathetic issues seemed like nothing compared to what we all just went through.

I pointed over my shoulder. "I didn't know what you wanted to do with her."

He pushed off the ground, very naked, and went to his twin. Within seconds she was removed from her hook and in his arms. She didn't fight or kick or scream. Instead she buried her head in her brother's chest and wept.

They walked to the door, but before Julian crossed over the threshold he stopped. "I've got to deal with the repercussions. There's going to be a fallout in the pack. I promise I'll come see you when things calm down. I still owe you that explanation."

He turned and I watched his glorious naked ass leave.

The humans were safe, Reaper was safe, and the bad guy was gone. Maybe not forever, but I couldn't focus on the negative.

Reaper touched my shoulder. "I have to call Coleman. He needs to know what happened here."

I handed him my phone. "Get it over with."

Reaper glanced back at the man I'd killed. "Maybe you should disappear."

"I'm sick of running." I planted my ass in a chair. "It's time to face the consequences of my actions."

Reaper dialed and asked for James Coleman and I sat and waited for my fate to be decided.

Chapter Thirty-One

The sound of sirens got closer to our current location, carrying with them my judge, jury, and executioner. The urge to run, to hide, to escape judgment, moved my feet against the chipped grey floors.

The man I'd killed lay just a few feet away, his dead eyes accusing me of the vilest crime. Guilt over the man's death twisted its fingers in my soul, and rang out any bit of hope I had that I wasn't the monster the world believed me to be. Life wasn't worth living anymore, knowing what I did, what I could possibly do again.

Reaper sat with the other victims, the ones I'd managed not to kill. Helping them come to terms with what they'd just witnessed. Nathan stayed close to me, offering his comforting presence without any inane chit-chat.

The sirens stopped out front. Gravel crunched under the heavy tires of what sounded like multiple vehicles. Footsteps and shouted commands joined a few moments later.

Time to let Detective Coleman and the VAU have their way with me. Time to do the right thing.

I pulled my chair back farther into the shadows, not wanting to be on display when the VAU walked in. I'm pretty sure they had a stake first, ask questions later policy. If anyone was going to take a stake to my heart, it would be Coleman or maybe Reaper.

Reaper patted a young man on the back and made his way over to greet the cavalry. The first officer on the scene walked through the door, took one look at the pile of guts, bottles of blood, and dead man, and promptly fled through the door and puked.

"Get it together, Rookie." Detective Coleman's voice preceded his body through the door.

Coleman marched into the room followed by a barrage of paramedics and uniformed officers. He stood in the center and surveyed the scene, never once flinching at the horrors that upset the rookie.

The others scurried around, pulling together the survivors. While the paramedics checked their vital signs and patched up the fang and knife marks, the officers asked questions, and took notes.

The youngest officer in the group motioned for Detective Coleman to come over during his interrogation. He showed Coleman his notepad. The detective nodded, then knelt down so he was face to face with one of the humans I'd saved. They talked for a few moments; Coleman rubbed her shoulder, and stood.

Standing in the center of the room, his gaze roamed over the gore, but settled on the dead man off to the side, now surrounded by several people examining my bite marks.

My partner moved to stand at his side, but remained quiet until Coleman spoke one word, a word I hoped he wouldn't have gotten to until much later in the investigation. "Alexis?"

Reaper followed his line of sight to my victim, "She couldn't help it."

"Is she here?"

Reaper scrubbed his hands over his crew cut, then pointed in my direction.

Coleman headed my way, side stepped several busy medical personnel, and took a seat in the metal chair next to me. "You killed a man."

"Yep." There was no use denying I was the vampire that caused his death, they already had my DNA on file. And Julian would be the one to extract it.

"That makes you an enemy of the VAU."

"My lack of heartbeat makes me an enemy of the VAU."

"True, but I could have overlooked the lack of a beating heart. I can't overlook the death of an innocent."

I held out my palms. "Do what you have to do."

The solid silver handcuffs clinked when he removed them from his belt. The bracelet snapped around my wrist, the metal burned into my skin. He stood, hand on my arm, ready to help me up, but before I got out of my chair, the officer he spoke to earlier interrupt him.

"Sir." He cleared his throat. "My witness would like to speak to the...ummm." His face paled when he looked in my direction.

"Vampire?" Coleman finished for him.

Red crept into his cheeks. "Yes, sir."

"Bring her over."

Coleman helped me up. "Don't try anything." His fingers dug deep into my flesh.

"If I wanted to leave, I'd be gone."

A woman in her forties, covered in blood, with a bright yellow blanket wrapped around her small frame approached with the officer. She held out a shaky hand between us and waited.

I looked down, unclear on her intention.

"I wanted to say thank you." She noticed the handcuffs, reached over and took my hands in hers, then pulled me close in a tight hug. "You saved us."

She let go of my hands and turned to face Detective Coleman. "Without her we would have all died."

The rest of the survivors left their various positions around the room and joined our little party. They circled around me, all murmuring their heartfelt gratitude.

A tall, balding man, covered with tattoos glanced at the cuffs. "What are you doing with her?"

"She's a vampire. The law's simple. She killed one of ours, she must be executed." Detective Coleman tried to be the voice of reason.

The man put a barrier between the heavily armed VAU agents and me. "That monster would have killed us if it wasn't for her. She deserves a medal, not death."

The woman wrapped in the yellow blanket took the vacant spot next to the man. "Vampire or not, she's a hero." Her warm hands found mine. "There's plenty of evil vampires in the world, we've all seen the proof, but there's evil humans too. What you are doesn't make you evil, or wicked, it's who you are on the inside. What's in your heart and soul that makes you the person you truly are." She wrapped her arm around my shoulder and pulled me close. "She's a good vampire, a good person."

My eyes welled up and the tears began to tumble at her words. I wanted to believe her. To believe I wasn't evil or wicked or a bad egg. But seeing the man I had murdered in cold blood being loaded into a body bag made it impossible.

How ironic, Eddie, who I've loathed for the past two years was the one thing that gave me the strength and power to save a room full of humans. Power to get us all out of one hell of a situation. How ironic that a group of humans who less than an hour ago had been horribly abused by a vampire, now stood in a line. Protecting me. Fighting for my life. Even though I killed one of their own.

"It's not my choice, ladies and gentlemen. It's the law, but I will do my best to see that she is treated fairly. This way, Alexis." Coleman grabbed my arm and escorted me past the line of survivors, out the door and into the night. We stopped by Reaper's car. He didn't remove the handcuffs, but he did release his hold on me. Then he leaned against the hood.

"Those people owe you their lives." He paused, swallowed deep, and added, "I owe you an apology."

"For what?"

"For the way I treated you."

"You had your reasons." I brushed off his apology.

"Not good ones." He rubbed his chin. His eyes. His forehead. The man standing in front of me was tired. "The truth is I needed your help. I knew it and I used you to do what the VAU couldn't. I planned on taking you into custody when this was all over and executing you. That's what the VAU does."

I picked at the holes in my now bloody tank top. "Is that still the plan?"

"I don't know." He lowered his chin and stared at his shoes. "We couldn't have saved the victims without you. Officers would have died. More innocents would have died. Unnecessary bloodshed."

I wet my lips and swallowed hard. "I have some bad news. Terrance wasn't Terrance. He's Delano Melazi."

Detective Coleman stood up and closed his eyes.

"He's still alive. Injured, possibly close to death, but alive."

He slumped back down onto the hood of the car. "Then we need your help more than ever. I need your help. The VAU can't fight this fight alone. We can't go up against a vampire like Delano and expect to win"

"Over one hundred trained military men and women aren't enough to battle the Chicago vampire population?" I cocked my head and my brow.

"Not even close. I need someone who knows the vampires. The way they think. The way they move. From what Reaper tells me, you're already doing your part to help us, just without the official title."

"I do what I do for my own reasons and I only go after the creatures that hurt others."

"Then help the VAU and get paid for fighting evil." He met my eyes. "You would still work alone, but you'd be a consultant. My little secret."

Coleman's little secret. His chance to move up in the ranks of the VAU, take out more vampires than any other agent, and make a name for himself.

Laughter erupted from my mouth. "I've already got one boss I can't stand, and you expect me to have another."

Coleman placed his hand on my shoulder and pressed down. "Not a boss, a partner."

"What makes you think I want to help?" I lifted my chin and looked into the starry night.

"Because tonight you stepped up and saved a room full of people." His words were complimentary.

"I didn't have a choice. Terrance had Reaper."

One of the officers peeked his head out of the door and called for the Detective. Coleman removed the handcuffs and then handed me Reva. "You're free to go, but I really hope you consider my offer. I'll call you in a few days to hear your decision."

I rubbed the charred skin on my wrist, happy to be rid of the shackles, and slipped Reva into her sheath. It wasn't a bad offer. It got the VAU off my butt, plus it gave me the opportunity to satisfy my contract without hunting on my own. With the added perk of taking out more of the bad guys. But could I work with the VAU? With Coleman?

That was a problem for another night. Right now I wanted to go home, take a hot bath, and forget about contracts, the VAU, Delano.

I walked into the warehouse, approached Reaper and Coleman. As I walked up I heard the tail end of their conversation.

"I owe you an apology too," Detective Coleman said to Reaper. "I thought you were insane to be working with a vampire after what happened to Lorelie. But after meeting Alexis, and seeing what she can do, I understand why. She's a powerful weapon to wipe them out."

I cleared my throat. Both men looked at me. "Ready, Reaper?" Without looking back I marched to the front door. The good detective's words ringing in my ears. *A powerful weapon to wipe them out.*

Some prejudice ran too deep. Some words hurt to hear.

On the way out, Reaper said, "He told me about his offer. Are you going to take it?"

I shrugged one shoulder.

"Would it really be that bad to help them out?"

I ignored the question and slid into the car, slammed the door and settled my head against the window.

The drive to my apartment was long, quiet, and strained. I didn't feel like talking for once. Nathan didn't feel like talking. And Reaper never felt like talking. The mood was somber, and the air was heavy with unspoken words.

The car slowed in front of the warehouse, and I went to open my door. Eager to be inside. Alone. Reaper's hand on my arm stopped me.

"Thanks for coming back for me."

"Did you think I would leave you?"

"After the way I've treated you, I wouldn't have blamed you."

"That's the difference between us Reaper. I would never leave a man behind."

I stepped out of the car and slammed the door. He didn't pull away for several seconds, and I didn't look back. He deserved to carry his guilt around with him.

I looked at my ghostly companion. Reaper could take a few lessons from him. Hell, I killed Nathan. Ran a stake through his heart, and he found a way to forgive me.

I opened the door to my apartment, stripped off my boots and flopped onto the couch, still in my tattered blood-covered clothes. Nathan took the spot next to me. Raja curled onto my lap, purring. I stroked her fur.

The air in front of me blurred and a chill crept through the room. Caleb filled the space.

"I see you're still around to be a pain in my ass."

Chapter Thirty-Two

C aleb stood in front of me, hands on his hips, lips curled in a smile that belonged on a devil, not an angel, and his expansive black wings blocking my view of the television. After saving the day, I didn't have the energy to exchange witty repartee with the angel of snark, but I doubted my opinion mattered.

I leaned to the side and placed my head on Nathan's shoulder. "Could you move to the left? I like this part."

Caleb stood his ground. "Is he dead?"

My eyes never left the TV screen. "Define dead."

Caleb snapped his fingers and the TV went dead. "A large pile of smoldering ash on the ground."

Since I couldn't actually answer his question, I decided to volley one of my own. "Did you know that Terrance was Delano?"

"We heard rumors, but didn't know if they were true."

I tossed the remote control on the table and Raja jumped. "And you didn't feel like sharing. Warning me about what and who I might be going up against?"

Caleb took a seat in the overstuffed leather chair, fluffed his wings, fixed the cuffs on his shirt, and adjusted his pants before crossing one foot over one knee. Once his primping was done he said, "Would you have left your partner to die if you thought that you were fighting Delano? Would that knowledge have changed your decision or altered your course?"

"No. But I would have been a hell of a lot more prepared."

"Sometimes knowing everything up front causes fear to make you react differently in a stressful situation."

"So your lack of communication was for my benefit?"

He waved off my comment. "Do you know that you

are the only Assassin who has come close to taking out their mark?" He didn't wait for my answer before continuing on. "But your success didn't come without a casualty, did it?"

My stomach clenched, rolled, and then dropped.

I had managed to avoid death by Coleman and the VAU, but somehow I doubted that I'd be that lucky where Caleb was involved. My contract made it clear, the death of a human by my fangs, meant the death of me.

Time to pay for my slip-up.

"It was an accident, totally unintentional." And for some reason I felt compelled to explain my situation. "Without the blood I was dead. Without the blood everyone in that warehouse would have died. I did what I did and will live with the consequences of my actions."

Caleb studied my face before answering. "That's why I went to the council on your behalf and asked for mercy."

I tilted my head to the side. "You've been looking to get rid of me since I started this gig. Why would you ask them to give me a second chance?"

Caleb leaned forward, elbows on his knees. "All the others are struggling and innocent people are dying because of it."

A tiny voice in my head warned me to tread carefully into this conversation because I wasn't going to like the outcome. "Your point?"

"We would like you to help out a few of the others, lend your expertise."

"Why would I want to do that?"

"To be helpful. Not for me, but for the queen." Eddie perked up at the mention of his daughter.

I tried for my best who-me look, but I only had enough energy for a half-raised eyebrow.

"I'll take more time off your contract."

Now he had my attention. "How much?"

He tapped the tip of his nose with his index finger. He had

me and he knew it. "Give me an answer and we'll discuss the terms."

Great, not only did I have Detective Coleman wanting to use my talents, but now Caleb wanted to loan me out as an assassin-for-hire. When did I become so in demand? On the bright side if I helped Caleb, I could get out of this life of servitude faster and I'd be one step closer to getting my soul back.

"Do I get time off for good behavior?"

"I haven't seen any yet."

"In that case, I need a few days to think about my new job offer."

"Then I will leave you to enjoy the rest of your evening." Caleb stood and waved his hand at Nathan. "But before I go, I have some information on your ghost situation here."

Nathan turned his gaze away from the television and perked up. "You know how to help me?"

Caleb walked over next to me. He picked up my hand and played with the platinum band on my finger, twirling it around and around. "It seems this simple piece of metal is what bonds the two of you together."

I pulled my hand from his. "I don't understand."

"When Nathan sacrificed himself for you, the combination of his death, and your hands touching created a bond between you. When you wear this band on your finger Nathan is yours to command, he is stuck with you. Now if you were to remove this band." He grabbed my hand once again and slid the ring off my finger. "Nathan, try to leave."

Nathan stood in the center of the room, and started to fade away. I waited for the sonic boom that came every time we did this, but it never happened. Instead, the solid spot over his heart turned translucent and then disappeared altogether.

Nathan was gone, without a shaky reentry.

"Holy shit," I said. "That ring is the reason Nathan hasn't been able to move on?"

"Such a simple thing."

Nathan popped back into the room before the conversation moved on any farther. "I just popped over to London. Bloody fantastic."

Guilt bubbled around my heart. "Nathan, I'm sorry. I had no idea."

"No sweat, Luv."

"I guess you're free now." I tried to hide the sadness that clouded my words.

Caleb cleared his throat. "There are a few items I must tell you before you make that decision." He stopped talking to me and turned to Nathan. "It is true that if Alexis takes off the ring you are free to go. Move on. But it won't be in this world. You will move on completely, and not be allowed back on this realm."

"Move on where?"

"Heaven. Hell. That is not an answer I can give you. You would find out when you leave for good."

"I would never see Alexis again?"

"No." Caleb looked my way. "Not that I see how that would be a problem." He then continued. "I must tell you this is a one-time offer. If you choose to stay you will be here as long as Alexis is alive."

I wanted to voice my opinion. I wanted to yell, "No, Nathan, don't leave." I wanted to keep him with me. But in the end I have already done enough to him, and it had to be his choice.

Caleb looked at the watch on his wrist. "You have five minutes to make your choice."

Nathan floated around the room, his fingers steepled in front of his lips. Back and forth, back and forth. Through the furniture, the walls, the doors. In and out of rooms and the elevator. I was relieved he was thinking this over, taking his time to make a decision, but I was also surprised. If the option had been mine, I would have jumped at the opportunity to leave.

He stopped in front of Caleb. "If I stay will I have freedom?"

"If Alexis takes off the ring you will have one hour before you start to fade away completely. After one hour you will be removed from this realm, but you will not enter heaven or hell. Your soul will be gone for good."

I wasn't sure I was ready to be responsible for Nathan's life again. I had complete control over him, and that wasn't fair. But I also knew I wasn't ready for him to be gone forever either.

Nathan continued his rotation of the room, before finally settling in front of me. "I love you like a daughter."

The words showered my innards with a downpour of joy. "I love you too." But then my heart plummeted at the thought of losing Nathan forever.

He turned to Caleb. "I'm staying."

My heart flipped. "Are you sure?" I asked.

"Who else can give you relationship advice and keep you and Reaper from tearing each other's throats out?" He reached out and touched my chin with his finger. "Besides, heaven won't have me, and I'd be ruling hell in a matter of days. I'd rather stay here and see how things work out with Doctor Hottie."

Caleb walked towards us. "This decision cannot be undone. Only once Alexis dies or completes her contract will you be free. Do you understand this?"

"I understand. I'm not ready to move on. I missed my China Doll for the two years we were apart. Now that I have her back I'm not letting her go again."

Caleb looked between the two of us, walked to the coffee table, picked up the ring and slipped it on my finger. "As you wish." He walked back to the center of the room. "Now I must be off. I will be back soon for your decision."

"I'll be counting the hours." No one could miss the sarcasm in my words.

The angel narrowed his eyes at me. "Why did I get stuck

with the biggest pain in the ass of the group?" And with that he left the room in a cloud of smoke.

"Looks like we're going to be together for a while." I nudged Nathan with my shoulder.

"There's no place I would rather be," he said, and then added, "unless you include the strip club down the street. How do you feel about giving me some time off?"

I removed the ring and placed it on the table in front of me. "Enjoy your hour."

Chapter Thirty-Three

For the first time in weeks I was alone. No Nathan to disrupt my peace. No monsters lurking in the shadows that occupied my mind. No worries. It felt good. I was going to enjoy every single minute of this time.

Or I thought I was until the gears on the elevator started whirring. I took a deep breath to find out who was bothering me. Julian. Multiple emotions raced through my body. Excitement. Anger. Nervousness.

We needed to have a conversation about his lies by omission, but I wasn't sure I was in the right frame of mind to have that talk tonight. I tried to evaluate how I felt about his furrier side before he got to the second floor. Honestly, it wasn't a big deal that he was werewolf, unless he skipped a dose of his homemade brew and Eddie sensed it. Then I'd have to kill him. That could put a huge kink in our relationship.

The elevator gears stopped and the cage slowly opened. He stood in the center of three walls, in a pair of perfectly tailored linen pants and a cream-colored dress shirt. His grim expression, and lowered eyes let me know he wasn't sure if he was welcome in or not. I could let him stew, but I didn't want to.

I stayed on the couch, but motioned for him to enter. "Come on in."

He stepped into the kitchen and leaned against the kitchen table. "I'm sorry I left the way I did. Things with Julia have been complicated to say the least."

I smiled, not sure what to say to him. "Are we alone?"

"Nathan has a one hour pass. He's at the strip club down the street." I patted the cushion next to me. "It's just you and me and the pile of secrets between us."

He took the seat next to me, careful to keep his hands to

himself, although I noticed his fingers twitched to touch mine, but he pulled back before he did. "I'm not very trusting by nature, the whole solitary wolf thing. And you being who you are, I just wasn't sure I could trust you."

The sad thing was I understood. If I was a supernatural that could hide their ability, I might not trust a vampire whose existence existed on killing my kind.

"You made the serum for yourself?"

He pulled a tube out of his pocket; a black stopper plugged the top. It held a thick orange liquid. "Yes. And Julia."

I took the tube from his hand, and held it up to my face. I couldn't smell anything through the glass. "I surmised you are hiding from your pack?"

"We're hiding from all werewolves." He paused and let out a frustrated breath. "I take that back. *I'm* hiding from all werewolves. Julia isn't." He took the tube from my hand and placed it on the table in front of us.

"Why?"

"My choices are limited, either hide, lead, or die."

"Since we've had sex, I think I deserve a better explanation than that."

Julian grabbed a lock of my hair and let the strands slip through his fingers before he settled back into the couch. "Ready for a long story?"

"I've got an eternity to hear it."

"My father was the pack leader of the Chicago pack. For twenty years he led the pack, did the right thing, was fair and honest. When the vampires came out, the pack wanted to step out into the world with them. My father refused. He spoke to the Elders and convinced them that letting society know of our existence would be our downfall. In the end the younger members of the pack felt like my father was too old fashioned to lead the new generation of wolves. Ten of them showed up at our house, ripped through the door and kidnapped my mother." He sank farther back into the couch and picked at a loose thread on his pants. "They used my mother to control my father. When he showed up to save her, they killed them both. Gunned down with silver bullets to the heart."

I pulled air between my teeth in a hiss, memories of the death of my own family floating to the surface as he talked about losing his. Looked like Julian and I had more in common than I thought. "They spared you and Julia?"

"We're only alive because we were in college and our execution would have been too public."

"What did you do?" I leaned in closer, letting my leg bump into his.

"Pack law dictated that as next in line I was to lead the pack. I was still in college, young, untrained, and not interested, but none of that mattered. It was my right to take over. If the wolves that had killed my parents had been punished, and I felt that it was safe for Julia and me, I would have stepped up. But, I agreed with all the reasons that my father refused to let us come out, and because of that I was still standing in the way of their plans."

"They have to know by now that it was a horrendous idea for the vampires to come out." I nudged his shoulder.

He nudged me back. "They do. The subject is now off the table."

"So why aren't you leading the pack?"

He slumped back into the couch cushions and let his head fall back on his shoulders. "When I forced Julia and me into hiding, we became an enemy of the pack. Now they want us, well, me, dead for deserting."

"Who is running the pack now?"

"Officially no one. Until I am defeated in a battle for leadership, I am still leader by law. But for the past four years, the man who orchestrated my family's death is running things."

I took the vial of serum off the table and held it in my hand. "You created the serum so you could hide in plain site?"

"I had to find a way to hide our scents from the werewolves.

I happen to be a very talented chemist, and was able to create this little gem." He took the vial from me and swirled the liquid in the test tube. "It's the only thing that has saved our lives."

"What happens if they find you?"

"I'm not sure anymore. Death. A Challenge. Full on war."

"Is he still hunting for you?"

"He's been quiet for years. But now, thanks to Terrance and Julia, he knows about the serum." He tossed it back on the table and watched it roll to the edge. "He also knows we still live in the area. According to Julia he is planning on issuing a challenge."

"I wish you would have told me all of this sooner."

Julian reached up and touched the underneath of my chin, his soft fingers lingering on my skin, causing a wave of heat to puddle between my thighs. He tilted my head so our eyes met. "I was scared to death the serum wouldn't work the first time you walked into the morgue. Afraid I had just met my end. I never imagined I would end up falling for you." He leaned in and kissed me.

His lips warmed mine. His tongue entered my mouth, and found mine in an erotic tango. And just like that all the anger, disappointment and thoughts of secrets vanished.

Heat poured off him through the thick fabric of his shirt, and realized I wanted to feel it on my bare skin. I grabbed the edge of his shirt and pulled it off his head, separating our mouths, but seeking his again the instant the fabric was gone.

He followed suit and removed my shirt, my bra, anything that separated us. His hand cupped my breasts, his finger teased my nipples, and then he bent his head low and took the sensitive flesh between his teeth. Small teasing pulls that sent shivers down my spine.

When I was wrapped in Julian's arms, all my problems faded away into a sea of skin and sex.

I licked along his neck, stopping just over the pulsing vein. For a second Eddie flared with the smell of the blood rushing under the surface, but instead of biting him I sucked on the skin just over the vein, and felt my lips curl with the groan that escaped his lips.

His hands worked at the zipper on my pants, sliding them down my long legs, and pushing them to the floor. His head roamed lower, teeth grabbing the thin fabric of my thong, and pulling it off. His fingers found their mark, rubbing gently before diving deep between my folds. I moaned. It felt so good, and I wanted more. Wanted all of him. He must have read my mind because his head crept lower and his mouth replaced his fingers. I moaned again, my body arching. He placed his hand on my stomach.

His tongue darted in and out, he licked, he teased. He was very attentive. So attentive that the orgasm came on hard and fast. Relieving the stress of the past week in the most glorious way.

After the last tremor left my body, he kissed his way up my body, stopping at my neck. "You're the most amazing woman I have ever met." He breathed into my ear. Then he entered me, slow and smooth at first, but then found a rhythm and he rode me hard.

That's one advantage to being a vampire, rough sex was not a problem. He could take me hard and fast, pound me into the ground, and my body could take every second of it. He did. Our bodies fused together. His eyes stared into mine, and for a brief moment they changed from his normal deep blue to the amber of his wolf.

We both had our inner monsters to fight.

My second orgasm came just moments before he growled with his own release.

He tucked me against his body, flesh on flesh, gaze on gaze. His hand pushed my dark waves away from my eyes and tucked it behind my ears. Leaning forward he nipped at my bottom lip, ran his tongue along the soft curve. "I've fallen for you. Hard. Think we can make this work?"

"It's not the most conventional relationship in the world. Beside the whole mixed species thing, one wrong skipped dose of your magic wonder drug and I might end up having to kill you."

"Let's hope it never leads to that."

"Let's hope," I mumbled, but deep inside the thought scared the shit out of me. I already off'd Nathan, but he came back to me. I might not be so lucky the second time around. Speaking of Nathan.

I looked at the clock on the wall. "Shit. I've got to get the ring back on. Nathan only gets an hour before he fades away to lands unknown."

Julian stood up and pulled his clothes back on. I watched all this beautiful muscles and perfect skin get covered by cloth and knew I couldn't wait for the next time I saw him. I followed suit and got dressed. Nathan didn't need to see what I looked like naked.

Once everything was in place I picked up the ring and placed it back on my finger. Within seconds he was standing in front of me. He eyed us suspiciously.

"It smells like sex in here."

So much for hiding the evidence.

Chapter Thirty-Four

I t had been two weeks since I fought Delano and walked out with my life. Two weeks of changes and decisions and growth. Reaper and I still trained and hunted every night, because Eddie still needed to be fed. Nathan and I spent our time together watching cheesy movies and reminiscing about the old days. And Julian and I, well, we spent our evenings naked and happy.

Eddie and I had come to an understanding. I didn't kill humans and Caleb would allow me to come visit the queen. On those visits, Eddie would be in control. He tried to get me to agree to call him Vlad, but I still liked Eddie.

I contacted Coleman and agreed to help him on some of his more difficult cases, but he hadn't called yet. Caleb and I came to an agreement, five years off my sentence and I helped the other Assassins when needed. He tried to get me to agree to being less difficult, but I refused.

Every night, when my day was done, and it was just Nathan and I, we hunted for one vampire in particular.

Because, a promise is a promise.

Twenty-four hours ago, I found him and now it was time that he paid for his crimes.

I stood outside in the cool night air and waited for Reaper. The Chevelle turned the corner and Reaper pulled up beside me. "Ready?" he called through the open window.

I slid into the seat next to him, leaned forward and punched an address into the GPS unit. "That's where we're headed tonight."

"You have a lead?"

"A hot one." I settled back in my seat. "Now let's get going."

Reaper and I sat in our usual silence while he followed the

directions. Instead of being two people without anything to say, we were two people who enjoyed the fact that we didn't need to fill up the silence with nonsense chatter.

The landscape became familiar and I wondered if Reaper noticed that he'd been here before? The knowledge of what was going to come made me grin.

Reaper stopped the car in front of the same dilapidated house where we found the first nest, right next to Julian's car. He cut the engine. "Care to explain?"

He recognized the house, but then again who could forget. I didn't answer. Instead, I got out of the car and stood by the hood. He followed and stood next to me. I whistled and Julian, in his wolf form came through the front door, passed us by and walked into the woods.

"Your boyfriend?"

I watched the wolf disappear behind the trees. "Yep." I reached into my boot and pulled out two stakes. I tossed one to him and he caught it without a problem. "You're going to need this."

Then I reached into my back pocket and pulled out a black silk scarf. "Bend down."

He took one look at the fabric, held up his hands, and began to back away. "No way."

"Trust me, it's worth it," I teased.

He sighed and then stepped forward. "Fine."

Before Reaper and I battled for our lives I would never have attempted this, but things were so much easier between us that I enjoyed being able to tease him.

He eyed me for a moment before following my direction. Then I tied the scarf around his head, making sure his eyes were covered nice and tight.

He picked at the edge of his blindfold. "Is this necessary?"

"You don't want to spoil the surprise, do you?"

I wrapped one hand around his upper arm and folded my fingers around his. We took slow steps and I guided him through all the potholes and loose boards on the front steps. I opened the creaky front door and pulled him over the threshold. A quick look let me know that his surprise was still subdued and where I had left him. Thanks to my guard wolf.

The vampire chained to the radiator looked frozen. Probably because there was a stake lodged in his chest cavity, and one wrong move and his life would be over. His clothes were torn and covered with blood; I might have been a little rough when I found him. His eyes widened when he saw me walk in. It had been just over twenty-four hours since I captured him and left him. I'm sure he was wondering what I had in store for him.

I positioned Reaper so he was standing right in front of him, and pulled the scarf away from his eyes.

His heartbeat sped up at the sight of the vampire who murdered his family. The monster responsible for all his pain and anger and suffering. "You caught him?" His voice barely above a whisper.

"I never break a promise."

Reaper stalked over to the hog-tied vampire, stake in his hand, knuckles blanching as he crushed the wood. His breath slowed and he swallowed. He knelt in front of him, noses almost touching. "Do you remember me? Do you remember the pregnant woman you killed?"

The vampire looked at him, back at me, and then at Reaper again. I saw the fear flitter through his eyes the moment he recognized the man in front of him. The moment he realized his fate.

"You ready to kill this undead asshole?" Reaper growled.

Eddie wanted to jump forward and stake the vampire, but this wasn't my kill. It was Reaper's.

His chance for revenge. His chance to cleanse his soul. His chance to move on. I shook my head nice and slow, and walked next to him. I touched the stake in his hand. "Not me." I pointed to his chest. "You."

Reaper met my eye for a brief moment before he smiled.

The first true smile I'd ever seen grace his lips. He walked over to the vampire, a little more spring in his step than I was used to. He leaned forward and I heard the words he whispered. "This is for you, Lorelie, and our baby." His arm pulled back and the stake went straight through the vampire's heart, clinking as it hit the metal of the radiator at his back.

We stood together as the vampire burned away, his body ending up as a pile of ash. Reaper walked over and slid his foot through the pile, scattering it across the room. The only sign of anger he let crack through his tough guy persona. Then he turned and walked back out into the night.

I followed him to the car, noticing that Julian had left. Reaper cranked the engine and we drove away from the house that started us along this path. I'm not sure what I expected to happen after I gave him the one thing in the world he wanted, but it wasn't the suffocating silence that we drove back to my place in.

Silence that allowed me to reflect. In less than a week, I'd gained a roommate, a maybe boyfriend, and Reaper and I had entered a new place in our usually strained relationship. In other words I'd gained an odd sort of family. Something I hadn't had in so many years.

Not since the day Andre and I escaped from Xavier and gone our separate ways. And even though my twin brother wasn't dead, at least I didn't think he was, his absence in my life left a gaping hole that I had only begun to fill.

With these new additions to my life, I've realized I would do absolutely anything to protect them. The people I cared about. The people I loved. The people that made me feel that I was more than a bloodthirsty monster that caused nothing but pain to those around me.

In other words they were mine to protect, but no one was safe until I got rid of Delano and all of his protégées. And I needed Vlad to do that, something I had come to terms with since Delano disappeared. Because, as much as I liked to pretend it wasn't so, the vampire and I were one in the same, always had been. I just couldn't deny the fact anymore.

Reaper pulled in front of my apartment, and without a word I opened my door and stepped out. I was almost to my front door when the window rolled down and Reaper yelled my name.

I turned to look. He leaned over the seat, one hand perched on the window frame.

"You're not half bad for a blood sucker." And for once his words didn't carry a hint of sarcasm. In fact, I detected a hint of respect. Just a hint.

———————

I SINCERELY HOPE you enjoyed reading this book as much as I enjoyed writing it. If you did, I would greatly appreciate a short review on Amazon or your favorite book website. Reviews are crucial for any author, and even just a line or two can make a huge difference.

Acknowledgments

This book is the first book I had ever written. It's my baby. The world that I love to write in, characters who I adore. To see it finally published, I can't even put into words what that means.

As always, there are so many people who helped get this book out to my readers.

James, there were so many highs and lows with this book. From the my very first writing group, to the many rejections and the many contest wins, but you never let me quit, even on the worst days. Love you!

Sage and Syndee never give up and never let anyone tell you that you can't do something. Nothing is unobtainable. I think I've more than proved that to you with this crazy journey.

To the READerlicious girls, Brinda Berry, Kelly Crawley, Christina Delay, Kathleen Groger, Susan McCauley, Abbie Roads, Jennifer Savalli, Carol Michell Storey, NK Whitaker, and Sandy Wright, this book is the reason I met all of you, no wonder it's so special to me because you guys are too.

To all the vampire authors out there that made me fall in love with the genre, without all your amazing stories, I would never have been inspired to write this story.

ABOUT THE AUTHOR

Jenn Windrow loves characters who have a pinch of spunk, a dash of attitude, and a large dollop of sex appeal. Top it all off with a huge heaping helping of snark, and you've got the ingredients for the kind of fast paced stories she loves to read and write. Home is a suburb of it's-so-hot-my-shoes-have-melted-to-the-pavement Phoenix. Where she lives with her husband, two daughters, and a slew of animals that seem to keep following her home, at least that's what she claims.

Find out more about Jenn and her books at:
www.jennwindrow.com

Join my **newsletter** to keep up on upcoming books and receive a free Alexis Black Prequel Short story, **Blood and Orgasms.**

ALSO BY JENN WINDROW

The Redeeming Cupid Series

Struck By Eros

Pierced By Venom

Pricked By thorns

The Alexis Black Novels

Evil's Unlikely Assassin

Evil's Ultimate Huntress

Chapter One

My nightly vampire hunts used to be all wham-bam-thank-you-ma'am, but lately they've been more can-you-keep-up-bitch? Two months ago, I nearly killed Delano Melazi, an ancient bloodsucker hell-bent on eradicating the human race. But I failed. And ever since, he's been trying to return the favor. One pointy-toothed motherfucker at a time.

His latest kill-Alexis weapon, a vampire amped up on screw-with-me serum and armed with dripping fangs and a serious case of undead halitosis, had me pinned against a chain-link fence. Hands firmly planted on my breasts. Fangs snapping at my neck. I wasn't sure which pissed me off more.

Nathan, part one of my two-part band of merry misfits and my own personal punk-rock poltergeist, huffed and puffed from his safe spot on the swing. "You about done getting felt up by that tosser?"

"Happy to switch places." I dodged the vampire's teeth aiming for my jugular.

I head-butted the Dracula wanna-be trying to turn me into a chew toy. He stumbled backwards, giving me time to sweep my hand through the early October snow and find my stake. I grabbed the ultimate vampire killing tool and wedged it between us. Pressed the pointy tip against his ribcage and pushed, using all my she-vamp strength. Half a second later, I heard the satisfying crack of the stake breaking through the ribcage and straight into Chester the Molester's heart.

Flames sparked from the left side of his chest where I had

shish-kebabbed his heart, slowly burning through his flesh and bone, lighting up the playground. Within moments the ground and most of my clothes were covered in dead vampire ash.

I dusted off my leather pants and assessed our situation. Not good. At least ten new vampires were lining up to take their dead buddy's place.

"Reaper?" I yelled for my too-human, too-stubborn, vampire-hating partner. Another fun bi-product of my do-it-or-die contract with Caleb, the Angel with Attitude. A contract that required me to hunt and kill one supernatural creature every night for fifty years. At the end of my servitude, I got my humanity back. Seemed like a good deal at the time.

"He's tossing a wanker over at the seesaw." Nathan's voice carried over the sound of the approaching lynch mob.

I really hoped that was some sort of British slang for "fighting a vampire," but with Nathan, who knew?

No time to ask. Two vampires broke away from the pack and ran over for a meet-and-greet. I borrowed a bit of super-speed from my inner beast, the unwanted soul that had hijacked my body. I named him Eddie, but everyone else knew him as Vlad the Impaler, the Father of All Vampires. Lunging to the left, I skidded past the first pair of blood suckers, but my maneuver put me in the path of two more. They slapped their weapons against their palms like they were rival gang members in a 1950s movie.

These guys had cliché down to a cheesy vampire film.

They were too close and too quick. I slammed into their legs, hoping to knock them on their asses, but they didn't fall. Grabbing my arms, they pulled me to my knees. One placed his hand on the top of my head and forced me to watch the rest of the fang and clueless gang form a half-circle in front of me.

Most of the vampires who surrounded me looked like new vamps, two or three days past their first meal. Skin still semi-human looking. A little bit of blush in their not-yet-sunken-in cheeks. Fangs pointy, but not quite something to write to their sires about.

Then there were the pus-filled sores, a lovely side-effect of the serum their sire injected into their system to keep Eddie and me from being able to detect them. Typical of what we had been encountering since Delano decided to expedite his revenge and complete the total annihilation of anyone with a beating pulse.

But there was one vampire standing in the center of them all, a Grandpa compared to the rest. Skin the color of marshmallows, eyes almost solid black, and an impressive set of fangs hanging over his bottom lip. His clothes were a cross between drunken pirate and frat boy. Tight grey jeans and a red and black coat with lots of blingy buckles and buttons. No sores covering his skin.

This one made Eddie angry. *Tonight's main course.*

My blood lust kicked into hyperdrive.

Captain Pirate Pants swung a massive machete with some serious rust spots in a figure eight in front of him. I guess I was supposed to be intimidated.

No chance. I still hadn't let my inner killing machine off his leash. And oh, how Eddie loved to maim and destroy.

"I don't know why everyone in the vampire society is so afraid of you." Captain Pirate Pants sounded so confident. How cute.

"Come on over and I'll show you." I snapped my own impressive set of fangs at him.

He smiled, all teeth-and-serial-killer-like. "Do you think I'm stupid?"

"You're dressed like a pirate. What am I supposed to think?"

*Ask a stupid question...*Eddie spoke up from his cozy corner in my mind.

Captain Pirate Pants rushed forward and wrapped his hand around my neck, giving it a nice, tight squeeze. Guess I poked a fang hole. "Too bad Delano wants you alive." He licked my cheek, leaving a trail of slime.

I dry heaved.

He pointed his rusty-ass machete into the center of my throat. For a second, I wondered when I had my last tetanus shot. Oh, yeah, they didn't have those in the 1800s when I was born.

"I might be scared." Total lie. "If you hadn't just told me that you're not allowed to kill me."

"When Delano tortures you, you'll wish you had been staked." He tried for a menacing grin, but ended up looking constipated, which was more frightening than his words.

"I've already tangled with your boss once, he barely survived." Neither had I, but I didn't mention that. Those memories were safely buried under a load of guilt and shame.

He pushed the machete deeper into my neck, drawing a bit of blood. It ran down my cleavage, staining my favorite tank top. "He's ready for you this time, now that he knows Vlad's soul inhabits you."

For a covert operation, Delano sure picked a Chatty Cathy.

"Alexis, are you going to kill this prat soon?" Nathan whined like he wanted me to remove the platinum ring that bound him to me so he could enjoy his free-from-Alexis hour at the local tits-and-ass club.

I yawned and smacked my lips. "Are you about done? I'm completely bored playing with you."

Captain Pirate Pants' blade dug a little deeper and the two goons holding me down gave my arms a turbo twist. Vampires were so touchy.

"Take her away, lock her up tight." Captain Pirate Pants pointed to their no-window van in the parking lot. "If you need to subdue her, use the poison."

Oh great, we've moved on to the abduction part of the evening. Not the first time Delano had tried this trick.

Are you finally ready to kill these monstrosities? Eddie's blood lust was about to consume us both. My fangs grew. Molten lava rushed through my veins. The branded angel wings on my hip burned. The world became a hazy crimson. I lowered my head and hid the red glow of my eyes, another tell-tale sign that Eddie was taking over.

I now looked and felt like the monster who resided in my soul.

Maybe I like being manhandled by goons.

About as much as I like being stuck in your carcass. Eddie's daily bitch about having to play passenger to my driver.

Trust me, having you playing Invasion of the Body Snatcher isn't a joy for me either.

I groaned at the reminder that unless we killed Caleb, the asshole angel who stuffed Eddie into my body, we were stuck together until my sign-or-die contract was up. Only forty-one years, thirty weeks, and four days left. And that was a reduced sentence.

I rolled my shoulders, stretching like Raja, my Bengal cat, after a long afternoon nap. *Ready to school some blood suckers in the proper way to abduct and kill?*

Eddie dragged his claws down my insides, playing my ribs like a harp. Guess that was a yes.

With a quick peek, I searched the park for Reaper and found him playing peeping-partner from behind a large oak tree about ten feet away, waiting for my come-hither-and-kill-vamps gesture. He didn't like my new keep-Reaper-alive tactic, but a grumpy Reaper was better than a dead Reaper.

Eddie gave my insides a vicious poke. *Let's get this over with.*

And he wondered why I refused to call him Vlad.

Having Eddie's soul inside of me gave me the extra boost of power I needed to kill the supernatural creatures I hunted. But every day I lived in fear that he would grow stronger, more powerful, and take control. Control he craved. Control he once used to break my biggest vow.

Don't. Drink. From. Humans.

But a few sips from a live vein wasn't what woke me up every day, sweat-soaked, lying in my sheets. It was trying to outrun the nightmares that tormented me. Relentless memories of a dead man in my arms. An unwilling sacrifice that saved me from my own death-by-cremation.

A sacrifice that helped save other human lives, but almost destroyed me. A sacrifice that I would make worth it by doing what I could to hunt and kill vampires like Delano and his army.

Fists tight. Teeth clenched. I fought the fear that raced through my body like an out of control L-train ready to plunge off the tracks at the next sharp turn.

Eddie and I still had some trust issues to work through.

But...without his strength and speed and superior fighting skills, my photo would end up on the back of a bag-o-blood with the word "Missing" over my head.

Eddie's rage rolled through me like a steel-wheel roller over asphalt.

Ready? He sounded strong and fierce and everything the Father of All Vampires should sound like.

Let's kill some blood suckers.

Using all of Eddie's I-am-King-of-the-Undead power, I wrenched my arm from the first vampire's grip, then smashed my elbow into his nose. Blood gushed. He hit the ground screaming like a little bitch. One gone. One still clinging to my arm like a pathetic parasite. With my newly freed hand, I grabbed him by his severely out of style shirt and tossed him toward Reaper's hide-a-tree. The vampire hit with a bone-crunching thump. A present to my partner.

"Stop her." Captain Pirate Pants screamed at his flunkies, but there was a gigantic dollop of desperation in those two words. "If she gets away, Delano will kill us."

He didn't have to worry about Delano's wrath. In five minutes, he'd be a pile of ash.

With Reva, my trusty blade, in one hand and a stake in the other, I gave Captain Pirate Pants a wink. "Ready to play?"

He scooted behind what was left of his squad, using them as a vampire shield. "Eight against one, the odds are still in my favor."

I had always been fast and strong, but with Eddie on board, I was supersonic and unstoppable. Eight vampires? Just a warm up.

"Surround her." His voice was filled with a butt-load of fear.

The vampires formed a circle around me. Fangs bared, drool sliding down their chins. Weapons protecting their hearts. Like that could keep them alive.

One got stupid and ran toward me, his war cry echoing through the bare trees. I slashed open a large, blood-red, oozing gash in his stomach. It wouldn't kill him, but it was hard to move when your innards became outards.

The other vampires watched their buddy fall to the ground in a pile of gore. I stalked over to the fallen vampire and slammed my stake into his chest.

Seven. Eddie liked to count his victims. It was sick and sadistic, but what did you expect from the man they called Vlad the Impaler?

Two vampires broke rank and took off in the direction of the playground.

I called out to Reaper. "Two coming your way." That would keep him busy.

Five.

Easy-peasy.

"You guys going to play ring-around-Evil's Assassin all night or are you going to attack me?" I wiggled my fingers in a come-and-eat-me gesture. No one moved. WTF? I was bored and hungry and late for a date with a hunky werewolf.

I blew a few strands of my dark hair out of my face and tightened my grip on Reva's hilt. The remaining vampires took three steps in, closing the gaps.

"I will be the one to capture you and take you to Delano." Captain Pirate Pants was as confident as he was stupid.

Eddie, let's end this.

His power unfurled, almost consuming me. I took a steadying breath and ran around the circle, Reva's blade slicing through flesh and bone, leaving a gaping hole right over their non-beating hearts. Blood sprayed in an arc around me. A macabre fountain.

Four vampires hit the ground. All except for Captain Pirate Pants. I grabbed my stake and zipped past the incapacitated baddies, slamming a life-ending blow to their exposed hearts. Flames sparked from their bodies, lighting up the area before they burned to ash. A charred vampire bonfire.

One left.

With his army gone, the ringleader fell to his knees, his hands smashed together like he was praying, and started to babble. "Don't kill me. I can tell you about Delano's plans."

"I already know Delano's plans. Kill me, then take over the world." But I hesitated before driving the stake through is heart.

What are you waiting for? Eddie's blood lust rose to unbearable. *Maybe Captain Pirate Pants knows something we don't.*

Eddie groaned, but gave me my way, knowing I would give him his kill when I was done with my interrogation.

I crouched down next to him. "Talk."

"You won't kill me?"

I looked at the night sky and pretended to ponder his dilemma for a second. "Depends on what you tell me."

"Delano has a big surprise for you. Something you'll never expect." Guess he figured that was a "yes."

I twirled my stake at him. "Care to elaborate?"

"There have been whispers of a new second-in-command. An old, ruthless vampire whose only mission is to hunt you down and bring you in."

"Name?"

"I'm not high enough in the chain of command to know all the details." He gave me a look so full of hope, I almost felt bad for what was about to come next.

"Then you've used up your usefulness." I raised my stake over my head and slammed it into his heart.

The blood lust receded. My fangs went back to normal, the brand stopped throbbing, my blood cooled, and the world went back to technicolor. I felt like Alexis, The Good Vampire again.

We work well as a team. A now-content Eddie started to fade away to wherever Eddie went when he wasn't tormenting me.

I didn't want to agree with him, but being a cooperating part of Team Psycho was better than fighting him every day of my undead life.

Nathan golf-clapped from the swings. "I would have helped, but I'm made of bloody mist."

I slapped him on the shoulder, sending blue and purple sparks shooting into the air. "That's okay, I just like having you around."

"Reaper's staking the last vamp who tried to pull a David Copperfield." He pointed to a group of evergreens.

With Reva in hand, I went to see if my partner needed backup. When I got there, Reaper was ramming a stake into the last vampire's heart. The vamp burst into flames and then turned to ash.

"We good?" He wiped the dead vamp off his standard-issue black t-shirt.

Eddie?

My inner vampire searched with his own supernatural radar for anything of the non-human variety.

Only thing left with fangs and an attitude is you.

"Eddie says we're all clear." I slid my weapons back into their sheaths in my thigh-high boots. "We killed another twelve tonight."

"At least." Reaper dusted the vampire's remains out of his Marine crew cut and side-stepped a pile of dead blood-sucker. "Delano is making them as fast as we can kill them."

"It's one way to keep us off his ass." I wiped a spooge of

semi-dried blood off my leather pants. "I think I'm killing more vampires than the VAU these days."

The mere mention of the Vampire Apprehension Unit, a group of highly-trained ex-military created shortly after the Eradication, sent a chill skittering up my spine. A group whose only mission was to root out the evil undead scourge and kill them. A group created after some rogue vamps decided to have an all-you-can-suck buffet on live TV. I had managed to evade the VAU my whole undead life until a few months ago. Now, I worked for the one detective who found me useful. Better that than dead.

"At this pace, we'll never have time to search for Delano." Reaper headed through the park to his midnight blue 1970 SS Chevelle.

"Pretty sure that's the point." I scanned the area for anything with fangs that might pop out and try to attack. But the night seemed vampire-free.

The winter wind picked up, leaves swirled on the frozen ground, tree limbs swayed, and a scent from my past smashed into me like a tombstone.

A mixture of bergamont oil and cedarwood.

A smell so familiar, so welcoming, yet so wrong, it sent a belfry of bats flapping through my tummy. I stopped walking, eyes and nose searching the area for the person who owned that sniff down memory lane. Then something caught my eye. Something that hadn't been there before and didn't belong there now.

An object in one of the bucket swings inches from where Nathan had sat just moments ago.

I pointed to the still-swaying swing. "Was that always there?"

Nathan floated over for a closer inspection. "Nope."

"What is it?" I wasn't sure I wanted the answer.

"A doll." Nathan's words sounded odd, like he was trying to figure out a puzzle.

I walked over, ready to remove a child's toy from the swing, but when I saw it, I pulled my hand back and wrapped my arms around my stomach, squeezing tight, hoping to stop the battering in my belly.

The doll was an antique porcelain replica of an eight-year-old little boy. Wavy hair the color of midnight. Freckles dusting the cheeks and nose. Blue eyes one shade darker than mine. The face a more masculine image of my own.

I picked up the fragile porcelain and turned it over, my hands trembling. Traced my fingers over the cracks caused by age. Pulled at the sage green vest, tucking it back into place.

Memories of happier times flashed through my mind like a mini-movie. Our eighth birthday. Papa, mama, and Lysette handing André and I identical burlap wrapped boxes. Pulling off the bow, the wrapping falling away. The excitement of seeing a tiny version of myself in the wooden crate. Pulling her out and hugging her tight.

André's toothy grin when he held up his matching doll to show me. A doll that looked just like my twin brother, my best friend, the other half of my soul.

The moment we decided at the same time to switch, each wanting the other's.

For the rest of our lives, André's doll stayed with me, mine stayed with him. They traveled on Xavier's boat with us, another prize to add to our sire's collection. And when we fled for our lives, we were forced to leave them behind.

With a small shake of my head, I tried to erase the memories of the last time I had seen this doll. Memories that dragged me down the path of regret and loneliness I fought to escape from every day. I opened my eyes, shutting out the past.

"Not possible," I said in a whisper that floated away on the wind.

"Alexis?" Reaper's tone had an Alexis-is-about-to-be-stupid sound to it.

I didn't answer him.

His combat boots crunched the gravel and broke through

the whistle of the wind through the trees. "What's that?" Reaper stood next to me.

"A piece of my past." I turned the doll back over to show him the face. "And something that shouldn't be here."

Nathan hovered close, placing his hand on mine so he could solidify, the only way non-vampires could see him. "Thought you said those were left at Xavier's when you escaped?"

I held the doll up to my nose, inhaled, and closed my eyes. Two different scents clung to the clothes, the hair, to every fiber. The first, I never thought I would smell again. France. The farmhouse I was raised in. The lavender scent of the soap mama made by hand. The smell of my childhood buried under another, stronger odor. André's. It clung to the fabric as if he had hugged the doll before placing it in the swing.

"They were." I looked up to meet my friend's eyes, not sure what emotion they would see in mine. Anguish? Confusion? Disbelief? Despair?

There were only two people in this world that could have left the doll. One who I wanted to hold and hug, the other who I wanted crucify and kill. My twin brother, André. Or Xavier, my sire.

Killing Delano had just been bumped from the number one spot on my to-do list.

Made in the USA
Middletown, DE
17 August 2023

36498869R00163